D1524124

YELLOWSTONE DECEPTION

YELLOWSTONE ROMANCE SERIES

PEGGY L HENDERSON

ISBN: 9781096697732

This book is dedicated to all my wonderful readers. I wish I could thank each and every one of you personally. Some of you I've gotten to know through interactions on forums, facebook, and from emails you send me. Maggie, Hazel, Joyce, Diane. Just to name a few. Thank you for sticking with me through this series, and giving this new author a chance. I wrote Yellowstone Deception because of the many requests I received for Jana and Dan to have their story.

INTRODUCTION

Dan Osborne has one ambition in life. He wants to be a permanent park ranger in Yellowstone National Park, a place where his family roots run deep. He'll do just about anything to make his dream a reality. When a pretty tourist tells him an incredible story about his ancestors, his dreams might be realized sooner than he hoped.

Jana Evans' best friend traveled back in time for true love. Not only is a weathered diary proof that she survived, so is the handsome park ranger standing before Jana now. Her immediate attraction to Aimee's descendant leaves her disturbed and confused, and she rushes back home to the safety of a normal life. An unexpected phone call months later from the very man she wanted to put out of her mind forces her back to Yellowstone. He has news that Aimee met with an untimely death. Is she willing to follow him 200 years into the past to save her best friend's life?

Dan is convinced that Jana holds the key to finding the device that makes time travel possible. He hasn't stopped thinking about her since their one brief encounter months ago. A journey into the past could not only set things in place for his own future, but it might also bring Jana back into his life. Will the truth about his motives shatter any chance they might have at love?

CHAPTER ONE

*J*ana Evans groaned loudly, and rolled onto her stomach. She pulled the covers up over her head and buried her face in her pillow. None of her efforts managed to drown out the shrill ring of her cell phone. Reluctantly, she lifted her head and squinted to check the time on her alarm clock. Five-thirty in the morning!

Jana worked her arm out from under the covers and reached for her phone. Another ring or two, and it should go to voice mail. Other than someone from work, she couldn't imagine who would call her this early in the morning. Today was her day off. She didn't relish the idea of being called in if they were short staffed, but she knew she would go to work, if asked. Doctors didn't like to rearrange their surgery schedules and nurses were expected to be available at a moments' notice.

"Hello," she mumbled, her voice raspy from sleep. Jana rolled to her side and brought the phone up close to her ear.

"Jana. Jana Evans?" The deep male voice at the other end of the line startled her and her heart actually skipped a beat. It was not a voice she recognized, but something about him sounded familiar nevertheless. She was instantly more alert. It was definitely not someone from work.

Jana rolled fully onto her back and raised herself to a sitting position. She didn't know any male co-workers who would be calling her. And she certainly didn't have a boyfriend at the moment. This had better not be a sales call.

"Yeah," she grumbled sleepily, rubbing her eyes with her free hand. She scooted backwards on her mattress and leaned against the bed's headboard.

"I hope this isn't a bad time," the man said.

Bad time! Of course it was a bad time! Where the heck was he calling from?

"Who is this?" she asked and scrunched her eyebrows together.

"Dan." His reply sounded more like a question than an answer.

Dan who? Jana waited for him to give his last name. Seconds passed in silence. She frantically searched her mind for any Dans that she might know.

"Jana, it's Dan Osborne. From Montana."

Adrenaline jolted her, and her arms went numb. She sucked in a lung full of air. *Dan Osborne!* She hadn't thought about him in a while . . . she had wanted to, needed to, forget all about him. She'd put her brief and bizarre encounter with the ruggedly handsome park ranger out of her mind almost immediately after their one and only chance encounter a few months ago. Her chest heaved in a long sigh. Yellowstone National Park. A place that held both fond and bittersweet memories for her.

A wave of sadness swept over her and she blinked at the sudden stinging sensation behind her eyes. It was not a place she cared to visit again. It just wouldn't be the same anymore without . . . Jana's best friend's face flashed before her eyes.

Aimee Donovan. No, wait. She shook her head slightly. Her name was Aimee Osborne now.

How long had Aimee been gone? Ten months now, leaving a deep void in Jana's life. Aimee had made a choice to follow her heart and leave everything she knew behind and begin a fantastical new life. *In this time, Aimee is long dead, Jana.*

"Jana? Are you still there?" The voice on the other end of the line jolted her out of her thoughts. Jana cleared her throat.

"Yes . . . um, hi. What a surprise." She laughed nervously. Her voice rose cheerfully. She rolled her eyes.

God, I sound like some silly high school bimbo.

She slapped her palm against her forehead. *Can you sound any more lame, Jana?*

She had a distinctly annoying habit of getting tongue-tied around men she was attracted to. And she'd certainly been attracted to Dan Osborne. Instantly. The moment she'd first seen him. That was the main reason she'd left in a hurry after their surprise meeting two months ago. The circumstances had been too bizarre for her to take in at the time.

"Listen, Jana, I need to talk to you about something," he said, and from the way he hesitated with his words, Jana had the distinct impression he sounded uneasy. "It's kind of important."

"Well, since you're calling me at five-thirty in the morning, I expect it's important," she retorted, biting her lower lip. What on earth could be so urgent that he would even call her now, after two months? They barely knew each other. Of course, the approximately three hours they'd spent in each other's company over dinner had probably forged a bond that wasn't so easily broken. Not after the story Jana had told him. More like a family secret that he obviously knew

3

nothing about. Had Aimee ever passed on her secret to her descendants?

Jana chuckled quietly. She'd certainly let the cat out of the bag two months ago. He had probably regretted asking her to dinner, probably thought she was some deranged nutcase. It had taken more than a few bottles of lager before Dan had seriously started listening to her tale and read some passages from the weathered old diary Jana shoved under his nose. Why on earth had she even told him? The shock of seeing him when he casually sat down next to her in the lobby of the Old Faithful Inn, thinking at first he was someone else, had prompted her to talk faster than the waters spilling over the Lower Falls of the mighty Yellowstone River. She'd needed to talk to someone about the things she knew.

At first startled that a park ranger had tried to engage her in conversation, she'd been completely taken aback after she'd gotten a good look at him. The fact that he was simply gorgeous had nothing to do with it. Seeing Dan, who looked so much like another man with the same name, he had seemed the obvious choice to spill her secrets to.

"Yeah, sorry. I forgot about the time difference," Dan answered.

"It's only an hour's difference," Jana reminded him. Why did she feel compelled to act so disagreeable? Dan Osborne was her living link to Aimee. Why the need to keep her distance? Aimee was her best friend. They'd grown up together like sisters. Done everything together. Maybe that's why it felt so creepy. She had been attracted to her best friend's descendant. Jana shuddered.

"Look, if it's a bad time, I'll call back later. I'm sorry to have bothered you." The sincerity in his voice dissolved her annoyance.

"No, wait . . . Dan. It's okay. It's not a bad time. Really." Jana pushed herself from the bed and onto her feet, and ran her fingers through her shoulder-length hair. She began pacing the floor, suddenly nervous. Why was he calling her, after two months?

"Jana, I really need to see you," he said quickly.

It was the last thing she expected. She stopped in her tracks. "Excuse me?" Was this some kind of joke? Men didn't call her out of the blue, from a thousand miles away, asking to see her.

"Can you come to Yellowstone? I know this is rather sudden, but it really is urgent."

Jana's eyebrows shot up and she laughed. A sudden thought caused her limbs to flood with adrenaline. Her heart rate increased. "You didn't lose the journal, did you?"

There was a slight pause at the other end before he answered. "No. Nothing like that. It's safe."

Jana expelled her breath in relief. Aimee's journal. The accounts of her life in Yellowstone . . . 200 years ago. Her unbelievable experience with time travel, falling in love with a mountain man and her decision to live her life in the past. It was all there, documented in her journal. For a brief moment, Jana wondered what had compelled her to give it to Dan. She'd read it several times, and committed some passages to memory. After meeting Dan Osborne, she thought he deserved to have it. It had belonged to his ancestors, after all. Jana laughed nervously. "I can't come to Wyoming, Dan. I have a job--"

"Aimee is going to die," he interrupted, speaking forcefully into the receiver. Jana imagined his dark eyes glaring and his jaw clenched as he spoke. Another Dan - Daniel's face - came to mind. What was he talking about? Of course Aimee would die. In fact, she was already dead.

"She's already dead," Jana said quietly, echoing her thoughts. Her eyes pooled with tears.

"No, Jana. You don't understand." If Dan had the power to

reach through the phone, Jana was sure he would be gripping her shoulders right about now. "Aimee is going to die, in the past, very soon."

If she were having this conversation with any other person, Jana would have called for a psychiatric check-up at this point. Strangely enough, his words made perfect sense to her. She shook her head and pinched the bridge of her nose with her thumb and index finger. She felt a massive headache coming on.

"And how do you know this?" she asked, her hands suddenly sweaty. How could Aimee have died prematurely in the past? If that were so, there would be no journal. In fact, Dan wouldn't exist.

Her eyes widened. His urgency suddenly became clear to her. But again, how could he know something like this? Had time altered again? What things in history had changed because of Aimee's time travel? Had something else occurred to alter her future . . . in the past? Jana groaned in frustration. This was too much to wrap her head around.

"I did some investigating after you gave me that journal. I've been hiking the Madison Valley and the surrounding mountains, trying to find clues to my ancestors' past. The area where their cabin stood is a parking lot now, as you know. But I finally found something." He hesitated.

"What?" Jana felt compelled to ask, even though she knew he would tell her at any moment.

"Jana, I think I found Aimee's grave. And it's dated 1811."

DAN SPOTTED JANA INSTANTLY. He could easily pick her out of a crowd, just like that first time he saw her. She walked quickly through the glass doors into the lobby of the Old Faithful Visitor Center, her long slim legs accentuated by the form-fitting jeans she wore. In one fluid motion, she removed the sunglasses from her face and shook her head slightly. Her chestnut hair tumbled around her face. It was longer than he remembered when he'd met her that one and only time two months ago. She'd looked so sad at the time, sitting in one of the couches positioned around the large fireplace that took up the center of the Inn.

He'd just returned from a day hike, taking several of Yellowstone's first visitors of the season on a trek to Shoshone Lake, south of Old Faithful. Dan enjoyed those hikes. They made his job as a seasonal park ranger and inter-preter more pleasurable than duty at the Old Faithful Visitor Center Information Desk that he was assigned to at the moment. He would rather be out on the trail, backpacking the wilderness, or leading a group of eager hikers to learn more about Yellowstone's ecosystem.

Thankful that his colleague, Art Tanner, was dealing with the only visitor asking questions at the moment, Dan stepped out from behind the desk and moved across the hall to meet the pretty girl from California. His heart rate actually increased. He'd only seen her once, but the memory of her face had been engrained in his mind since that day and he hadn't been able to stop thinking about her.

"Jana," he called, a wide smile on his face. She turned her head in his direction. Recognition filled her eyes and she hurried toward him. God, she was as gorgeous as he remem-bered her. He held out his hand. She hesitated for a second, then placed her dainty hand in his. She smiled, but it looked forced. Why did he get the distinct impression that he made her nervous? He'd gotten a similar vibe two months ago, but it was much more pronounced now. He wondered what her reaction would be when he brought up his reason for asking her to come back to Yellowstone.

"I'm glad you could make it," he said, leading her away

from the middle of the lobby. Everyone wanted to talk to a ranger, and his uniform drew people to him quicker than bees to honey. After Old Faithful went off in about ten minutes, this place would be packed. Better to duck out of here now, while he still had the chance.

"I'm taking a break, Art," he called to his colleague at the desk. Art glanced up briefly. He held up his hand, indicating he had understood, then returned his attention to a map splayed out before him, pointing at various things to a tourist with a squirming toddler riding on his shoulder.

Jana followed him silently out the back doors leading to the paved path to Old Faithful. Hundreds of people had already gathered to watch the famous geyser erupt. Dan guided Jana to one of several park benches overlooking the path in front of the visitor center, and motioned for her to sit.

They sat in awkward silence for a few minutes, watching people rush by. Moms pushed strollers with screaming toddlers in them and dads fumbled for their cameras. Just another day in Yellowstone. What he wouldn't give for some peace and solitude. His days off were spent hiking the back-country, usually alone, but sometimes with fellow seasonal rangers who preferred the lesser traveled paths as much as he did.

Someday, after he finished his master's degree in Wildlife Biology at the University of Montana, he hoped to gain permanent employment in the park, not merely seasonal. Then he might not be relegated to desk duty most of the time. It was a nice dream. Full time ranger positions were few and hard to come by.

"Okay, Dan," Jana broke the silence. She held her hands clasped together in her lap so tightly, her knuckles turned white. She was definitely uncomfortable. "Where is this grave you say you found?"

"Up on Purple Mountain. I can take you there, if you'd like." He smiled and waited for some sort of response. She shook her head almost imperceptibly, confusion in her eyes. Did she even know the hike he was talking about? He'd made an assumption that Jana was a hiker, based on the boots and hiking pants she'd worn two months ago. But what did he really know about her?

"I've got the next two days off, so you and I can discuss what to do," he continued. "Traded with one of my colleagues after you told me you'd be here today. How was the flight into Jackson?"

"Fine." Jana's forehead wrinkled. "Thanks for getting me a room here at the Lodge. I've never actually stayed in a hotel in the park. Aimee and I usually . . ." She didn't finish her thought.

She met his eyes briefly and inhaled deeply. She looked past him, presumably to watch the herd of people rushing to see Old Faithful go off. At this point, the view would be so obscured by the hundreds of souls who had secured front row seats since the last show, it was hardly worth it. But that was just his opinion.

The faraway, painful look in her eyes when she mentioned Aimee's name spoke volumes. She obviously still missed her friend dearly. Hopefully he could use that to his advantage. He should just get right to the point with Jana, rather than make small talk. She might just walk away if he told her what he proposed to do.

He cleared his throat. "Jana, I'm still trying to wrap my head around this time travel business. If Aimee . . . my great great great great grandmother . . ." He paused. Jana sucked in a deep breath. Perhaps he shouldn't have referred to her friend as his ancestor. "If she died shortly after she went to the past, how can I be alive? How is it that I even exist?"

Jana shook her head. "I've been wondering that myself,

Dan. There has to be some mistake. That grave you found, maybe it's not a grave."

"What if time altered again? What if something else happened than what should have happened originally?" He ran his hand through his short hair. "This time travel stuff is really hard to make sense of. But if time got changed somehow, when Aimee dies in the past, I won't exist anymore in this time. Does that make sense?"

"Yes, I see what you're saying, but there's absolutely no way of knowing anything. There's nothing we can do." Jana met his stare for the first time. She didn't look away for once, and concern was evident on her face. Dan's gut tightened involuntarily.

He took a deep breath. He reached for her hand, and held to it when she stiffened. Her hand was so small in his, her skin a much lighter shade than his natural olive complexion. Without thinking, he caressed her palm with his thumb. A subtle tingling sensation crept up his arm, originating in his fingers.

"Yes. There is something we can do," he said, clearing his throat. She cocked her head slightly, her brows narrowing in a silent question.

"Help me find that time travel device, Jana. Go back to the past with me and help me save my grandmother, your best friend. Help me save my life . . . my future."

CHAPTER TWO

*J*ana paced the floor in front of the large king sized bed in her hotel room. She'd never stepped foot inside the Yellowstone Snow Lodge before, much less spent the night in one of the rooms here. She could only imagine how expensive one of these rooms was, and Dan had already paid for her to stay a full week. She wondered how he could afford such luxury on his seasonal park ranger salary. When she'd offered to reimburse him, he'd quickly declined.

The rustic wooden table, chairs, and matching bed frame accentuated the wildlife artwork that hung on the wood-paneled walls. The bedspread was an earth-tone woodlands pattern of alternating pine trees and moose silhouettes. The entire room looked like a miniature cabin.

Jana gazed out at the wooded landscape beyond her window. The brief conversation with Dan earlier had left her head spinning. The way he'd held her hand, and his thumb stroking her palm, had sent odd chills along her spine. She was glad when several inquisitive tourists had interrupted them a few minutes into their conversation, and Dan returned to duty. He'd told her he'd pick her up after his shift and they could continue their discussion over dinner.

Alone for the moment, Jana's mind reeled with everything he'd said. She still couldn't imagine how it was possible that Aimee could have died so soon after her return to 1810. Daniel, her husband, was with her. Surely, he wouldn't have let any harm come to her. The man was so deeply in love with Aimee, Jana was sure he would have lain down his own life before he'd let her get hurt. And how was it even possible? The few sketchy historical accounts Jana had been able to dig up on the internet revealed the descendants of Aimee and Daniel as being prominent in the founding of Yellowstone as a national park.

It just didn't make any sense. Jana shook her head. Then again, time travel didn't make any sense, either, but she couldn't deny the fact that it was real. That weird-looking magical device that made it all a reality – who knew where it came from? Jana's mind conjured up all sorts of ideas about aliens or some ancient higher power.

She'd never been a superstitious person who believed in all that hocus-pocus. She'd always been firmly rooted in science and fact. Supernatural forces just didn't fit into her orderly world. But since time travel was undeniably real, then maybe something had happened to change the historical time line again. Even Einstein's theory of relativity proved that time travel, at least moving forward in time, was a possibility. According to Einstein, time was simply a direction in space. Time was relative. Therefore, things could change. Time could change. Jana sank onto the bed and stared at the ceiling.

Dan's idea of going back in time to . . . to do what? How could they save Aimee when they had no idea what they needed to save her from, or when exactly she died? And how were they ever even going to find the time travel device in the first place? It could be anywhere. And if history had changed again, would the time travel device still be where Aimee had left it originally?

Jana groaned in frustration. Right now, she simply wanted to be back home, in her bed, and wake up from this nightmare. There would be no time traveling, no magical snake heads, no gorgeous mountain men from the past, or their equally gorgeous park ranger descendants. She and Aimee would go to work at the hospital each day, and plan their semi-annual backpacking trips.

Aimee had probably looked forward to those trips more than Jana, but her best friend's sense of adventure had always been infectious. While Aimee was the bold and adventurous one, Jana was rather quiet and reserved. Too serious about everything, Aimee had always said.

Smiling softly, she stared at the patterns on the wooden ceiling. Jana had certainly had a lot to say in Aimee's defense months ago. Once, when confronting Zach Osborne at the hospital, after he'd come back from the past suddenly after forcing Aimee's return to the twenty-first century. Aimee had been heartbroken after she'd been wrenched away from Daniel, and Jana remembered giving the old mountain man – Daniel's father – a piece of her mind.

Another time Jana had actually confronted Daniel Osborne himself. A rather unwise move, she thought now. If she hadn't been so mad at the injustice dealt to Aimee when Daniel had coldly rejected her and had accused her of lying to him, she would have realized that threatening a dark and formidable man like Daniel was not a good idea. Both times, Jana had been defending her best friend. She knew without a doubt she would do anything for Aimee. Jana inhaled deeply and squeezed her eyes shut.

How on earth am I supposed to help you now, Aimee?

Jana and Aimee had been best friends since early childhood. They complemented each other well. Aimee was pretty, outgoing, and popular with the boys. Everything seemed to always come natural to her. While Jana'd had her share of boyfriends in high school and college, she always felt it was more because she was Aimee's friend.

Aimee's leaving had created a deep void in Jana's life that she hadn't been able to fill. Several break-ups with guys she had no interest in was all she had to show for her ten months of living on her own. She hadn't even been able to get out of the city to do some hiking. The backpacking, the wilderness adventures, those were all Aimee's passions.

Not that Jana didn't like the outdoors. She loved camping, hiking, and doing all the crazy survival stuff Aimee enjoyed, but she wasn't quite as passionate about it. She could just as easily find thrills and excitement sitting at a beach somewhere, soaking up the sun and reading a good book.

In short, she was a boring person who liked doing boring things. She hastily swiped at a tear that rolled down the side of her face. She certainly lived an unexciting life now, since Aimee began her new life with Daniel.

Jana shook her head. Her quiet existence was certainly upended once again. The farfetched idea of going back in time didn't scare her half as much as spending time with Dan Osborne. Chills of dread and apprehension ran down her spine. He was too ruggedly good-looking, and he was Aimee's descendant. She couldn't be attracted to him. It just seemed so . . . wrong.

Jana scoffed. She shouldn't worry too much about it. Dan had only called her because of Aimee and the journal. Once they figured out what to do, if there was even anything they could do, she'd go back to her condo in California, and he would live his life in Yellowstone. *Just like Aimee.*

Jana squeezed her eyes shut, trying in vain to get the images of Dan's heart stopping smile when he'd greeted her earlier out of her mind. Her palm where his thumb had stroked her began to tingle at the memory.

DAN STEPPED out of the tiny shower that was no larger than a phone booth, and lifted a towel to his head as water ran down his face and chest. The dull ring of his cellphone interrupted his attempt at drying off. He hastily wrapped the towel around his waist. His two roommates weren't home yet, but just in case, he didn't need to be running through the tiny barrack buck-naked. Pulling the door open to the bathroom that was barely the size of a closet, he stumbled to his room across the narrow hall. It took all of four strides from the bathroom, across the hall, and into his room to reach his bunk. Fumbling for his pants that he'd tossed on the floor earlier, he pulled his cellphone from the back pocket. "Yeah," he answered, putting an end to the incessant ringing.

"Is the girl here?"

Dan frowned. He'd only answered the call because he thought it might have been Jana, wondering what was keeping him. He was already late. Tourists at the visitor center had him detained way after his shift, and he'd told Jana he'd pick her up at seven. It was well past that time already.

Dan clenched his jaw and dropped his pants to the floor. "Yeah, she's here," he answered slowly.

"And? Is she going to help you?" The voice at the other end sounded much too eager.

"I'm not sure yet." Dan drew his eyebrows together.

"Well, just use your charm and good looks to win her over. She's not married, is she? Or has a boyfriend?"

Dan paused. He didn't remember seeing a ring on her finger. "No, I don't think so." The thought bothered him. It wasn't something he'd even considered before. He was fairly sure she wasn't married, but did Jana have a boyfriend? Maybe if she did, she would have brought him along. If she were his girlfriend, he certainly wouldn't let her rush off to meet another man a thousand miles away.

"Well, then it should be no problem. Remember, your future depends on this."

Dan clenched and unclenched his jaw, running a hand through his damp hair. He yanked open the drawer of the nightstand next to his bunk, pulling out a fresh pair of boxers. The caller was getting on his nerves. Dan was well aware what was at stake here. He didn't need to be reminded. He inhaled deeply, and expelled the air through his mouth, then ran his hand through his hair. "Yeah, I know," he said slowly. "I gotta go."

Dan didn't wait for a reply. He tapped the disconnect button on his phone and stared out the window, absorbing the tranquility of the lodgepole pines beyond his barrack. Here at least, at the residential compound for the seasonal rangers, things were relatively quiet, as opposed to the city-like hustle and bustle around the commercialism of the Old Faithful visitor area.

Last summer, he'd been assigned to Canyon. He much preferred it there, even though it was also a busy tourist hub. Here at Old Faithful, it was even worse. He'd applied for a backcountry ranger position for the last three years in a row, but hadn't been successful in landing one of those coveted positions. Four months of complete solitude, living in a cabin miles and miles away from anyone, would be a dream come true, almost as good as landing a full time ranger position.

Dan heaved a sigh. If things went the way he hoped, he just might get to experience peace and solitude real soon. His heart rate accelerated at the idea. To go back in time, live like his ancestors for a few days, or a few weeks. It all seemed too good to be true. And once he came back to this time, his future here in the park would be secure.

Quickly, he pulled on his boxers, jeans, and a green t-shirt, and ran a comb through his hair. For a moment, he stared at his reflection in the small mirror hanging over the equally small bathroom sink.

You're nervous, Osborne.

He grinned and shook his head. Hell, yeah he was nervous. The last time he remembered his heart pounding faster, thinking about going out with a girl, had been seven years ago when he asked Cindy Weston to the senior prom. This was a different nervous, he told himself firmly. Everything was riding on convincing Jana to help him find that time travel device.

Dan chuckled and pulled his well-worn hiking boots on. When was the last time he'd gone out on a date? He didn't have time for dating. Or the money. He was up to his eyeballs in student loans and in a major that didn't guarantee him a well-paying job later on.

Girls wanted to be wined and dined, and he couldn't afford that. He couldn't remember the last girl who held his interest for more than a couple of dates. Until now. He hadn't even actually gone out with Jana, but he hadn't been able to get her out of his mind for the entire two months since he'd met her, and that had never happened to him before.

Most of the girls he'd dated in college could never see themselves with a guy whose idea of an exciting date was a weekend backpacking trip into the Yellowstone interior. The majority of the female seasonal rangers he met were either in relationships, or lived too far away once the summer was over to consider dating any of them.

Even if it was an informal date, having dinner with Jana put his nerves on edge. The last time he'd asked her if she wanted to grab a bite to eat was on the spur of the moment two months ago. From the first time he saw her, something had stirred in him, something he couldn't explain. He'd singled her out from all the other people in the lobby immediately, as if she'd leaped in front of him.

He hadn't even given himself time to think about his actions when he'd sat down next to her on the couch by the Inn's great big historic fireplace, asking her why she looked so sad. He certainly didn't make it a habit of asking pretty park tourists out to eat. He definitely couldn't have known that his impulsive behavior would change his life forever.

During their short time together, she'd abruptly told him she had to leave after dropping that bomb on him about his ancestors. He'd barely had enough time to get her phone number, and cursed his dumb luck that she lived so far away. If he hadn't been on duty the following morning, he would have had a lot more to drink to help him swallow everything she'd told him. She'd offered him the journal of a woman whom she claimed was his ancestor, and how Aimee Donovan had time traveled to marry his mountain man ancestor, Daniel Osborne.

Dan had committed most of the pages of that journal to memory. There were descriptions and personal accounts about Daniel Osborne in that journal, bringing the man he'd heard family stories about to life more vividly than the tales his grandfather used to tell him.

Dan had always been proud of his family's history here in Yellowstone. The fantastical idea that none of his family tree would be around if not for the impossibility that a woman from this time had traveled to the past was still something he couldn't quite wrap his head around. He'd long given up wondering where that time travel snakehead could possibly come from. He didn't want to know the answer.

What he really did want to know, what he needed to know – where was that device now?

Dan ran a hand through his hair, and headed out the door. Jana Evans was his key to finding that device. She had to be. His entire future depended on it.

CHAPTER THREE

$\mathcal{J}$ana stood in front of the bathroom mirror and ran her brush through her hair. She didn't know whether to just let it hang free, or put it back in a ponytail. Dan hadn't mentioned where they would be going for dinner. Not that she expected him to wine and dine her, but if he had plans to go somewhere other than the informal restaurants here at Old Faithful, she didn't want to look like a bum, either. She hadn't changed out of the jeans and simple cotton t-shirt she'd worn on her flight here. Casual dress was her preference, and if she didn't have to leave the room anymore this evening, she would be lounging in her pajamas right now.

A loud knock on the room door broke the silence. She dropped her brush in the sink with a loud clank.

"Good grief, Jana. Get a grip," she mumbled. Her heart sped up as if she'd just run a marathon, and her legs turned to jelly. She glanced at her reflection in the mirror one last time. Too late to gather her hair in a ponytail.

"Jana, you need to smile more. The world doesn't always have

to be so serious. You are beautiful, and I wish you'd stop thinking so negatively about yourself all the time."

Aimee's words echoed in her mind. Aimee had always told her the right man would come along someday. For a fleeting moment, the thought entered her mind that Mr. Right stood outside her hotel room door this very minute.

Ridiculous! You know nothing about him, other than he's Aimee's great great great great grandson.

Jana inhaled a deep breath and expelled the air slowly through parted lips. No matter how much she tried to relax, her heart would not stop hammering away against her ribcage. She raked her teeth across her lower lip and opened the hotel room door. Dan Osborne stood before her, his hand held up in a fist, apparently ready to knock again.

"Sorry I'm late." He lowered his hand, and his mouth widened in a grin that made Jana groan silently as her heart fluttered in her chest.

"Oh, no problem," she blurted out and smiled nervously. She quickly took note of his clothes - jeans and a t-shirt that hugged the contours of his physique much too well. While his ranger uniform had hinted at broad shoulders and a well-muscled chest, the green shirt he wore now left no doubt he was lean and well sculpted. Jana's mouth went dry. Dan's eyebrows rose and his forehead wrinkled as he sent her a questioning look when she didn't say anything else.

"So. Are you ready?" he asked, breaking the awkward silence.

"Um, sorry. Let me get my shoes," she stammered, and turned hastily into the room. She hoped he hadn't noticed her face, which must be flaming red at this point, judging by the heat creeping up her neck. Dear God, she would never survive this evening without making a complete fool of herself.

Too late, she realized she should have invited him in. Her

nerves were getting the better of her. Maybe she could feign a sudden illness and tell him she couldn't go out to dinner after all.

"Can I come in?" he called, still standing in the hall.

"Oh . . . sure." Jana cringed. The door closed behind her with a soft click.

"Did you bring hiking boots?" Dan asked. She turned, and chanced a look at him. He stood, eyeing his surroundings. Apparently, he was just as impressed with the nice room as she had been earlier.

"Yes. I figured I'd need them to go see Aimee's . . . the spot you thought was her grave." She turned to face him. She noticed the daypack he had slung over one shoulder.

"You might want to wear them," he suggested when she reached for her sandals at the foot of the bed.

"Now?" she echoed. "Isn't it too late to hike Purple Mountain?"

"It is. I'm taking you to dinner, remember?" His smile sent renewed adrenaline through her veins. He pulled the pack from his shoulder, and held it out. "Dinner's in here," he said before she had time to wonder at the gesture.

"We're eating trail mix?" she asked, hoping her attempt at following Aimee's advice to lighten up didn't come across as too stupid-sounding.

Dan laughed. "I may be a cheap date, but hopefully not that cheap. Local burgers were all I could come up with. But for my lack of gourmet fare, I hope the ambiance will make up for it."

"Ambiance?" Jana swallowed nervously. His inference that this was a date sent another rush of warmth through her system.

"Yeah. I hope you'll like it."

Curious, but afraid to ask what he was talking about, Jana sat on the bed and pulled on her hiking boots. While she tied them, Dan continued to survey the room. "I hope this is comfortable enough for you," he said, pushing aside the curtain to look out the window. He had slung his pack over one shoulder again.

"This is really too much. I could have just as easily stayed in a motel room outside the park." Jana stood and grabbed for a wool sweater she'd hung in the closet earlier. She stared at Dan's back. His shirt hugged him like a second skin along his shoulder blades, defining the muscles along either side of his spine. He turned, and her eyes quickly darted to the ground, hoping he hadn't caught her staring.

"Ready?" he asked and moved to open the door for her. She realized he hadn't responded to her comment. He stood aside, and waited for her to step out of the room ahead of him. His hand lightly touched her lower back as he followed her into the hall. She suppressed a gasp. His warm hand might as well have been a hot iron as it sent coils of heat radiating up her back, down her legs, and around her waist, to settle in the pit of her stomach. She fumbled in her pocket for the room key.

With her nerves on edge at her heated reaction to his simple touch, Jana followed Dan as he walked briskly down the hall, through the lobby, and out into the bright early evening sunshine. He cut a sharp right along the sidewalk, and headed across the parking lot toward the visitor center. She broke into a jog to keep up with his long, confident strides.

"Where are we going?" she finally asked when they skirted the visitor center and headed for the boardwalks leading to the Upper Geyser Basin. He seemed to be in quite a hurry.

Dan slowed, and glanced over his shoulder. He waited for her to catch up with him.

"If we hurry, we'll be able to see Old Faithful erupt."

There was a boyish enthusiasm in his voice. *Aimee's enthusiasm*. No matter how many times she'd seen Old Faithful erupt, the idea of seeing it again had excited her every time.

"But we're right here." Jana swept her arm to their left. Old Faithful's sinter cone stood like a solitary sentinel several hundred feet away, steam and occasional sprays of water belching from the opening. The benches that lined the boardwalk were already filled with people, but at this hour, the number of spectators was far fewer than earlier in the day.

Dan grinned and his eyes lit up like a little boy at Christmas time. Jana's mouth suddenly went dry.

"Have you ever seen it go off from Observation Point?" he asked.

Jana emitted a short laugh. "I've probably been on almost every hiking trail here in the park, and more backpacking trails than I can count. Aimee was obsessed with this place."

Dan's eyebrows rose and the gleam of admiration in his eyes sent a flutter through her chest. His lips curved in a lazy grin. He let his shoulders slump in a feigned defeated gesture.

"Well, there goes my surprise then. But since I don't have a Plan B, could you please act impressed when we get to the top?"

His easy-going manner and natural smile were infectious. Jana nodded. Dan reached for her hand and pulled her along with him. Her palms began to sweat. She couldn't extract her hand free from his firm grip. Some small part of her enjoyed the gesture as she noticed several women they passed flash appreciative looks at him.

Get a hold of yourself, Jana. He's not your boyfriend. He's merely trying to hurry you along.

He walked briskly down the asphalt walk toward the boardwalks that led to the back geyser basin and turned right toward the river. They crossed the wooden footbridge over the Firehole River, and instead of following the path to the left that led to the geyser basin, he turned right up a dirt path where a trail marker indicated that this was the Observation Point Trailhead.

The trail began up a gentle incline, heading up and into a lodgepole forest, and Dan slowed and motioned for her to walk ahead of him. He released her hand, and Jana rubbed her damp palms together. Her hand still tingled from his touch.

The trail switchbacked up the mountain and became gradually steeper. Jana picked her way up the incline, determined not to slow him down. The high altitude air left her feeling dizzy and winded. She inhaled deep, steady breaths. The fragrant scent of pine, damp earth, and sweet grass overpowered the more acrid sulfurous odors the nearby geysers emitted. Every now and then when they hit a particular steep section, Dan's hand on her lower back propelled her to greater effort to navigate the half-mile of switchbacks, simply to avoid him touching her. His light touches as he assisted her up the hill sent her mind spinning, and left her nerves on edge.

They reached the top of the hill in silence. Trying to take enough of the thin air into her demanding lungs, she breathed as hard as if she'd just completed a five-mile run at home. She took in the breathtaking view of the valley before her. It had been a while since she'd last stood in this spot, and certainly not at sunset. The entire geyser basin was visible from here through the tops of the pine trees, the bright orange sun on the horizon magnifying the brilliant colors of reds, oranges, and greens of many of the geyser run-offs. People walked the boardwalks, and several of the smaller geysers suffused the air with their steam and jetting water sprays, veiling parts of the valley far below in a misty white.

"At this time, there's rarely anyone up here," Dan said. "I

figured this would be a better place to talk than in a crowded restaurant." Jana turned, startled to find him standing directly behind her. His lips curved upward. "And you can't beat the view."

His eyes held hers, his last words spoken in a low tone. Jana's heart rate sped up anew, having just recovered from her trek up the hill. She inhaled a lung full of air, drawing in his clean scent. She got the distinct impression he wasn't referring to the scenery. Jana blinked, and merely nodded. A rustle in the nearby brush was a welcome distraction to the man standing before her. A marmot scurried off a large boulder, emitting a loud whistling sound in apparent protest of the human invasion to its territory.

Dan's deep brown eyes lingered on her face. Jana found it difficult to breathe. Her throat constricted almost painfully, and she tried to swallow away the imaginary lump. Finally breaking eye contact, he headed for a downed log that had obviously served as a resting place for countless other visitors, and peeled his pack from his shoulder. He pulled out two cardboard boxes, and Jana's stomach grumbled in answer to the delicious smell of burgers and fries. The odor of deep fried food seemed so out of place here, among the pine and sage.

"Did you know that the Shoshone that lived here considered marmots a delicacy?" he asked, handing her a plastic soda bottle. Jana sat on the log, and took a long drink. "They called them whistle dogs."

"I can hear why they called them that," Jana said. "And no, I didn't know they were a delicacy. I don't think I could bring myself to eat something as cute as a marmot." She unwrapped the cheeseburger Dan handed her. About to take a bite, she stopped and eyed the food in her hand. "These are beef burgers, right?"

Dan grinned. "You'll never know the difference," he said

26

conspiratorially, kneeling beside her. "You'd be surprised what you might eat in a survival situation."

"I've eaten my share of nasty stuff," Jana said between bites. "The survival courses Aimee and I took were pretty demanding sometimes. But I never resorted to killing something cute and fluffy."

Dan stared up at her. His eyes visibly darkened. There was something familiar in their depths. They were the same color she remembered Daniel's eyes to be, but the intensity and seriousness were missing in this modern version of that feral mountain man.

In desperate need to focus on something other than the man squatting next to her, Jana readjusted the paper wrapper around her burger, and took a bite. She chewed and forced the food down past the lump in her throat. Fearing she might choke, she reached for her soda that she'd set on the ground in front of her. Dan got to it first. Her hand grazed his for a mere second, but the contact was like an electric jolt. Tingles raced up her arm, and she shivered when the sensation shot down her back. How could he affect her so deeply? Apparently unperturbed, Dan handed her the soda.

"Would you have done it?" he asked suddenly.

Jana's forehead wrinkled. She took the bottle from him, careful to avoid touching him. "Done what?"

"Stayed in the past." Dan placed his hand on her knee, and Jana took a hasty drink from the bottle.

"I . . . I don't know," she stammered. *If I had met a man like you, I might have.*

"Jana, I have to find that time travel device." His grip on her knee intensified. His facial features took on a surreal intensity. For a split second, it was Daniel who knelt beside her.

In the valley below, the collective oohs and aahs of the crowd pulled Jana's gaze away from him. Old Faithful was putting on its timeless show. The enormous fountain of water shot high up in the air, enveloped in a veil-like cloud of steam in the cool evening breeze. From their high vantage point, it seemed even grander than watching the spectacle from ground level. Dan removed his hand from Jana's knee, and stood to his feet.

Although her eyes focused on one of nature's most amazing displays, her awareness remained fully on the man beside her. He was asking the impossible, but how could she not try and help him?

CHAPTER FOUR

"*I*t's right around here somewhere. It's been well concealed for two hundred years." Dan swept a large stick through some dense brush and foliage from the overgrown vegetation, pushing aside the tall grasses with his foot. Jana stood right behind him. She'd been looking around with wide eyes when he'd suddenly left the trail just before they reached the top of the mountain.

They'd made good time coming up the steep Purple Mountain Trail. Dan continued to be impressed with Jana. He'd been pleasantly surprised yesterday when he'd found out that she was not only a hiker, but had backpacked in the park extensively. After watching Old Faithful go off last night, they'd strolled the back geyser basin until the sun finally dropped behind the mountains. He still couldn't put his finger on the reason why she seemed so edgy around him.

Jana had relaxed somewhat when she began to tell him about his ancestor, how Aimee had loved Yellowstone, and had found her destiny when she went back in time. The way

Jana talked about her gave Dan a deeper understanding of his own love for this park.

Your gut was telling you something that first time you saw her.

He still couldn't explain what had drawn him to Jana that afternoon at the Inn. Fate. Karma. Whatever it was, the more time he spent with Jana Evans, the more he liked her, and not just because she was a pretty girl and looked good in tight jeans. She was different from other girls he'd dated. Quiet. Reserved. Serious. Maybe a bit too serious. Over the years, he'd gotten so tired of women acting flirty and pretentious, painting their faces with makeup and changing the color of their hair more frequently than the clothes they wore, it seemed.

Jana was down-to-earth. Natural. With the sun shining on her auburn hair just right, some strands shimmered almost copper, like the coat of a sleek chestnut horse. Her amber eyes were as soft and expressive as a doe's, and he got the impression that there was a lot behind those eyes that she kept hidden. That she was an experienced backpacker was like icing on the cake.

Dan cursed silently. He had his future to think about. He couldn't allow his hormones or romantic notions interfere with what he had to do. Memories of the most pleasant evening he'd spent in the company of a girl in a long time sent heat creeping through him now. On their walk the night before, they'd passed several couples – both young and old - holding hands, and some openly showing their affection for each other. Twilight in Yellowstone seemed to bring out the romantic in a lot of people. Dan had firmly kept his arms at his sides and his hands stuffed in his jeans pockets. The urge to hold Jana's hand while they talked and took in the scenery, to pretend he was on a real date, had hit him with such force, he finally cut their stroll short and headed back in the direction of the lodge.

How many times over the past two months had he dialed her number, only to lose his nerve and hang up after the first ring? Visions of her had tormented him late into the night for weeks after their one meeting, visions of her sitting alone and sad amongst a sea of people at the Inn's lobby. He simply hadn't been able to get her out of his mind, and not because they shared a common link. He'd found the perfect excuse to finally bring her back here, and guilt nagged him to no end. After spending a nice evening in her company, his initial feelings for her from their first encounter had only intensified.

He couldn't allow himself to act on his attraction to her. At least not at the moment. Once he knew his future was secure, then perhaps . . .

"How did you ever find this spot?" Jana asked from behind him. "I mean, we're off trail, and there's overgrown brambles everywhere."

Dan turned to look over his shoulder at her. Shrugging, he said, "Luck? Something just drew me here."

He straightened, and gazed out at the vast valley far below them. In this location, they stood higher than National Park Mountain on the other side of the valley, and could easily see the smoke plumes from the lower geyser basins ten miles to the south. The green-carpeted Madison Valley appeared below them to the west. Dan's gaze followed the Gibbon River as it swept in a large U-shape arch into the valley. The Firehole roared out of the canyon to the south. The two rivers looked like tiny ribbons of shimmering blue, then met up to converge into the slightly wider Madison.

"This looks like a spot where I'd want to be buried," Dan said, grinning at Jana. Somehow she didn't seem convinced that he had found Aimee's final resting place here. She glanced around, doubt etched on her face.

"You don't think Aimee would have wanted to be buried

somewhere where she could oversee this entire valley?" he prodded.

Jana slowly shook her head. "I can't believe Aimee wanted to be buried anywhere," she said softly.

"What do you mean?" He frowned. An alarming jolt of adrenaline shot through his system at her words. What if he couldn't convince her?

Jana shrugged. She looked at him, but only briefly before her focus returned to the dense shrubbery behind him. "She always talked about having her ashes scattered over the Lower Falls. That's what she would have wanted. I think Daniel would have known that."

"Maybe it's not something they discussed," he suggested quickly. "Two young people, recently married, wouldn't have their minds on death and dying so soon into their relationship, would they?" He raised his eyebrows at her.

"I don't know," she muttered.

In an effort to divert her attention away from her thoughts of doubt, Dan resumed his scouring of the underbrush.

"There," he called suddenly. He pried apart the heavy undergrowth to give Jana a better view. She scrambled up next to him to stare into the shaded area he'd uncovered. Dan drew in a deep breath. The air was infused with the pungent, rich smell of earth mixed with the soft scent of lavender from Jana's hair. He knelt to the ground and swept his hand over some rocks that had obviously been placed there. They were not random, as one would find them in nature, but placed in a neat cluster butted up against the trunk of a lodgepole pine. Decades of decaying vegetation had left behind a rich soil, which now covered up most of the area, but he managed to clear away enough dirt for Jana to see the carved inscription in one of the rocks. Natural weathering had obscured the writing, but the name *Aimee*, and the number *1811* was clearly legible. There appeared to be more carving, but age had weathered the rock to the point that it was illegible. Jana gasped.

"I left it as undisturbed as I found it the first time," Dan said. "I didn't want someone else to stumble onto this spot."

Jana held her hand over her mouth, and her eyes pooled with tears. Quickly, she stepped away from the spot and turned her back. Dan rose to his feet. Hesitating, he placed his hand on her shoulder.

"Hey," he said softly. Jana stiffened. She took a step forward, away from him, and his grip tightened in an effort to make her stay. She froze. What would she do if he pulled her into his arms? Turning in his direction, her large amber eyes stared up at him. Dan swallowed, and he dropped his arm. Involuntarily, he took a step closer. He breathed in the lavender scent of her hair, the clean smell of freshly laundered clothes, and a subtle hint of a flowery fragrance he couldn't name.

"You still miss her, don't you?" he whispered. His hands clenched into fists at his side. God, he wanted to pull her to him, wipe away the pain in her eyes, kiss her full lips. He couldn't risk it. Not now.

Get your mind on straight, Osborne. You can't lose your focus.

Jana nodded almost imperceptibly, and inhaled a shuddering breath. Abruptly, she moved around him and scrambled up the slight incline back to the trail. He stood, rooted to the spot, and simply watched her. What was going through her mind? Did she believe that this could be Aimee's final resting place? He'd been quite surprised himself when he stumbled onto this spot a couple of weeks ago. He didn't know whether to believe if this was a grave, but it was the perfect story to lure Jana back to Yellowstone. She seemed quite skeptical.

Is your future worth deceiving her?

He heaved a sigh, and followed Jana up the hill, his mind wracked with guilt.

"How do you know that's even a grave?" she asked, her voice raspy, when he'd barely caught up with her. She swiped a hasty hand over her eyes. "It could be something else entirely. Maybe Daniel simply carved her name in a rock, and dated it."

"You're right," he conceded. "But what if it is a grave? I don't want to gamble with my life like that. If I have the means to secure my own future, I want the chance to do that, Jana." At least that last part wasn't a lie. He stepped in front of her, and gripped her upper arms for emphasis. "Can you understand that?"

"Yes," she said, after a prolonged silence. He reluctantly released her arms. She glanced down the incline, toward the now-trampled brambles. Finally, she looked up at him, and said, "I'll help you find that device. I just don't have a clue where to even begin to look."

Dan closed his eyes for a split second, and drew in a breath of relief. He smiled down at her, and silently formed the words *thank you* on his lips.

"Why did you leave so quickly?" he asked before he could stop himself.

Her forehead wrinkled. "Leave?"

"Two months ago. Why didn't you stay another day?" He almost reached for her hand, but stopped himself just in time by shoving his own hand in the back pocket of his jeans instead.

This isn't the time, Osborne.

"I needed to get back home. I only took a few days off from work," she said quickly and avoided looking at him. He didn't believe her for a second, but decided to let it go for now. He stepped away from her and peeled his backpack off his shoulders.

"Let's put our heads together and see what we can figure out," he suggested casually, hoping to hide the turmoil inside him, and motioned for her to sit on a downed log to the side of the trail.

He handed her a water bottle from his pack, and a bag of trail mix. When she shot him a surprised look, he couldn't help but grin.

"You suggested trail mix last night, remember?" His grin widened.

For the first time since he met her, Jana's face lit up in a bright smile. The breath left his lungs. She was radiant when she smiled. The sun high above them reflected in her amber eyes, making them appear almost golden. Dan sat several feet away from her on the log and placed his backpack on his lap. It wouldn't do for her to see the effect she had on him. He took a long drink from his own water bottle.

"I didn't tell you this last night, but I hate nuts," Jana said, obviously trying to suppress a giggle.

Dan frowned. "Excuse me?" He nearly choked on his water. He kicked himself mentally. *She's referring to the food, you idiot.* Dan groaned silently. Jana was playing havoc with his mind, and this was only the second day spent in her company.

"Well, ah. . ." He cleared his throat. "You can always pick out the raisins and other bits of dried fruit." Not even as an awkward teenager had he felt like such a bumbling fool. He ventured a glance at the girl sitting a few mere feet from him. She cradled the plastic bag between her hands in her lap, and stared out at the distant mountains. Although the smile had left her face, Dan sensed she was more relaxed than she had been the night before.

His eyes followed her line of vision, and minutes passed in silence. The swooshing sounds of ravens flapping their wings as they flew from tree top to tree top, their deep clucking sounds amplified by the peaceful tranquility of the mountain, mixed with the rush of the wind through the tops of the tallest lodgepoles. In a nearby tree, a couple of squirrels chattered loudly. They seemed to be engaged in a heated argument, probably over territory rights.

Dan stuck his hand in Jana's trail mix bag, and pulled out a handful of peanuts and almonds. "Maybe Aimee left the device somewhere along Hellroaring Creek, just like the journal," he finally ventured a guess, breaking the silence.

"No," Jana said immediately. "She wouldn't leave it somewhere that obvious." The plastic bag rustled as Jana dug through the nuts and seeds to find some morsels of dried fruit. She stopped abruptly, and looked at him. "Do you realize this is more impossible than trying to find a needle in a haystack?"

"What is?" He gestured at the bag in her hand. "Finding the raisins in the bag, or the time travel device somewhere within two million acres of wilderness?" He grinned at the annoyed look she shot him.

"Aimee mentioned in her journal that the device would never be found again. She didn't want anyone to find it for good reason. Imagine what could happen if someone got a hold of that device. The problems it could cause in the wrong hands."

Dan coughed, nearly choking on the nuts he was chewing. After taking a long drink from his water bottle, he stared straight at her.

"You're my only chance, Jana. You knew her the best, and if anyone can figure out what she might have done with that device, it's you. I have complete confidence that you'll figure it out." Their eyes met and held, and Dan wished for the thousandth time that he could have asked her back to Yellowstone under different circumstances.

CHAPTER FIVE

*J*ana pulled the covers higher up to her neck, and shifted her body on the unfamiliar mattress. Somewhere in the chasm between sleep and wakefulness, her body shuddered involuntarily. Aimee's presence was so vivid, Jana didn't want to wake just yet, and lose the dream she was dreaming. She relaxed her head into the pillow, and drifted back to sleep.

In her dream, Jana inched slowly toward the mesh-wire fence that guarded the overlook of the raging waterfall. Aimee stood on her toes, leaning over the fence, staring straight down into the gaping scar in the earth more than three hundred feet below. Her long blonde hair whipped wildly around in all directions from the wind generated by the rushing river. The loud roar of the mighty Lower Falls of the Grand Canyon of the Yellowstone drowned out her laughter.

"Come on, Jana. Just try it once," Aimee called over her shoulder. Jana stood a few feet back, the tremendous power of the river as it plunged deep into the earth making her head spin with dizziness.

"You can feel the spray of the water. It's really quite refreshing," Aimee yelled, coaxing her onward. Jana took a tentative step closer to the edge. She was being silly, she knew. The fence was there to guard anyone from accidentally losing their balance. She'd always been a bit scared of heights, and the movement of the fast-flowing water was playing tricks with her mind. The entire cemented viewing platform felt as if it was floating, ready to tumble over the brink.

Jana grabbed for the fence and slowly peered over the edge. It was an awe-inspiring view. Millions of gallons of water spilled over the yawning cliff, plunging straight downward. The icy wind created by the river left thick patches of snow and ice clinging to the rocks of the canyon walls, even though it was well into July. Far below in the canyon, the turquoise water of the Yellowstone River continued its journey north after it's mighty plunge. The blue ribbon was in sharp contrast to the earthy hues of yellows and reds that adorned the canyon walls as if an artist had painted them there with broad brush strokes.

The cool air was a welcome reprieve from the warmth of the afternoon, and from the four-mile hike they had just completed along the canyon rim to reach this spot.

"No one could survive going over this waterfall," Aimee commented as they stood side by side, taking in the view. Odd how all surrounding sound suddenly ceased, including the deafening roar of the river. Aimee barely spoke above a whisper, but Jana heard her loud and clear. "The weight and force of the water alone would crush someone before they hit the rocks that are no doubt under all that spray."

The thought of accidentally falling into the river and being swept over the edge made Jana shudder.

"I bet a body would never be recovered here," Aimee continued. "Going over the edge would probably bury a person or object at the bottom of this fall forever. The weight of the water would pin you to the rocks for all eternity. It's the perfect final resting spot, don't you think? You'd never be found again."

Jana stared at her. Sometimes her best friend had the wildest imagination.

Aimee smiled brightly. "When I die, I want my ashes scattered over the falls," she said softly. "You'll make sure that happens someday, won't you, Jana?"

Jana merely nodded. This was not the place to be talking about death and dying. She took another brave step closer to the fence, and ventured to lean over like Aimee was doing. Her heart sped up. It was an exhilarating feeling. Her attention was focused on the heavy white spray of water as the river met with the rocks below, when a movement along the canyon wall caught her attention.

An Indian stood, balanced perfectly on a shallow outcropping near the very bottom of the falls. The dense mist enshrouded him, making him almost invisible. Jana leaned over further to get a better look. Were her eyes playing tricks on her? The Indian raised his hand, beckoning to her. Leaning even further over the fence, Jana lost her balance. She screamed as she went tumbling over the edge. She hit the frigid water of the falls, the force of the river dragging her under.

The sensation of millions of gallons of water crushing her like a tin can overpowered her. She couldn't move her arms or legs. She'd never reach the surface. If she didn't die crashing into a rock, the force of the water would finish the job in less than a second.

Suddenly she felt nothing, heard nothing. A serene quiet and calm overtook her senses. She was light as a feather, floating through the air. Jana raised her head. Slowly, the sound of the river and falls once again penetrated her mind.

She opened her eyes. Large rocks materialized before her, water lapping against them, leaving behind a foamy spray reminiscent of a bubble bath.

Groaning, Jana lifted her head. She stared up at the gaping walls of the canyon. She could barely see the very top. It was as if the earth had swallowed her up. She was lying along the shore of the fast-moving river, her feet dangling in the water. She could feel the current trying to reclaim its hold on her and pull her back. How had she survived? The waterfall was at least a hundred yards upstream. It wasn't possible that she could be alive.

She gasped. A few feet from the edge of the water stood the old Indian she thought she had seen from above, just before she tumbled over the railing. She blinked. He was not an illusion. His face looked weathered and ancient, and his leathery skin held more deep creases than the canyon wall. He suddenly smiled a toothless smile at her, and extended his arm. He pointed toward the water.

Jana's eyes followed where his fingers led. Still lying on the rocky ground, she spied a leather pouch lodged between two rocks, some long strings trailing away and floating in the water. The pouch was half-open, and gleaming at her from within were two ruby red eyes. The air left her lungs, and she gasped.

Jana woke with a start. Her body's first reaction was to bolt upright in bed. He arms and legs were tangled in the sheets, holding her to the mattress. She tried to suck air into her lungs, as if she had actually been deprived of oxygen. Pulling her arms free of the sheets that acted like anchors, she clutched at her chest. She swore she could still feel the crushing sensation of the water as it sucked her under the waterfall. She swiped a trembling hand over her face. Drenched in sweat, she threw the covers aside, and struggled to pull her legs over the edge of the mattress. She cupped her face in both hands, then ran them through her damp hair.

"A dream. It was only a dream," she mumbled, trying to calm her racing heart.

Everything that had happened recently had put her brain into hyper drive. That had to be the reason for this vivid nightmare. She recalled standing at that very ledge with Aimee on their trip to Yellowstone together the year following their high school graduation. Aimee's words, wanting to have her ashes scattered, and that someone going over the edge of the falls would be buried under the water forever had been real. The Indian, her fall, seeing the time travel device, those things had crept into her dream by an overly stimulated brain.

Jana stood on trembling legs, raking her teeth over her lower lip. She'd heard of people having visions. She'd never bought into that. Until now. With a start, she realized she knew where the time travel device was. Suddenly there was no doubt in her mind. Aimee thought that by tossing it over the waterfall, it would lay buried under the rocks in the water for all eternity. In her journal, she'd mentioned it would never be found again. Was it possible that it had come loose and washed ashore several hundred yards downriver?

Jana glanced at the clock on the nightstand. It was only six in the morning. She shrugged. Dan had called her earlier than that. Surely, he'd be awake at this hour. She stumbled toward the bathroom, peeling her pajamas off as she went. There was no time for a phone call. She had a desperate need to see Dan in person. He'd shown her where he lived after their return from Purple Mountain the day before. Quickly, she pulled on her jeans and a sweatshirt, and barely took time to lace up her boots to dash out of the hotel room.

~

THE BARRACK DOOR opened on Jana's second knock. A bare-chested man in his early twenties stared at her through sleepy half-closed eyes.

"Is Dan awake yet?" She tried to ignore the fact that the guy wore nothing but boxers. He had to be freezing cold in the frigid morning temperature.

A lazy grin swept over his face. He cocked an eyebrow, and assessed Jana from head to foot.

"If you're done staring, could you please tell Dan I need to see him," she said in exasperation.

He scratched under his right armpit, then stepped aside. "He's down the hall, first door on the left," he motioned with his hand. "Can't miss it." Loudly, he yelled, "Hey Osborne, you got company."

Jana scooted hastily past the guy. This cramped trailer bungalow reminded her of the college dorm she and Aimee had lived in, only this place was much smaller, if that was even possible. A loud voice, Dan's voice, came from within the room the other ranger had indicated. The door was half-open, but she knocked tentatively and remained standing in the narrow hall. Dan stood by the window, his right hand clutching at his short hair, a cellphone held to his left ear in the other. He was also half-nude, but at least he wore pants.

"I'm working on it," he growled into the phone. "This is going to take some time. It's not as easy as you make it sound." He threw his hand in the air, clearly agitated about something. He obviously hadn't heard her soft knock.

Jana's heart pounded in her chest. She was still shaken up from her nightmare. She knocked again, unwilling to simply step into Dan's room. She felt like an intruder already.

Dan turned, and the angry look on his face startled her momentarily. A fleeting memory of Daniel entered her mind, the murderous look in his eyes when he'd nearly killed Aimee's former fiancée. Abruptly, Dan's hardened facial features softened, and he smiled at her, his eyes filled with surprise. He motioned with his hand for her to enter.

"Yeah, yeah, I'll keep you informed. I have to go." He quickly pocketed his phone, apparently cutting the person on the other end of the line off, and stood in front of her in a single stride. Dan's large physique made the tiny room appear even smaller. Jana shivered involuntarily.

"I'm sorry for interrupting."

Dan ran his hand through his hair. "No, it's fine." The hard edge to his voice from a moment ago was completely gone as he spoke to her. "Just my boss on my case about a project he needs me to complete." He gave a short laugh. "The man's a tyrant."

Jana looked past him toward the window. She didn't want to openly stare at his nude chest and corded arms, even though she was sorely tempted. He stood so close to her, the heat from his body, and the clean scent of soap sent her mind spinning in turmoil.

"Jana? Is everything all right? You look . . . like something happened." Dan reached for her hand, his forehead wrinkled, and concern evident in his eyes. She shuddered, and wrapped her free arm around her waist before she ventured a glance at his face.

"I think I had a vision, Dan," she blurted.

He held still, and didn't immediately respond. His forehead wrinkled. "What do you mean, vision. You had a dream?" He reached around her and pushed his bedroom door shut.

"More like a nightmare." Her voice cracked.

"Here, sit down," Dan pulled her to his bunk, which didn't look big enough to support him comfortably if he stretched out on it. "You're obviously quite upset. Tell me about your dream."

The bed springs squeaked when Jana sat, and her body

dipped toward him when he eased himself down beside her. Her outer thigh rubbed against his. Dan held her hand in his lap, making it impossible for her to scoot even a few inches away. The warmth and concern in his eyes was mayhem to her already frayed nerves.

"I think I know where the time travel device is," she said softly, almost in a whisper. She hardly believed her own words. Dan's grip on her hand tightened and he tensed. She turned her head to look him in the eyes. Soft chocolate eyes that drew her in like a magnet. She sat so close to him, his fresh, clean male scent was intoxicating. Jana trembled involuntarily.

"Hey." He turned toward her, and wrapped his arm around her shoulder, pulling her against his solid chest. "This dream has you all shaken up, doesn't it?"

Jana couldn't breathe. It was not so much the dream at the moment as his nearness. Her hand reached up to push against his chest, and adrenaline infused her limbs, making her quiver even more. His heart beat strong against her palm. Had she imagined him shudder when her palm touched his bare skin?

Dan's warm hand moved slowly up and down her arm in an almost sensual motion. When she ventured a glance up at his face, his dark eyes startled her. No longer soft and brown, they held a certain deep intensity. Full of longing, and . . . want. All the air left her lungs as if she'd been punched in the stomach. She couldn't move. His hold on her arm tightened, and he pulled her even closer.

"Care to talk about it?" he whispered. His other hand reached up to gently swipe calloused fingers along her cheek, brushing loose strands of her hair behind her ear.

Jana blinked. She didn't want to break the spell she was under. Had it been like that for Aimee, when she'd first fallen in love with Daniel?

Oh my God! No. This isn't happening.

Her mind jolted back to awareness of what she shouldn't be feeling. This was completely crazy.

Jana somehow found the strength to push away from him, and she stood to her feet. She wrapped her arms around her waist, hoping he couldn't see her tremble. She sucked in as much air as she could into her starved lungs. Dan's scent - rugged, masculine, and clean - suffused his room. It was a scent Jana was sure she'd never forget.

Composing herself, she turned to face him. Dan remained where he sat, his eyebrows furrowed as he looked up at her. His eyes revealed a hint of confusion.

Jana inhaled another deep breath. She hoped her voice sounded steady. "In my dream, Aimee and I were standing over the brink of the Lower Falls. She talked about wanting her ashes scattered there, and how someone - and I believe she would include that to mean something - could be lost forever if it went over the falls. It's a conversation we actually had a few years ago."

Dan stood to his feet. "Wait a minute." He frowned. "Are you telling me you think she tossed the time travel device over the falls?"

"I'm convinced she did." Jana held his gaze. Dan clenched his jaw. He walked away from her. Jana watched the muscles along either side of his spine tense. He cursed, just before he turned to face her again.

"Aimee was right. We'll never find it." All softness had left his eyes. He looked as hard and weathered as she remembered his ancestor at the moment.

"That's not all of my dream," Jana said slowly.

Dan laughed. "This is worse than trying to find a needle in a haystack."

"Maybe not." It was her turn to laugh nervously. "This is

going to sound ridiculous." She stopped, unsure whether to tell him the next part of her dream.

"What?" Dan reached for her arms, his grip firm. He had an almost desperate look in his eyes. Jana could well understand his anguish. Without the time travel device, there would be no hope of saving his own life.

"I saw something in my dream. An old Indian was somehow standing in the canyon, right next to the falls. It startled me, and I went over the railing. The next thing I knew, I was hundreds of yards downriver along the shore. The Indian was there, too. He pointed at the time travel device. It was wedged between a couple of rocks." Jana talked quickly, wanting to get her surreal dream out in the open. She still didn't truly believe the time travel device would be where she had seen it. The supernatural was not something she bought into.

Dan released her and ran his hand through his hair. "Unbelievable," he muttered.

"What?" Did he actually believe her dream was real?

Dan paced in front of her, which meant he had to turn back the other way every two strides in his cramped quarters. He appeared to be deep in thought. Finally he stopped. His features were as tense as before.

"There's an old Shoshone legend," he said, as if to himself. He didn't complete his thought, but rather started a new one. "The mountain Shoshone who inhabited the park hundreds of years ago were very spiritual. Everything in their physical world was classified into water, earth, and sky spirits. The most powerful, most spiritual member of each clan was called a *puha,* and was said to hold great power over natural forces." He looked at her abruptly. "Jana, what if those spiritual people were real? Maybe that's where that device came from. It's a snakehead, right? The Shoshone were often called Snakes."

Jana shook her head. "Are you suggesting some ancient spiritual Indian came to me in a dream to tell me where to find the device?" She stared at him, wide-eyed.

"It's one possibility," Dan said. He reached for a t-shirt draped over the lone chair in the corner of his sparse room and pulled it on over his head. "Hell, it's the best explanation I can come up with at the moment." With a determined look on his face, he added, "give me a couple of hours. I'll get us down into the canyon."

CHAPTER SIX

*J*ana sat on the rocky ground, leaning against a tree trunk, her knees drawn up to her chest. She stared out at the gaping canyon before her, a firm grip on the two-way radio Dan had given her. She hadn't heard from him in nearly an hour. She'd long given up trying to spot him. If she took one step too far, she'd surely lose her footing in the loose, gravelly yellow earth, and fall to her death. She opted to wait him out, sitting against the closest tree to the canyon rim, trying in vain to relax.

Earlier today, Dan had pulled the National Park Service truck he'd borrowed into a spot at one of the parking lots close to the Lower Falls. He'd sent her back to the lodge after her dream revelation, and told her he'd pick her up later in the day. Climbing down into the canyon was strictly forbidden by park regulations, and he needed some time to call in a favor or two. Jana had been surprised when he'd shown up at her door in official dress, looking stunning in his ranger uniform. If anyone asked, he was on official park business. Jana was grateful he hadn't asked her to make the climb into the canyon with him.

"I told my boss if he wanted me to get his project completed that I'm doing as a favor to him, he'd have to scratch my back, too. But he can't look the other way when a civilian's involved, so I'll need you to stay up along the rim, and we'll communicate via two way radio."

What if she was wrong? That climb into the canyon was dangerous. What if the device wasn't where she'd seen it in her dream? What if it wasn't there at all? Jana chewed her lower lip. They'd walked off trail along the rim, out of sight from curious tourists, until she'd pointed out the area she thought was close to where she had washed up along the river in her dream.

The sudden static noise from the radio startled her. She scrambled to her feet.

"Jana, I found it." Dan's excited voice came through the radio on a weak signal. The roar of the river in the background drowned out most of his words. "I'm heading back up."

Jana was too stunned to even respond. Her heart slammed against her rib cage. He'd found the device! An icy chill crept up her spine. How was this possible? Had she really received a spirit vision?

Jana's legs turned to rubber as she stood. She leaned against the tree trunk for support. This whole situation was getting creepier all the time. Had some mystical ancient power intervened, wanting Dan to find that device so he could travel to the past to save Aimee? To save himself? Jana vowed that when she returned home she would start attending church more regularly.

To pass the time and to calm her frayed nerves, she paced a short distance back and forth along the rim. She hoped Dan would get out of the canyon safely. There was good reason why climbing was forbidden here. The volcanic soil was brittle and weak and gave way easily. She'd heard horror stories of people falling over the edge to their deaths. She convinced herself that Dan would be okay. He'd told her he was an experienced climber. He'd strapped himself into a climbing harness and had all the ropes and tools needed for a safe descent and return. Still, it gave her an uneasy feeling.

A full moon rose slowly from behind the millions of lodgepole pinnacles on the other side of the canyon. Stars began to appear in the evening sky and the orange glow from the setting sun only served to emphasize the already brilliant colors of the canyon walls. Another hour at most, and it would be dark. Even the full moon wouldn't give off enough light to safely climb from the gaping scar in the earth.

Jana glanced nervously at her wristwatch. How long had it been since Dan told her he was on his way back up? She hadn't checked the time when he contacted her. She had no idea how long it would take to make an ascent like that.

Suddenly, the sound of gravel and rocks sliding down the abyss several yards to her right made her jump.

"Dan?" she called, almost frantic and rushed to where the sound came from.

"Yeah," came a strained, muffled reply.

Jana's heart hammered in her throat. He was back, and he was all right. Seconds later, Dan emerged, and heaved himself onto level ground with a loud grunt.

"Geez, that was some workout," he said, panting as he stumbled to his feet. He dusted his hands off on his shirt, and unbuckled the climbing harness, dropping his gear to the ground.

"Thank God you're back in one piece," Jana exclaimed in relief and threw her arms around his neck. Too late, she realized her impulsive move, and tried to step away. Her overly charged emotions had gotten the better of her. Dan refused to let her go. He wrapped strong arms around her waist, and held her close. Her heart began to race, and her limbs flooded with adrenaline. Every inch of her skin where his arms touched her sprang to awareness.

"For a reaction like that, maybe I should put my neck on the line more often," he whispered into her hair. His warm breath tickled her neck, sending waves of electricity up and down her back and through her extremities.

Jana's legs turned to putty. He must have felt her knees buckle. His grip on her tightened, hugging her closer still. The smell of dirt and sweat mingled with the clean scent of his minty shaving cream. *This is so wrong*, her mind screamed. Oh, but why did it feel so good, then?

"I was worried you'd get hurt," she breathed voicelessly.

Dan eased his hold around her waist, but didn't let go completely. The grin he flashed her took her breath away. His face was too close.

"Well, truthfully, I hope I don't have to do that again," he said. Suddenly, his features turned serious, and his eyes roamed her face as if he was looking for something. His hands bracketed her waist.

"Jana," he whispered, just before he lowered his face closer to hers. She had no time to react.

The instant his lips touched hers, Jana was lost. Her body seemed to move of its own will and she leaned into him. Her lips parted as the pressure of his mouth on hers increased. Slowly, her arms slid up his chest, and she gripped his shoulders. A deep groan escaped his throat and the pressure of his hands spanning her waist increased, pulling her up against him. Heat pooled in her abdomen, and she struggled for breath.

An owl hooted overhead, followed by the distant bark of a coyote, the primordial sounds penetrating her senses. With the spell broken, her rational mind quickly intervened.

He's Aimee's descendant, what are you thinking, Jana?

She pulled her face back, and Dan relaxed his hold on her.

His eyes were as black as the forest closing in behind them. He cleared his throat and stepped away from her.

"Let's head back, and we'll figure out where to go from here," he said. His voice held a certain edge she'd only heard once when he was on the phone with his superior. Dan's face hardened and his jaw clenched. Did he regret kissing her? She certainly regretted that it had to end. No other man's kiss had ever drawn such an overwhelming feeling of desire from her.

He grabbed his climbing gear off the ground and word-lessly headed away from the canyon rim, up the incline toward the trail leading back to the parking lot. Jana touched trembling fingers to her lips that still tingled from his kiss, and wondered if he'd been referring to what had just happened, or about their plans to go back in time.

Dan drove back to Old Faithful in silence. Jana sat next to him, her hands balled up stiffly in her lap. Now why did he have to do such a stupid thing and kiss her? The way Jana flung herself at him had surprised him beyond belief. For the last day and a half, she'd acted like a skittish deer in his presence. Her unexpected reaction to his return from the canyon floor stirred a deep longing within him, and only served to intensify his attraction to her.

A herd of bison couldn't have stopped him from pulling her closer when she threw her arms around his neck. He'd dreamed of her for months, and when he'd held her in his arms and kissed her, he never wanted to let go. Damned if he could explain what was happening to him. He'd felt something strong and powerful tug at his insides the first time he saw her. It had drawn him to her like the proverbial moth to a flame, and the feeling only grew stronger by the hour, now that she was back. Especially now that he'd kissed her.

Dan cursed silently. If she knew the real reason he needed to travel back in time, she would never agree to go with him. Heck, she would most certainly try and prevent him from going. It was too late for that now. He had the time travel device. The thought had entered his mind that he should simply go on his own and leave her behind. No. He wanted her with him. He wanted to spend time with her. It would also be easier to explain his presence to Aimee and Daniel with Jana there. Somehow he would keep the truth from her.

"I've already put together a basic survival pack," he said slowly, breaking the awful silence. He stared straight ahead, concentrating on the dark road before him.

"That's good," she answered. She sounded relieved at the neutral topic. "And what are your plans? When do we leave?"

"Tomorrow morning." Dan laughed. "I'd like to take one more shower before I head into the wilderness."

"I wonder if the device is going to send us back to the time when Daniel and Aimee disposed of it, or exactly two hundred years from now," Jana said, talking almost to herself.

"From everything I've read in that journal, the device somehow makes sure that events don't overlap, so nothing ever gets repeated. I would think we would get there two-hundred years from right now, not before."

Jana sighed audibly. "I might be there when Aimee has her babies. I'll get to see her twins." She sounded almost excited now.

"Yeah, you just might." Dan turned his head and shot her a quick look, glad she seemed comfortable with the idea of going back in time.

"Jana . . . about that kiss." He hesitated. He wanted, needed, to talk about this. Even though he knew he was playing with fire. He should just leave it alone, and wait until they returned from this trip.

"We were both overcome with emotions." Jana quickly broke his train of thought. "I was so glad you were safe, and you've got to be happy to have found the device."

Dan slammed on the brakes. He eased the truck to the side of the road, and turned to look at the woman sitting next to him. Although it was dark everywhere, there was enough light from the truck's dashboard to make out her features, allowing him to gauge her reactions.

"Is that what you think it was?" he asked, more forcefully than he intended.

"I . . . yes . . . what else--"

Dan ran his hand through his hair in frustration. "Jana, I like you . . . a lot. I want to get to know you better." Damn. Couldn't he control himself? He shouldn't be saying such things to her. Not now. Not yet. Unable to listen to his inner voice of reason, he reached for her hand. She shrunk away.

"Jana, what are you afraid of? If you have a boyfriend . . ."

"I don't have a boyfriend," she scoffed. "But I can't get involved with you."

"Why the hell not?" He regretted his heated outburst immediately. Clenching his jaw, he inhaled deeply, trying to calm his frayed nerves. "Why not?" he repeated in a normal voice.

"Because . . . it's just not right. You're Aimee's grandson. Don't you get it, that this is just . . . weird."

He couldn't believe what she was telling him. "You won't consider a relationship with me because I'm related to your friend?" he asked incredulously. "What if Aimee had a brother in this time. Would you have gone out with him if he asked you?" She stared at him blankly. Obviously she hadn't considered that before.

"This is different," she argued in a firm voice.

"How? This makes no sense, Jana. I get that you're upset about losing your friend, and that I'm some kind of link to her, but . . . if I wasn't related to Aimee, would you consider going out with me?" He hoped he didn't sound too pathetically desperate.

"Yes," she whispered so quietly, he barely heard the word. Dan squeezed her hand, then let go. That was all he needed to hear.

"Just give me half a chance. That's all I'm asking." His pulse increased as he steered the truck back onto the road. Somehow he'd get past her hang-up that because he was distantly related to her best friend she couldn't enter into a relationship with him. At least now he knew the reason for her skittishness. Dan gripped the steering wheel.

She might just hate you by the time this is all over.

CHAPTER SEVEN

*D*an pried his backpack off his tired and stiff shoulders and tossed it onto his bunk. That was some climb. He and a few fellow rangers had often discussed what it would be like to scale the walls into the Grand Canyon. Every year, some foolhardy mountain climber tried it, and more often than not, a rescue team would have to be sent in to retrieve a dead body. Dan unbuttoned his dirty shirt and tossed it on the chair in the corner. His white t-shirt followed. If his entire future wasn't at stake here, he wouldn't have made such a climb.

His future. Dan laughed and shook his head. In the last two days, he'd thought less about his future and more about the woman sitting in a hotel room a couple of miles away at the Old Faithful Snow Lodge. The picture in his mind of his ideal future seemed to be changing. One chestnut-haired beauty with the soft amber eyes of a doe, stood front and center.

He glanced at the pack on his bed. Hesitating, he unzipped the main compartment and carefully removed the soggy old leather pouch from within. It felt slimy and soft, the dark color of the leather tinged with green algae from two hundred years in the water. Incredibly, it had been right where Jana described. The idea that she had dreamt about its precise location had startled him more than he let on this morning, when she'd told him of her vision. His great-great grandfather, Josh Osborne, had been part Shoshone, and Dan had always been fascinated by the old legends of the people who inhabited the park hundreds and thousands of years ago.

Dan stared at the pouch in his hands. He didn't dare open it. He'd already checked to make sure it contained the snake-head when he'd first found it. Clenching his jaw, he cursed silently. He held his future in his hands, but at what price? He'd made a deal with the devil, and it was too late to back out now. Somehow he would make everything right again. The power to change history was in his grasp. What he'd agreed to do could be undone again later, he convinced himself firmly.

Dan admitted that he hadn't thought this through very carefully when he'd agreed to John Hasting's terms. Maybe he could just tell him he hadn't found the device, and that it would be impossible to ever recover. The man had always been a thorn in his side. Dan was convinced his applications for backcountry ranger had been rejected every year because Hastings played a hand in the decision. And all because Dan had been outspoken against allowing a private concessioner into the park, which Hastings had wanted approval for. His management policies here in the park bordered on corrupt and illegal, but no one ever dared challenge his authority. Anyone who spoke up usually found him or herself without a job for some obscure reason. A seasonal position was hard to come by. A permanent one, Dan's dream, was virtually impossible.

Dan sighed and set the leather pouch on the nightstand

beside his bunk. He couldn't face the rest of his life knowing that he had sold out Yellowstone National Park, a place so rich in his family's history. His ancestors certainly wouldn't approve. He cursed under his breath. In order to secure his own future, he was jeopardizing the future of the park.

He drew an odd comfort from the knowledge that an ancient spirit had apparently led Jana to the device. His meeting with her two months ago was more than mere coincidence, he realized with sudden clarity. Somebody wanted him to attain his goals here in the park, and without Jana and the time travel device, that might have been impossible.

A plan slowly formed in his mind. He would do what he'd been asked to do, but the minute he returned from the past, he would undo it all, right after he sealed the deal to secure his future.

With one final glance at the pouch on his nightstand, Dan headed for the bathroom. He inhaled a deep breath, imagining smelling Jana's subtle perfume. He needed a long, hot shower. Hell, maybe he needed a cold shower.

Once this whole mess was dealt with, he'd be free to pursue Jana Evans. She felt the attraction, too. He was sure of it. The way she'd responded to his kiss . . . Somehow he'd chisel away at her ridiculous apprehension. Under no circumstances, however, could she know the reason he needed to go to the past. It wouldn't be too difficult to keep it from her. She'd be too preoccupied with meeting up with Aimee again to pay any attention to his activities.

Dan stripped off his pants and stepped into the shower. For now, he had to keep his desires under control. That kiss had been a mistake. It had only left him wanting more. He hadn't realized what a distraction she would be to his objective. Jana had no idea how desirable she really was. Spending a week or more alone with her in the wilderness might be another big mistake.

JANA SANK onto her bed with a weary sigh. Tomorrow she would be traveling back in time. Her head spun at the very idea, but not nearly as much as with the memory of Dan's kiss and their subsequent conversation earlier. He was right. She was being ridiculous. Maybe she should be more open-minded to the idea of a relationship with him. Her attraction to him was undeniable. She'd felt it the first time she met him.

Aimee had told her the perfect man would come along some day, for both of them. Aimee had found her perfect match in the past. She couldn't have known that she would be directly responsible for providing Jana with her ideal man. Why was she fighting what was right in front of her?

She rolled onto her side. In the morning she would tell Dan she was open to the idea of something more than a casual friendship. Obviously the attraction was there. They needed some time to get to know one another. Traveling back in time might just give them the time they needed.

Get some sleep, Jana. Tomorrow is a huge day.

She made a mental list of the things she wanted to take with her. Obviously, she couldn't bring her suitcase, and she hadn't brought a backpack. When she'd packed to come to Yellowstone, she'd never imagined she would actually be going back in time.

Dan had said he'd already prepared a basic survival kit. Hopefully there was enough room in his pack to stash some spare clothes. Traveling light would be essential. Maybe they could avoid other people while they traveled through the wilderness to get to Madison. She wondered how far from their destination they would be once they arrived in the past.

According to Aimee's accounts, and what Jana remembered Zach Osborne telling them, the device would take them in the general vicinity of where it had last been in 1810. With a jolt of adrenaline, she realized suddenly that they might end up in the canyon after touching that snake eye.

Everything would be all right, she assured herself. She'd be with Dan. He was a skilled ranger, and she was a competent nurse. Anything that happened, they could deal with it. Comforted by that thought, she closed her eyes. Her lips began to tingle and Jana drifted off to sleep with the memory of Dan's kiss fresh in her mind.

JANA WALKED up to the front door of Dan's barrack the next morning. Loud voices came from inside. After dropping her off at the lodge last night, Dan had told her to meet him at his place at eight. His roommates would already have gone to work by then.

She was a few minutes early. Someone was having a heated argument inside. Jana hesitated. Should she knock anyway, or wait outside? The door wasn't closed completely and Dan's loud and angry voice reached her ears.

"You want me to do what? Are you out of your goddamn mind?"

Curious, Jana slowly pushed the door open further. She clutched the bundle of clothes she'd brought firmly under one arm.

"That was never part of the deal, Hastings."

"I thought you might say that, Osborne, so I'll make it easy on you," another male voice said, his tone much calmer than Dan's. "I'm relieving you of your obligation."

"What the hell is that supposed to mean?"

"It means I've changed my mind. I've had my doubts from the beginning that you would come through for me on this."

"You son of a bitch," Dan snarled.

Jana walked tentatively down the short and narrow hall toward Dan's room. Perhaps she should intervene before these two men resorted to violence.

"Dan?" she called loudly, hoping her presence would calm the situation.

"Jana, don't come in here," Dan shouted. Her heart rate suddenly increased. Whatever was going on, it sounded more serious than she'd first thought.

"Hand it over, Hastings," he demanded. Jana reached Dan's room. An older man in full ranger uniform stood by Dan's bed, holding something in each of his hands. Jana recognized the pouch that held the time travel device in one hand, and the snakehead in the other. He held the device up, inspecting it from all angles. No! How did this happen?

"Dan, what's going on?" she asked, her voice almost frantic. She stepped quickly into the room. Dan's back was turned to her, his attention focused on the other man. He wore dark green hiking khakis and a white t-shirt, his backpack slung over one shoulder. It appeared as if he'd been ready to leave, but had been interrupted by the other ranger. How had the man gotten hold of the device? Surely, he didn't know what it was.

Jana reached out to touch Dan's arm. At the same moment, Dan lunged for the ranger. His hand reached out to grab for the device. In the next instant, everything went black.

Jana blinked, trying to stave off the wave of dizziness that swept over her. She braced her hand against something wet and squishy. The bright sunlight overhead made it difficult to focus.

Once her eyes adjusted to the light, she was able to open them fully. She sat in a marshy meadow and her heart nearly leapt up her throat. It had happened! They had time traveled.

With the world still spinning around her, Jana slowly turned her head.

"Dan? Are you all right?"

There was no answer. Tentatively, she pushed herself off the ground, her pants soaked through with mud. The only sound was the loud chirping of crickets and various other insects in the grasses.

"Dan?" she called again. Her voice sounded out of place in the eerie stillness. She listened for an answer. Water trickled nearby, the sound mingling with the rhythmic chirping and humming of insects. Jana pulled her feet from the sloshy mud. The air was thick with mosquitos all of a sudden. Her heart pounded frantically and she turned in all directions, her eyes trying to focus, desperately searching for Dan's familiar figure. She ran several paces through the bog, her feet sinking into the heavy marsh.

"No," she whispered, shaking her head in utter disbelief. This couldn't be. In a near panic, Jana realized she was all alone.

CHAPTER EIGHT

*H*ow had this happened? Jana refused to give in to the thought that she had traveled back in time alone. With trembling hands, she reached for her bundle of spare clothes that lay a few feet from her. With any luck, most of them would be at least somewhat dry and clean from landing in the muck.

She hugged the bundle to her chest, her heart beating wildly. How was it possible that she had been hurled back in time, but not Dan? The last thing she remembered was touching his arm, and he was trying to grab the time travel device from the other ranger's grasp. He must have been successful in taking it from the man, and at the same time, touched the left eye of the snake.

What was she supposed to do now, stranded and alone in the wilderness?

When you're lost in the wilderness, your best chance of getting rescued is to stay where you are to make it easier for someone to find you.

Jana gave a short laugh. No one knew where she was. Heck, she didn't even know *when* she was. Another rule;

don't panic. She inhaled deep breaths to try and calm her nerves. Her heart pounded fiercely up into her throat. Her chest constricted, and breathing was almost painful. She wasn't quite sure she could follow the *don't panic* rule. She was on the verge of hysterics.

"Calm down, Jana," she said out loud and in a firm voice, forcing deep breaths of the freshest air she'd ever inhaled into her lungs. "This won't help you get out of here."

She had only one choice.

Find your way to Madison. Find Aimee.

Where was Dan? Perhaps he was nearby and she was worrying over nothing. It simply didn't make sense that she would be the only one to have time traveled. She knew from Aimee's accounts that touching the snake's left eye sent someone back in time, along with anyone touching that person.

You can't worry about all this now, Jana.

Her survival training began to kick in. Find shelter. That was her first priority. Then she could think about a course of action. A cold night spent in Yellowstone could be her death. Especially since her clothes were wet.

Jana finally ventured a closer look at her surroundings, and at the mountains looming all around her. Where was she? Nothing here looked familiar. One thing she was sure of. She was nowhere near the canyon area. At first she had thought she might be in the Hayden Valley area, but this landscape did not resemble those vast green rolling hills.

She glanced at the sun overhead, trying to get a sense of direction. She definitely stood in a vast valley, and forested hills beckoned to her toward what she guessed had to be south. In the opposite direction, jagged snow-capped mountain peaks jutted toward the sky.

It was just her dumb luck that she had to land in a marshy puddle. Her waterproof boots offered some protection, and the mud wasn't deep enough for her to sink further than a few inches, but it made the going difficult as the dense mud reluctantly released its claim on the soles of her boots. The back of her jeans was soaked, though, clinging to her skin and making her shiver.

"It could be worse, Jana," she said. "You could have landed in a geyser basin."

Cold fear trickled down her spine. She had nothing with her, except the clothes she wore, and the ones firmly clutched under her arm. This was possibly one of the worst survival scenarios she could think of. Several times, she called Dan's name, only to be met with the complete absence of another human's voice. Her calls managed to startle a few birds to take flight from the brush several feet in front of her. Their wings flapped wildly, and they screeched in protest. The insects continued their cadenced chirping, but the one sound she desperately wanted to hear did not come.

As she trudged on, the mud finally gave way to hardened soil. Countless animal prints were baked into the clay-like earth. The familiar oval shaped tracks of bison were everywhere. Taking a deep breath for strength, Jana inhaled the pungent odor of those massive beasts

and hoped she could avoid a bison encounter. The valley she was in wasn't flat. The ground was uneven, marred by deep ruts and dips. Sagebrush and grasses covered the many rocks that jutted from the ground, adding to the difficulty of her walk. The brush was high enough in places to conceal even a wallowing bison.

The rushing sound of a large, fast-flowing body of water soon replaced the trickling sounds of a nearby stream. Jana headed toward the sound of the water, her direction taking her up a gently sloping incline. Once she reached the top, she stared into a gaping narrow canyon, where the water flowed fast over large boulders and rocks.

She gazed toward what she assumed was south, judging by the flow of the water. The canyon appeared to widen into a valley further ahead. The rolling hills to her right were mostly carpeted with grass and sagebrush. Small groupings of pine trees, rows of cottonwoods and aspens made up the rest of the landscape. Her gaze lingered on the pine covered forests in the distance. They appeared to be further away than ever. She inhaled a deep breath for courage.

Just keep moving forward.

Jana trudged on over the uneven terrain, following a safe distance along the rim of the canyon until she reached the open valley. Spread out before her as far as the eye could see was a vast herd of bison, their grunts and bellows audible now against the rushing waters of the river. Their bodies in the distance looked like nothing more than brown dots spread out along the water's edge.

Jana named off as many of the large rivers she could remember in Yellowstone. It would be helpful if she at least knew what river she was staring at. The water before her was moving swiftly in the direction she guessed was south, eliminating it as the Yellowstone River as one of her choices. The Yellowstone flowed in a northerly direction. This particular body of water moved in a parallel direction to the timberline that she'd chosen as her destination.

Even without the presence of the bison, she would have to ford this river if she hoped to find shelter near the forest. It was too risky. The current looked fast and strong, and the water was no doubt frigid. Jana knew she had no alternative but to change her plans. All the survival classes she had taken with Aimee seemed tame in comparison to what she faced now. She'd sometimes been a reluctant accomplice when Aimee dragged her off to yet another wilderness course, but she was suddenly glad she's paid attention.

From her vantage point up on the rise, she could see for

miles. A short distance up ahead, the river she'd been following joined with another. She chose to follow the wider river from a safe distance.

Hours passed as she walked. There was still no end in sight to the bison herd, but an immense grove of aspen and cottonwood trees loomed ahead to her right. One of the places she recalled seeing aspens in any great number on her hikes through Yellowstone was in the Lamar Valley. With a jolt, she realized exactly where she was. She gaped at the river again. How could she not have recognized it before?

With certain clarity, Jana knew without a doubt she was staring at the Lamar River. How did she get transported here, to the northern-most corner of the park? Her initial thought that she was nowhere near the canyon area had been correct. From where she stood now, it would take weeks to find her way to Madison. Without a map or at least a compass, it seemed an almost impossible feat.

Jana was familiar with the trails in her time. Navigating them with a compass was fairly easy. There were no trails here now. She couldn't even get a good bearing on her location. An ominous feeling of dread consumed her. She sank to her knees amongst the shrubs of sage. Squatting, she held her head between her hands. Not even the fragrant scent of sage could offer her a small feeling of peace. Her confidence wavered. Her predicament was becoming more impossible by the minute. Even with a full pack of survival gear, how would she navigate her way to Madison on her own?

Don't give in to negative thoughts.

"Follow the river," she whispered. "Just follow the river. It'll take you to the Yellowstone." Jana laughed even as tears trickled down her cheeks. Nothing in all her survival courses with Aimee could have ever prepared her for this. She stared out at the endless land. Wide and vast mountains and forests loomed ahead with no end in sight. Was it even worth thinking about the wild animals? With her shoulders slumped, Jana pulled her gaze away from her insurmountable obstacles and stared at the ground. Her hands were caked with dried mud.

Go find shelter, and figure out what to do.

Gritting her teeth, Jana stood to her trembling feet.

You can't give up so quickly.

With a determined lift of her chin, she held tight to her bundle of clothes and headed toward the aspen and cottonwood grove. A small spring gurgled out of the ground before her just as she reached her destination, and she dropped to her knees again. Rinsing the dirt from her hands, she splashed cool water on her face and took a long drink. Staying hydrated would not be a problem here. She could even go a day or two without food.

"You'd be surprised at what you might eat in a survival situation."

Dan's words from a few days ago haunted her now. Her mouth began to water, thinking about the burgers and fries they had eaten that night. Her stomach growled loudly in response. His handsome face materialized in her mind, along with his dazzling smile.

"I like you, Jana . . . a lot. I want to get to know you better."

"I want to get to know you better, too. Dan, where are you?" she whispered. Before tears of despair threatened to overtake her again, she pushed on toward the aspen grove. To her delight, several large boulders jutted out of the ground among the trees, forming a small cave.

Cautiously, Jana inched toward the opening. She picked up a thick branch off the ground, knowing that if a bear made its home in that little alcove, a piece of wood would hardly serve as an effective weapon. She had to take a chance. This could be the perfect shelter to get her through the night.

Jana beat the stick loudly against the ground. "Hey, bear," she shouted, and waited.

There was no sound or movement from behind the rocks. With a pounding heart, she peered into the niche. Expelling her breath through parted lips, she quickly saw that it was unoccupied. Tufts of grayish brown fur lay strewn about, and several large splintered bones littered the ground.

At closer inspection, all the bones were bleached white and weathered, without a hint of flesh left on them. Jana felt confident that these remains were old, and the former resident of this small den had long moved away. Perhaps he would return come winter, but that was a long time off.

Jana dropped her clothes near the opening. She had shelter for the night, and she had water close by. Now she needed fire. The leaves of the aspen rustled melodiously above her in the early evening breeze. There was plenty of wood lying about on the ground. She gathered as much as she could carry, dropping her bundle in front of her temporary home. After multiple trips back and forth among the groves of trees, gathering large and small deadfall, she felt sure her woodpile would last her through the night. Hopefully a fire would ward off not only the cold, but any predatory animals as well.

"Ok, let's see if you remember how to do this, Jana," she spoke softly into the breeze.

She broke off a fairly long branch from one of the trees, stripping it of its smaller side branches and leaves, and testing it to see if it would bend without breaking. It gave in to the pressure of her hands just enough.

Satisfied with her choice, she settled herself on the ground in front of her shelter. Without a knife, her task would be a lot more difficult, but she found a pointed rock that might serve her purposes well enough. She glanced around on the ground until she found a fairly flat rock.

Laying these items aside, she stripped dried bark from several of the trees, and broke them into small pieces. Plucking some dried grasses out of the earth around her, and even a few tufts of fur from inside the cave, she added these to her pile of kindling.

Next, she untied the laces of one of her boots, pulling the string through the holes to free it from her boot. She dug through her pile of wood, picking out a fairly short branch.

"I managed to make a fire with a firebow before," she said, talking out loud to ward off the loneliness.

She recalled the task she and Aimee had been given during one of their survival classes. *Find anything available to you, and make a fire.* Of course, they had the advantage of having read several manuals on fire making before the course began, and each of them had a multi tool and knife at their disposal. With a soft smile on her face, Jana recalled Aimee's initial frustration with the task, and how she had shot mockingly annoyed looks at Jana's fire before she'd even managed to produce any smoke.

"One of the few times I bested you at anything, Aimee," Jana spoke fondly, thinking about the memory.

She tied the ends of her boot lace to either end of her long stick, in bow and arrow fashion, making sure her string was not too tight. Next she stripped a large chunk of wood of its bark, and using her pointed stick, carved a depression in the bark. She took her flat rock, positioned it between her legs, and set the bark on top. She twisted the shorter stick she'd picked out earlier around her loose string, and set the tip of the bow into the depression in the bark.

With fast motions of her hand, she began twisting the bow, sawing at the spindle, while pressing down firmly with the bow against the bark.

Jana's sense of time disappeared as she worked, concentrating on keeping the bow turning quickly. Her arms began to ache from the constant motion, and from pushing down hard on the bow. When she almost gave up hope, a small wisp of gray smoke swirled slowly into the air beside the deepening groove she had created in the bark. With renewed vigor, she kept sawing.

Finally, more smoke became visible, and she hastily tipped the bark onto her prepared bundle of tinder, causing the hot char she had created with the motion to fall onto the fur and parched grasses. The dry fine fur hairs ignited instantly, and Jana let out a yell of triumph. Bending over, she blew air onto the tinder, and hungry flames sprung to life, licking at her kindling.

Controlling the impulse to add wood too quickly, she chose the smallest branches first, adding more as her fire grew. With a loud spitting and crackling, her campfire lit up her darkening surroundings, casting the trees in ominous shadows. She sat back on her haunches, and breathed a sigh of relief. Fire meant life. It could make the difference between whether she would survive this night or perish.

With a loud sigh, she added a few larger chunks of wood to the blaze, and headed for the stream for one final drink. If anything, it would give her empty belly a feeling of fullness. When she returned, she stood for a moment, staring up at the ever-darkening night sky.

Millions of stars twinkled overhead, brighter than anything she had ever seen. Shivering, she crawled into her shelter, and slipped into another shirt. Bunching up the rest of the clothing, she curled into a fetal position, using the bundle as a pillow. The ground was hard, and coldness seeped up into her limbs, even though the flames from the fire created an ambient warmth throughout the little cavern.

Jana stared wide-eyed at the dancing flames. Sleep refused to come, even though her body was physically exhausted from her day-long hike. The events of this morning kept playing over and over in her mind. Who was that man Dan had been arguing with? And how had he gotten hold of the time travel device in the first place? Why had Dan left it lying around so carelessly?

Dan. Where was he now? Had he also time traveled? And if so, why hadn't they arrived at the same place? She imagined his strong arms around her, holding her, keeping her safe. The fire's flames became a blur as tears filled her eyes.

Jana had no idea what the morning would bring. She angrily swiped at her eyes and sniffed. She'd simply keep moving in a southerly direction. That's all she could do. How long she could last before succumbing to the terrain, the elements, or the wild animals, she had no idea.

Her lids grew heavy, and Jana stopped fighting her weariness. Almost relaxed, the out-of-place sound of something moving in the brush in the darkness startled her fully awake. Listening for the sound again, she was sure it hadn't simply been the popping of burning wood. A tree branch on the ground snapped. Something was definitely moving beyond the light of the fire.

With a trembling hand, Jana reached for a large branch from her wood pile. She didn't believe for a second it would protect her from anything, but if a bear or wolf came at her, she wanted to get at least one swing at it before she became the predator's dinner. A large shadow moved into her line of vision, and with a pounding heart, she bolted upright, her stick held out in front of her.

CHAPTER NINE

"*J*ana?" A deep voice came from beyond the darkness. Jana's heart leapt into her throat. She recognized that voice instantly.

"Dan," she called, and scrambled from her shelter. She tossed the stick she clutched in her hand to the ground. "Oh my God! Dan," she cried. The tears flowed freely in relief, and her entire body shook as she threw herself at the solid form of the man emerging into the fire's circle of light.

"Jana," he whispered, his breath hot against her ear. He crushed her to him. "You scared the hell out of me when I couldn't find you. I didn't know if you were alive or not."

She wrapped her arms around his neck, clinging to him as if her life depended on it. She gave a short laugh between her sobs. Heck, her life did depend on it. Her body flooded with a feeling of relief. Everything would be okay now. Mere minutes ago she'd thought she might not live to see another day. Now, her world seemed whole again.

"I'm so glad I finally found you," he said close to her ear, his lips in her hair. He drew in a long, deep breath while his hands caressed her back.

"You knew I was here?" she asked, finally relinquishing her death grip from around his neck. She pulled her head back, straining to see his face in the darkness. The moving light from the flames distorted his features, but his dark eyes gazed down at her, filled with concern.

"I found your tracks hours ago to the north of here," he said. "At first I thought I was alone, that you'd been left behind. I felt your hand on my arm just before we traveled, but I wasn't sure if it would have been enough to bring you along with me."

"So why did we end up in separate places?" she asked.

Dan scoffed. "I don't know. Someone is toying with us, it seems." His teeth gleamed in the darkness when he smiled down at her. He released his hold around her middle, and cupped her face between his hands, caressing her cheeks with his thumbs. Jana closed her eyes for a moment, savoring his touch. Before she opened them again, Dan's lips were on her mouth.

For a split second, Jana stiffened, but then she remembered her decision from the night before. She would give this a chance. Slowly, she responded to his kiss, her lips moving against his. Heat suffused her body as she gave herself to the increasing demands of his lips. Dan's fingers raked through her hair, one hand cupping the back of her head. Jana's hold around his neck tightened, and she opened her mouth to his probing tongue.

Abruptly, Dan ended the kiss, and released his hold on her head. Breathing hard, he leaned his forehead against hers.

"Jana," he whispered. His hands framed her face again.

"It's okay," she squeaked, trying to find her voice. "I thought about what you said yesterday." She laughed softly, her pulse pounding in her lips in the aftermath of Dan's kiss.

He leaned back and tilted her head up. The sincere warmth and caring in his eyes took her breath away. "I'm just glad that you're okay," he said, clearing his throat. Smiling broadly at her, he stepped away and reached for her hands. He gave them a light squeeze. "I can't believe we ended up in Lamar. I was sure we'd be somewhere near the canyon."

"Me, too," Jana whispered. She raked her teeth over her lower lip, trying to dispel the beating of her pulse there. "What do we do now? Getting to Madison from here is going to take a miracle."

Dan's eyebrows rose, and he glanced from her to the fire near their feet. "This is coming from a girl who somehow managed to produce a fire without matches or a lighter? Or did you bring those things with you?"

Jana smiled broadly. "I'm pretty good with a fire bow," she said, lifting her chin.

Dan whistled. "Fire bow? Miss Evans, I've underestimated you. What other secrets are you hiding?" His last few words were spoken in a low tone, and he took a step closer. Jana sucked in her breath. He bent his head and lightly kissed her lips again.

"I'm sorry, Jana," he said. His grip on her hands tightened. "You have no idea how worried I was about you. Before I found your footprints, I thought you were left behind with that bast . . . I didn't know if you were okay or not."

Dan released her hands, and slid his pack from his shoulders. "I have food," he said, kneeling down to unzip the backpack. "In the morning, we'll figure out the best way to get to Madison."

Jana licked her lips. Dan's near reference to the man in his room this morning rejuvenated all the questions that had been floating through her mind earlier.

"Who was that man?" she asked, reaching for more wood to add to the fire.

Dan halted his motion of unzipping his pack. His shoulders visibly rose and fell as he drew in a deep breath. His back was to her, when he said, "That was the park's superintendent, John Hastings."

Jana had heard the name before, but hearing the man's title startled her. Why would the superintendent of Yellowstone National Park be in a seasonal ranger's barrack?

∿

DAN CLENCHED HIS JAW. *Damn!* Everything he'd feared over the last couple of days was coming to fruition. What was he supposed to tell Jana? He couldn't keep lying to her. He couldn't tell her the truth, either. She'd just kissed him. She said she was open to the idea of a relationship with him. Nothing else mattered to him anymore but the woman before him. He couldn't lose her now.

When he'd woken up alone, sitting beside a stream in the vast Lamar Valley, his first thought was of Jana. For a split second, he'd been relieved when she wasn't next to him, hoping she hadn't traveled with him when she was nowhere to be found. Then the thought occurred to him that it was far worse for her if she was left behind. Fear for her safety in John Hastings' clutches had consumed him all day. The reality that he was powerless to protect her if she was still in the future tore him up inside.

He couldn't begin to describe the relief that flooded him when he stumbled across the fresh tracks of someone wearing hiking boots. The telltale traction grooves in the prints from modern footwear were definitely not something an Indian or trapper would have made. Dan had picked up his pace, determined to catch up with her quickly. She'd been heading for the forest in the distance.

Smart girl, he remembered thinking, but he also knew that the Lamar River would present an obstacle. He hoped she hadn't decided to try a river crossing, and was once again pleasantly surprised when she altered her course once she reached the river.

Dan cursed John Hastings again. If he hadn't shown up this morning, all of this could have been avoided. Jana and he might still have ended up in different places coming through time, but he wouldn't be forced to come up with an explanation to what she'd seen. He'd hoped that by leaving early in the morning, he would have avoided Hastings.

The man was crazy. What Hastings had asked him to do this morning was insanity. It went far beyond what Dan had originally agreed to. Something he would never agree to. Even his original arrangement left a sour taste in his mouth. Now he had an entirely new problem on his hands.

Dan pulled several power bars from his pack. He had a few bags of freeze-dried backpacking food, but it was too late to cook a meal, and the odor might attract predators. If he were out backpacking, his cooking fire would be much further away from where he slept. Still squatting, he looked up over his shoulder, and handed a bar up to Jana.

"We can cook something better in the morning. I hope this'll hold you until then."

She quietly took what he offered. Even in the poor light, the questions in Jana's head were written clearly on her face. He stood, bracing himself.

The power bar wrapper crinkled loudly in tune with the crackling from the fire. Jana took a bite, chewed, and swallowed. She had to be starving at this point. She'd gone an entire day without food, and completed a long day hike to boot. She'd found shelter, and created fire. Dan was convinced she could hold her own with most of the seasoned rangers he knew. His admiration for her swelled out of control. He couldn't lose his chance with her now.

"Maybe we should leave, and rethink our strategy," Jana finally said between bites.

"Leave?" Dan's eyebrows rose. He reached for more wood from Jana's pile, and added it to the fire, then peered into the dark little cavern she'd found for shelter. It was probably an abandoned bear den. Usually the bear would return come winter when it was time to hibernate, but for now, it would be unoccupied. It looked big enough to hold them both.

"We could go back to the future, and perhaps try this again," she elaborated. "Maybe during the scuffle, the device hurled us in different directions." She shrugged. "I'm just thinking out loud," she mumbled as an afterthought.

Dan clenched his jaw and took a deep breath. "We can't leave, Jana." He stared straight at her. Her forehead wrinkled in confusion.

"Getting to Madison from here could take weeks, Dan. Maybe we should--"

"We can't leave," he interrupted, his voice loud and forceful, "because I don't have the device."

Jana stared, open-mouthed. She took a step backwards. Dan held his hand out to her, but she pulled her arm away. She shook her head in disbelief.

"I remember you reaching for it. You were trying to take it away from Hastings. You must have taken it. How else did we end up here?"

"Apparently I touched it in the right place to where it hurled us back in time. I never got the chance to actually take it from him."

Her soft eyes turned hard, filling with anger. "Why were you so careless with that device? Why would you leave it sitting out, where someone might see it? And what was the park's superintendent doing in your room in the first place?" Her voice grew louder and angrier with each question she threw at him. Dan ran his hand through his hair, waiting, hoping for her tirade to end quickly. Her questions were valid, and if he answered them truthfully, any chance he had with her would be lost.

"Now you're telling me he has the device. Please say he doesn't know what it does," she added heatedly. Dan simply stared at her. His silence would be his answer. He'd never felt so small, or more like a coward. He'd made the worst mistake of his life weeks ago, and he was paying the price for it now. It would cost him the girl of his dreams, and ultimately, it might cost him his life.

CHAPTER TEN

*J*ana stared at him through the dancing shadows of the fire. Disbelief, anger, and disappointment were clearly written on her face. Dan could deal with all of it, all except the disappointment. She had every reason to hate him. Hell. He hated himself more than anything.

"What's really going on here, Dan? There's something you're not telling me."

Come clean, Osborne. You can't go on lying to her. She's going to find out eventually. And she needs to know that . . .

"I was starting to . . ." She broke off mid-sentence, her voice cracking.

Dan slowly turned. He had to tell her the truth. The pleading tone to her voice tore at his heart. She was starting to . . . what? Care for him? Dan laughed bitterly.

Prying a long stick from the bundle of wood, he poked forcefully at the crackling coals. A gentle breeze stirred up the embers, sending wisps of smoke into the air. Jana stood stiffly off to the side, silently waiting.

"Sit down, Jana," he said, his voice lifeless. "I'll tell you everything."

Her eyes shimmered in the firelight. She swiped a hand across her face, then slowly sank to the ground on the opposite side of the fire. She stared blankly at the flames.

"What did you hope to gain by finding that device? By coming to the past?" She shuddered as she inhaled a deep breath. Her arms wrapped tightly around her middle, as if she was protecting herself from him. Dan clenched and unclenched his jaw. He couldn't bear the look of hurt and accusation in her eyes.

"Jana, I . . ." he scooted closer to her, wanting, needing to touch her, reach out to her and somehow make her understand that what he'd done was never meant to hurt anyone. He reached for her hand.

Jana's hands shot out defensively in front of her, her palms toward him. "Don't come any closer, and don't touch me," she said forcefully. Dan froze. "Just tell me the truth. Tell me why I am risking my life by being here in this time. Tell me it will all be worth it. Aimee was never in any danger of dying prematurely, was she?"

Her glare shot daggers at him, and at that moment Dan wished she would inflict as much and more pain on him as she must be feeling at the moment. He deserved nothing less. The forlorn drawn-out howl of a wolf in the distance resonated through his body. There was no answering howl.

"No, Aimee was never in danger," he conceded slowly. "Look, Jana, I made a horrible mistake. I admit that. I've been trying to figure out over the last few days how to make it all right again."

"How did John Hastings find out about the device? Who else did you tell after I confided a family secret to you back in May?"

Jana would have made an incredible lawyer. She bombarded him with questions without even giving him a chance to explain himself. Dan inhaled, and ran his hand over his face. His chin and cheeks felt rough from a day's growth of stubble. He tossed the stick he held in his hand into the fire. Orange glowing embers took to the air, floating like little miniscule lanterns toward the heavens before their fire extinguished. A sudden gush of wind blew smoke in his face, and he coughed. He changed his position, and was about to scoot closer to Jana. Her body tensed in response, and he stopped himself. He might as well let the fire choke the life out of him.

"John Hastings came by the visitor center about three weeks ago. I made the mistake of having the journal with me at the time. I must have been busy with a tourist, and left it on the desk. He read some of it." Dan ventured a glance at her. She stared back at him blankly. At least she kept quiet to allow him to explain.

"He sought me out days later, asking me about it."

"And you simply told him what it was?" Jana stood to her feet, glaring down at him. Even the crickets had stopped their chirping for a second at her heated question. An owl screeched loudly through the trees. Dan shifted his weight. He deserved her scorn. She'd be even more disgusted with him with what he hadn't told her. He pushed himself off the ground, and stood before her. When she took a step back, he reached for her arm. He needed her near him, to hear him out. Jana tensed under his touch. Their eyes met, and he refused to look away this time.

"Let me explain something about John Hastings," he said slowly. "The man has had it in for my family for a long time. My father was a state senator who fought against allowing more private concessioners in Yellowstone. Hastings wants more business, private tour groups, more winter usage. When he read that journal, he did some digging into my family's history. He came to the conclusion that everything in that journal is true."

Jana's arm muscles relaxed somewhat, and Dan eased his grip on her. He took a small step closer, encouraged that her eyes lost some of their cold anger. He waited for her to say something. She still glared at him, doubt and disbelief etched on her face. When she remained silent, he continued.

"Hastings has had a direct hand in the rejections I've received for my request for backcountry ranger for years. I almost got passed over for my seasonal position this summer. If not for one guy breaking his leg in a car accident, I wouldn't be working in the park this year at all."

"So what does any of that have to do with finding the time travel device and coming to the past?" Jana asked, her voice still sounding angry. The evening breeze blew some strands of hair into her face, and she hastily swiped them back behind her ear.

"Hastings saw it as an opportunity to change history."

Jana's eyebrows drew together. "How? What is there in the early 1800's that he could possibly change that would be to his advantage in the future?"

Dan's eyes roamed her face. A million thoughts raced through his mind. The one that kept coming to the forefront was that he had lost Jana before he even had the chance to build a relationship with her. A pack of coyotes yipped nearby. Their high-pitched barks sounded like laughter, mocking him for being the biggest fool to walk the earth.

"Have you ever heard of Robert Osborne?" he asked.

Jana shook her head from side to side.

"He was a senator who, in the 1880's, was able to pass legislation that would make it harder for the railroads, private enterprise, and concessioners to monopolize and exploit Yellowstone. He was also my great great uncle. One of his opponents was a man named George Hastings, John's great grandfather."

Dan studied her for any kind of reaction. Her mind was working, he could tell, trying to make sense of what he told her. His heart beat wildly, hoping he could make her understand why he'd agreed to Hasting's scheme.

"Hastings offered me a full-time permanent position in the park, with the condition that I find the time travel device and plant a document here, in the past, that would then be 'found' in the present. When I said I'd do it, he produced a fairly legitimate piece of paper, giving his ancestors certain grandfathered-in rights in the park. Anyone questioning the document's authenticity could have it dated, and since it would have been here for two hundred years, the dating would prove the document to be old. At least that was his thinking."

"Something like that could have devastating consequences for the park's future, Dan."

"I know that," he said forcefully, gritting his teeth. "I wasn't thinking when I agreed to his offer. A full-time ranger position. Do you have any idea how hard that is to get, how many years of work it takes to even be considered for a position like that? He also offered to pay off my student loans."

"So you were willing to sell out the park, everything your family has worked for for over two centuries, just so you can guarantee yourself a job?" Her eyes widened. She pulled free from his grip, and crossed her arms over her chest. In a tone of disbelief, she continued. "I don't believe what I'm hearing. I thought you loved this place. Like Aimee." She paused, and the cold, icy glare in her eyes sent a jolt of pain directly into his heart. Hearing what he'd done in her words made it sound a thousand times worse than how he'd initially perceived it. What made it even more loathsome was the knowledge that she was right.

"So basically I was just a pawn to find the device. Telling me you care for me, wanting to get to know me better, you were simply saying that so I'd agree to help you." Jana's accusation was completely accurate, everything except that she thought he didn't care for her. Dan flinched at the bitter tone in her voice as if he'd been slapped.

"You're right. I used you to find the device. But everything else I said, about what I feel for you, that's the God's honest truth."

"I can't believe you're even related to Aimee," she uttered almost as an afterthought, her eyes narrowing. Dan recoiled at the near hatred in her eyes. "Aimee would have never sold out the park for any reason, or lied to me. She was someone I could always trust."

"Dammit! I'm not Aimee," he blurted in frustration. He fisted his hands at his side. "But that doesn't mean you can't trust me now. I told you the truth. I'm trying to tell you I'm sorry. From the moment you came back to Wyoming, none of Hastings' promises seemed important anymore. I've given it a lot of thought the night before, after I dropped you off at the Inn. After I kissed you."

He took a hesitant step closer to Jana, and tentatively touched her arm. In the dim firelight, uncertainty registered in her eyes. Softly, he continued, "I planned to call him, and tell him we hadn't found the device, but he showed up unexpectedly this morning."

"Why were you all packed and ready to go then?" She pulled her arm away as if he'd burned her.

"I wanted to take you to the past. So you could visit with Aimee one more time. I could tell how much you missed her." Dan stepped around her, and ran a hand through his hair. "Hell, maybe I was a bit curious myself. What an opportunity, to come to the Yellowstone of the past." He turned, and sought her eyes again. "Jana, nothing's become more important to me, to my future, than you. I felt something two months ago when I first saw you, and my feelings for you are growing stronger every day." His fingers grazed her hands in a gentle caress. "I don't want to lose the chance to prove myself to you. Please. I need you to trust me. I need you to believe me."

Seemingly unaffected by his pleas, Jana asked, "What was that argument about this morning?"

Dan tensed. He drew in a deep breath. He might as well get it all off his chest. What did he have to lose that he hadn't lost already? "He changed his mind about what he wanted me to do."

"And what was that?"

"Planting a document was no longer good enough for him," he scoffed. "He wanted me to make sure that Robert Osborne would never make it to the senate to pass this law."

"And how were you supposed to do that?" Jana fired off the questions faster than bullets from a repeating rifle. To show her that he meant what he said about being honest with her, Dan didn't hesitate with his answers.

"He asked me to kill Robert's father . . . Matthew Osborne. One of Aimee's twins."

Jana gasped. "What?" She unfolded her hands, and took a step back.

Dan grabbed hold of her arms. She had to believe him, dammit.

"Jana, you can't believe I would agree to that. I told him he was crazy. That's when he picked up the device, and told me he didn't want my services after all."

"So, now he has the device," she said slowly. She glowered at him, then lowered her eyes to the hold he had on her arms.

"I don't think he knows how it works. But once he figures it out, John Hastings is going to come here to try and kill

Matthew Osborne. I'm sure of it. I am not going to let that happen."

Jana sucked in a long breath. She didn't say anything. He watched her eyes pool with tears. Silently, he swore that he'd do everything in his power to erase the horrified look on her face.

"Jana, I may have asked you back to Yellowstone under false pretenses, but now," he paused, gently rubbing her arms. He loosened his grip, giving her every opportunity to walk away. "But now, we really are here to save someone's life."

CHAPTER ELEVEN

*J*ana couldn't believe what Dan had told her. Never in her wildest dreams did she think it possible that he would have used the device for his own personal gain. She didn't know what to believe anymore. He sounded sincere and remorseful enough, but he'd been lying to her from the moment he called her four days ago in California. Everything he'd told her had sounded so convincing. Even showing her Aimee's supposed grave.

Jana fought hard to keep the tears at bay. Anger at Dan, and anger at herself consumed her. How could she have been so stupid? Silly romantic notions had overshadowed her rational thinking. All along, she'd been telling herself that she couldn't get involved with him. He'd worn down her resolve with a single kiss.

How was she ever going to face Aimee? Jana couldn't possibly tell her that her own descendant had sold out the place she loved so much. And now she had to worry about some deranged madman coming to kill Aimee's baby. Ironically, if John Hastings didn't come to the past, she'd be stuck here forever. He had the device. Without it, there was no returning home.

"Jana, say something." Dan interrupted her thoughts. His hands on her arms were suddenly much too warm. Jana looked up at him, her eyes unfocused, her vision blurred by the tears that she couldn't hold back any longer.

All the tender feelings, the notion of romance, of falling in love weighed on her shoulders like a ton of bricks. She sniffed. The harsh truth was that she had believed she was falling in love with Dan. After her decision not to fight her attraction for him, she'd realized just how fast she was falling. All it took was one touch from him, and her heart and mind were no longer her own. She scoffed in disgust. He had used her. Lied to her. How could she still entertain tender feelings for him?

Jana wordlessly pulled away from him, and hugged her arms around her waist. She turned her back, and stared into the absolute darkness beyond the trees. The cloudless sky was filled with millions of tiny twinkling stars. It was such a beautiful, peaceful sight, and so much in contrast to the inner turmoil in her heart and mind. The night air was filled with the sounds of countless crickets and other insects. In the distance, the haunting howl of a wolf sent shivers down her spine. Several coyotes yipped an answering call to the wolf, as if mocking him.

"Jana, we have to stick together, you know that, right?" Dan said from just behind her. She held her breath and squeezed her eyes shut. Hardening her heart would be one of the most difficult things she'd ever done.

"I know," she said quietly, then spun around. He stood closer than she expected, and she took an involuntary step backward, nearly tripping over her pile of wood. Dan caught her arm, and pulled her to him. His rugged male scent as she inhaled a breath sent her mind swirling. Quickly, she pushed her hand against his chest and stepped aside. If she didn't maintain some physical distance from him, how would she ever block him out of her mind? Luckily, he immediately released her arm.

"I know we have to stick together," she said between gritted teeth. "But it doesn't mean I have to like it."

Jana caught the pained look in his eyes. He appeared more like a little chastised schoolboy at the moment than the confident, easy-going man she had come to know.

He's a liar and he used you.

She quickly brushed aside any tender feelings, and ducked into her shelter.

"Good night, Dan. In the morning, we can figure out what to do." She pulled her bundle of clothes under her head, and turned her back to him, tucking her legs up to her belly into a fetal position. The heat from the fire seeped into her back. Dan must have added more wood. Jana squeezed her eyes shut, hoping for sleep to come and take away the pain of her aching heart.

Loud crackling and popping sounds intermixed with the chirping of birds penetrated her mind. The darkness was replaced by bright sunlight. For a moment, Jana wondered where she was. She moved her stiff legs, and flinched at the jab of pain the movement caused in her hip. She rolled onto her back, her spine meeting nothing but hard earth. The events of yesterday came rushing back. She opened her eyes, staring up at the jagged rocks that had provided a roof over her head all night. Slowly, she turned her head toward the light of the morning sun.

Dan sat by the fire, poking at the coals with a long stick. A small metal pot sat next to the flames. Jana inhaled deeply, sadness and anger consuming her all over again as last night's conversation replayed itself in her mind. The delicious smell of something sweet and sugary wafted to her nose, and her stomach growled loudly.

Discreetly, she watched Dan through half-closed lids. He looked to be deep in thought, his eyes dull and listless, staring into the fire. By his appearance, he'd spent a sleepless night. What did it matter to her?

Jana groaned, every muscle in her body sore from a night spent on a hard ground. She couldn't pretend to be asleep any longer. Her limbs demanded that she move around and stretch. Quietly, she crawled from the shelter, and stood to her feet, stretching her back. She forced herself not to look at Dan, but could feel his eyes on her. Wordlessly, she headed for the spring, and splashed some water on her face, gasping when the frigid liquid hit her skin. She headed further into the trees for some privacy, and found Dan waiting with a tin cup when she returned.

Steam rose in thin ribbons from the liquid within the cup, sending up the rich aroma of coffee. Jana reluctantly took what he offered. She could use a good strong cup this morning.

"I hope you like backpacking food. I'll try and catch us some fish at some point today. I didn't bring a whole lot of provisions." Dan's voice was as dull as his eyes.

What was she supposed to say to him? She couldn't think of anything at the moment. The pain of his deceit was still too raw. The almost hopeful look in his eyes when he handed her the cup was replaced by quiet acceptance when she didn't comment, and he turned to squat by his backpack. Rummaging through the bag, he produced a map.

"Let's figure out the safest and quickest way to reach Madison," he said, spreading the map out on the ground. Jana took a sip of her coffee, watching his broad shoulders. He turned his head to look up at her. The muscles along his jaw hardened.

"Jana, I know you're upset, and you probably hate me. But we need to cooperate and work together. I've tried to tell you how sorry I am, but right now, I also think time is of the essence. We need to reach Daniel and Aimee's cabin before John Hastings does."

The last thing she wanted to do right now was to cooperate with him, but she also knew he was right.

"Upset is probably the understatement of the century. Of two centuries." She glared at him. She refused to sit next to him. Standing while he squatted, forcing him to look up at her, gave her a small measure of power and feeling of being in control in a world of chaos at the moment.

"There's some oatmeal in the pot," he said, then turned back to study the map.

Anger made her think irrational thoughts. She didn't want to accept his food, but she knew she had to. She'd eaten only a power bar in twenty-four hours, and was in for another long hike today, through rough wilderness terrain. Common sense took over, and she squatted by the fire, as far away from Dan as she could get. She ate while he looked at the map, neither one of them speaking. In silence, she rinsed the pot in the spring when she was finished eating, and handed it to him, along with her empty coffee cup.

Neither one of them spoke while they broke camp. Dan stomped the fire out with his feet, and spread the ashes so they wouldn't ignite again, and Jana gathered her bundle of clothes. When he offered to carry it, she stubbornly refused. Shrugging his shoulders, he silently shouldered his pack and began walking, continuing to head in a southern direction.

Jana followed a few paces behind him. Although she wanted to ask which way he hoped would get them to Madison the quickest, her anger was still boiling at the surface, and she remained quiet. Dan set a moderate pace, choosing deer, or more likely bison trails through the grasses and sagebrush of the valley. He stayed within viewing distance of the Lamar River, and continued to head in a south-western direction.

"Look up ahead, Jana," he called eagerly after what seemed like hours of silence. Jana had been walking behind him, concentrating on the ground, and not so much on her surroundings. She was in a foul mood and realized that she really ought to pay more attention to what was going on around her. Even in modern times, a hiker needed to be aware of everything, or risk possible injury. Here in Yellowstone, the risks were even greater, what with the abundant wildlife and thermal features.

Admit it, you're comfortable that Dan will make sure nothing happens.

The thought annoyed her even more. When he called for her attention, she looked up, wondering what had him so excited. He'd stopped walking, and pointed into the distance. Squinting, she held her hand to her forehead to shield her eyes from the sun. Off in the distance, a multitude of small dots moved along the river.

"Pronghorn," he said, answering her unspoken question. "I've never seen such a large group in one place. And look over there. The sheer number of aspens in this area is phenomenal."

Dan grinned widely. Excitement and wonder replaced the dull look in his eyes from earlier in the morning. Jana couldn't help but stare at him.

So much like Aimee, when she discovered new things in the park.

"You're right," Jana said slowly. "I don't remember there being this many aspen trees here."

"The ecosystem as it was meant to be is intact and well," Dan said eagerly, surprise registering on his face. He looked at her, his eyes in constant motion. Abruptly, he turned his head to gaze once again into the distance, his arm outstretched, pointing toward the trees.

"The trees have a chance to grow, because the prey animals - the deer, pronghorn, and elk - need to be constantly moving. With these mountains teeming with wolves, it's not good for prey to remain in one place. What do you notice about the park's ungulates in our time?"

Jana's eyebrows rose in surprise. Suddenly, before her stood Dan Osborne, naturalist and park interpreter, leading a group of tourists on a discovery hike in Yellowstone. It came so natural to him, he reverted into that role now. He turned his head to look at her, waiting for an answer.

"Uh . . ." she stammered. "There are a lot of elk?"

Dan grinned. An indulgent grin. As if it was an answer he'd received many times. Her annoyance returned. Why were they discussing this? What did it matter anyhow?

"Ever since the wolves were brought back to Yellowstone, the aspen, willow, and the beaver have slowly returned as well," Dan said. "Simply because elk have had to change their behavior. With predators around, the grazers need to constantly be moving, and in our time, they had the luxury of staying together in large herds before the re-introduction of the wolf, moving or staying in one area as they chose, destroying young vegetation. Here we're seeing how nature intended it. I can't wait to see all the beaver dams I'm sure we'll come across in some of the tributaries."

Jana inhaled a deep breath. She hadn't noticed the strong, fragrant smell of sage, or the sweet buffalo grass. She'd been too absorbed in her anger. Dan's enthusiasm reminded her of the beauty of this place, how Aimee had found excitement in every little thing she saw on their trips. It had been infectious with her, and to her dismay, she found it to be infectious with Dan. She wanted, needed to stay mad at him. She had to guard her heart and anger was the only way she knew how.

"Would you like to rest here for a while?" Dan asked, breaking into her thoughts.

Reluctantly, Jana nodded, conceding she was tired. She dropped her bundle of clothes, and sank to the ground. Her feet pulsed in the confines of her hiking boots. The lush grasses looked inviting and soft. They would probably feel good to her hot, bare feet. She didn't act on her thoughts. Perhaps when they stopped for the night, she could finally remove her boots.

"Where are we heading, anyhow," she asked, plucking at some of the grasses, letting the blades glide through her fingers. Dan settled himself on the ground next to her and peeled his pack off his shoulders. He handed her a water canteen and a power bar. Gritting her teeth, Jana accepted what he offered.

"Well, since you wouldn't speak to me this morning, I made the decision to head toward the Yellowstone."

He didn't look at her when he spoke and unwrapped his own power bar. "By evening, we should reach an area where the Lamar and Slough Creek converge. We can camp there and cross in the morning. I'm hoping there's a safe place to ford the Yellowstone further to the west."

He took a bite of his bar, and chewed. "I thought about heading south toward Canyon, but I'm not keen on hiking the Washburn Range. It might take longer, but if we head west, toward Mammoth, then south, it'll be the easier route to Madison." He shot her a questioning look. "Unless you have another idea."

Jana glanced up. He wasn't mocking her. It was a sincere statement. She was surprised he was asking for her input.

"I think I'll defer judgment to the expert, Mr. Ranger," she said, and quickly looked away.

They sat in silence for a few minutes. Jana listened to the crinkling of her food wrapper. It seemed so unnatural amongst the sounds of the ever-present crickets chirping their rhythmic tune.

"Jana."

She glanced up quickly when he spoke her name. There was such longing, such remorse, in the tone of his voice, she swallowed nervously. His hand reached out, the tips of his fingers grazing her arm. She quickly shook her head.

"Don't," she whispered. "What you did . . . don't ask for my forgiveness." She stared straight ahead.

"At least talk to me," he said. "Can we just put aside our differences and get along? So that we both get out of this alive?"

Jana wanted to shout at him, make it clear to him that it was his fault they were in this predicament in the first place.

You were curious, Jana. You wanted to come. Even though he deceived you, you would have wanted to come here to see Aimee one more time.

"Yes," she said, taking in a deep breath. She scrambled to her feet. "I'll agree to that, but understand that cooperation in the name of survival is all you'll get from me." She glared at him one last time, then thrust the water canteen at him. She didn't wait for him to get off the ground before she started walking in the direction he'd been heading all morning.

CHAPTER TWELVE

*D*an didn't like the detour he'd been forced to take on their second day in the past, but a large bison herd had prevented them from reaching the confluence of the Lamar River and Slough Creek. He'd been left with no choice but to detour around the massive animals by leaving the valley and heading into some of the surrounding hills

They'd spent the last two days hiking out of the grasslands and marshes of the Lamar Valley, and Dan was looking for a place to ford the Yellowstone River after a fairly easy crossing of Slough Creek. He couldn't recall the Yellowstone's color ever being this turquoise before.

The river was tricky and treacherous in this area, narrowing through a steep canyon with sheer-faced cliffs. A crossing would be impossible here. As it was, there were only a few places he would chance to attempt a river crossing. If it were just him, he might do it, but Jana's safety was foremost on his mind. Not that she hadn't proven she could hold her own, but he wasn't about to risk her safety simply to save a few miles of travel.

Jana had kept up with the pace he'd set, never complained about anything, and wordlessly had helped set up camp at night, and torn it back down the following morning. She'd continued to remain distant and spoke to him only when necessary.

What had he expected? He knew all along that if she found out about his deception, she would hate him. His conscience had won out over his selfish needs that first night here in the past. He simply couldn't go on with the lie. He felt better, having told her the truth and being honest with her, even though the price he'd paid for his honesty tore him up inside. His feelings for her grew stronger with each passing hour of every day.

He'd never bought into love at first sight, but he knew now with absolute certainty that it had happened to him at their first encounter. He couldn't explain the overwhelming feelings that had come out of the blue any other way. Why had he let her leave so quickly that day when he'd met her at the Old Faithful Inn? Why had he acted like such a coward each time he dialed her number, only to hang up? Maybe none of what they faced now would have happened had he not allowed her to walk out of his life so quickly.

If he could turn back time, and had done one thing different, Dan would never have left that journal lying around for anyone else to see, and Hastings would never have known about it.

There was no sense beating himself up over it. He'd screwed up, big time, and the best he could do now was to make sure he got Jana safely home again. For that to happen, he had to confront John Hastings and also prevent the bastard from killing any member of his family.

That Hastings would show up, of that he had no doubt. He only hoped wherever the time travel device decided to send him, was as far if not further than the miles he and Jana had to cover. Dan simply had to get to the Madison Valley first, to warn his ancestors of the danger they were in. All of this was his fault, and he would make it right again, even if it killed him.

After hiking through sagebrush-covered meadows and hills for most of the morning, the river opened into a wide valley of woodland meadows and gently sloping hills. The banks of the river were comprised largely of weathered river rocks, and he kept a lookout for a good place to cross. The water level didn't appear to be any higher than mid-thigh on him, but he eyed the current warily.

"We'll cross here," Dan called over his shoulder, his mind made up.

He turned and waited for Jana to catch up. She'd walked silently behind him, lagging far back for the better part of the morning. Dan had silently wondered if his pace was too quick, and at one point he had slowed down to give her a chance to catch up. She'd changed her speed to maintain her detached contact. When he'd sped up, she'd had no problem picking up the pace as well. Dan cursed under his breath. How would he endure the next days and weeks ahead, alone in the wilderness with the girl he loved, knowing that she hated him?

"Is it safe to cross here?" she asked indifferently, looking toward the opposite shore of the river.

"I think so," Dan answered. "Why don't you put your spare clothes in the backpack?" he suggested. "That way they won't get wet."

Jana looked at the bundle of clothes she held protectively in her arms. She'd stubbornly refused to relinquish them for two days. She studied the river, and Dan could see her mind weighing her options. He wouldn't press her, but just one stumble over the slippery rocks in the river, and those precious clothes of hers would go floating downstream faster than she could swim after them. She was certainly aware of that. He hoped she wouldn't carry her damn stubbornness too far.

Jana's chest heaved in a sigh just before she nodded her head. Her lips were drawn in a tight line. Dan didn't say anything when he pulled his backpack from his shoulders, and unzipped the main compartment. She quickly stuffed the bundle into the pack, and backed away. He tried to meet her eyes, but she refused to even look at him.

"Let's find a couple of sturdy sticks to use for added leverage against the current." He motioned with his chin toward the trees. Without waiting for a response, he headed toward the timber, scanning the ground for a long branch or two that could serve as a walking stick. Testing the strength of several by leaning on them, he chose one for himself and one for Jana. She waited by the water, and gazed into the distance.

Dan stared at her, unable to pull his eyes away. The slight breeze in the air blew wisps of her hair around her face, and she shook her head, holding her chin up into the wind. She closed her eyes, and a look of pure contentment filled her face. He groaned silently, then clenched his jaw.

Suspecting she would probably greet him with hostility if he simply walked up to her, he cleared his throat and called out, "Found a couple." When Jana's head shot around to stare in his direction, he held up the branches, and headed toward her. Wordlessly, he handed her a thick branch, and waded into the water.

The current was as strong as he'd suspected, and he slowly set one foot in front of the other, testing the slippery river rocks by feel with his feet. When he stood halfway into the river, the cold water reached almost to his hips.

He turned his head to see how Jana was doing. She inched forward, putting one foot in front of the other, using her stick for leverage. Not once did she look at him, but concentrated on her task. She was waist-deep in water, and he could see that she was having a much harder time than he was. He could use his size and body mass to his advantage, whereas her slight frame battled the strong current.

Dan waited until she caught up to him. "Do you need help?" he asked loudly over the deafening roar of the rushing river. She briefly looked up at him, and with a determined set to her face, struggled on.

Dan shook his head, annoyed with Jana's stubborn demeanor, but conceding it was his fault. He decided to stay behind her just in case the current proved too strong for her, afraid she might slip. She may not want his assistance now, but if she lost her footing, he was ready to grab her before the water swept her away.

Dan breathed easier when she reached shore. She scrambled up the rocky banks, nearly stumbling over a slippery boulder. His hand reflexively reached for her, but he thought better of it and dropped it again before making contact with her arm. Out of breath, she leaned forward, her hands on her knees. He couldn't help but watch her chest rise and fall, noticing how well her wet clothes clung to every curve of her body like a second skin. Goosebumps formed on her arms, and her body shivered.

"How about you get out of those wet clothes. We'll rest here for a while until they're somewhat dry."

"Hand me my dry clothes," she said, gulping in quick lungfuls of air. Dan removed his pack from his shoulders, and set it down in front of her.

"I'll go gather some firewood. You need to warm up." The bluish tinge to her lips had him worried. It was easy to succumb to hypothermia in this climate. The river had been ice-cold, and he was eager himself to remove his shoes and slip into a dry pair of pants. He could think of only one more river they would need to ford, and he hoped by the time they reached the Gardner, Jana would be on better speaking terms with him again.

CHAPTER THIRTEEN

*D*an admitted that he was enjoying himself more than he could remember on any other backpacking trip, even though his hiking partner was cold and distant with him. He drew a small measure of satisfaction with Jana's aloof attitude in that she finally allowed him to carry her bundle of spare clothes in his pack. The natural beauty of the area lifted his mood regardless of her demeanor. Here, he was forced to forge his own trail instead of following in countless other men's footsteps. Nature was unforgiving, and he was ready to meet her challenges head on.

By evening of the next night after their successful river crossing, he chose a spot along a fast flowing stream that moved out from a sheer-walled narrow canyon. The forest was thick and dense in this area, overgrown with mosses and ferns, and the vegetation's canopies filtered out much of the sunlight. Birds of all species chirped and chattered high up in the trees. Shelter here was abundant in the form of thick vines and bushes. The weather had been good to them so far, and they hadn't needed anything more substantial than a warm fire at night.

"Where are we?" Jana asked, turning her head from side to side, staring up at the sheer canyon walls, taking in her surroundings with wide eyes. With a loud groan, she eased herself to the soft ground, and began to unlace her hiking boots.

"If you can make it just a bit further up into this canyon, there's a nice spot to soak your feet," he offered. "If I'm not mistaken, there's a little waterfall just up ahead."

She expelled a long breath of air through her open mouth, and pushed herself off the ground. Dan was about to hold out his hand, but thought better of it. She'd rejected all of his previous offers of assistance over the last few days, and he wouldn't expect her to reach for him now. He waited for her to stand on her feet, then headed further into the canyon. She looked tired, and he couldn't blame her. They'd covered a lot of ground over rough and demanding terrain, and she hadn't uttered a word of complaint.

The path along the creek was overgrown with thick mosses, and downed timber lay about everywhere, hidden by the tall ferns and grasses that grew in the shade of the canyon. Carefully, Dan navigated around the obstacles. It didn't take long before the sounds of a waterfall splashing onto rocks could be heard up ahead. Just around the bend, a long veil of water came tumbling from the canyon ledge high above them, splashing loudly into a rocky pool below.

"Beautiful," Jana murmured behind him.

"You mean, you've never seen this before?" Dan asked, turning his head in her direction. "I thought you hiked most trails in the park."

"Most, but apparently not all," she said wearily. She settled herself on a rock close to the crystal clear shallow pool below the falls, and with a sigh that sounded like she was in ecstasy, removed her boots and socks. Hiking up her pant legs, she carefully waded into the water.

Dan let his pack slide from his shoulders. His sweat-soaked shirt clung to his back. The water looked inviting, and he hadn't had a good shower in days. He ran his hand over his rough and whiskered face, and made up his mind. Rummaging through his pack, he found the bar of soap he'd brought.

He pulled his t-shirt off over his head, and tossed it on top of his pack. The cool breeze blowing through the canyon felt good on his damp skin. He reached for the button on his pants, eager to wash three days' worth of grime and trail dust from his body.

"What are you doing?" Jana asked, still wading in the pool. He glanced up, and couldn't suppress a grin when he caught her wide-eyed look of . . . what did he see in her eyes? Admiration? Desire? Dan hesitated, his thumb about to push the button through the button hole on his pants.

"I could go for a shower," he said, shrugging.

"Couldn't you warn me before you strip?" she asked, a high-pitched hitch to her voice.

He chuckled softly. Along with the note of alarm in her voice, her cheeks glowed a rosy red. He had every intention of giving her fair warning that he meant to strip down to his birthday suit, but she'd beaten him to the punch with her alarmed outburst.

"I'm sure in your line of work, you've seen plenty of naked men. You're welcome to join me if you'd like." He flashed her a wide grin in an attempt to dispel the sudden images in his mind of Jana standing under the waterfall with him, their wet bodies entwined in a passionate embrace.

Dan's throat went dry. He sat on one of the countless boulders surrounding the pool, trying to hide his physical reaction to his thoughts. Good thing he still wore his pants.

Jana's mouth drew together in a firm line, and her eyes narrowed. He'd definitely succeeded in making her even angrier with him. What would it take to get her to lighten up a bit? Splashing loudly through the water, she scrambled over the rocks to reach the shore. She snatched up her boots and socks, and shot him an icy look before heading back the way they'd come.

"Don't go too far. This is a nice place to stay for the night," Dan called after her. "I won't be long."

She didn't respond, but hurried off down the trail, stumbling once over some deadfall. Dan shook his head. He had no idea Miss Jana would act all shy around a half-naked man. For some reason, the thought made his heart drum faster in his chest, and his gut clenched almost painfully. He hurried out of his pants and boxers, and stepped into the ankle-deep pool and under the natural shower, welcoming the cool spray as the water pelted the sudden heat in his body.

JANA SETTLED under a pine tree nestled against the rocky wall of the canyon. The splashing sound of the waterfall behind her did little to drown out the rapid drumming of her heart in her ears. For three days, she and Dan had taken care of their personal needs discreetly apart from each other. Whenever they'd stopped along a creek, they'd gone their separate ways to wash the day's accumulation of dirt and sweat from their bodies.

Dan's bold move to almost undress right in front of her left her flushed and annoyed. Annoyed with herself at the sudden rush of desire flooding her senses at the sight of his beautifully sculpted body. She'd seen him nude from the waist up before, and her reaction had been the same, as she recalled.

He was right. She had seen plenty of nude men in her line of work, but she couldn't recall any of them with such a well-sculpted physique as Dan. Not too tall, but broad-shoul-dered, with corded arm muscles and well defined abs, Dan was certainly of much higher caliber than the men she saw on a routine basis in the surgery suites and recovery area at the hospital. For the most part, her patients consisted of middle-aged or older men. He was definitely a man in his prime, athletic and fit, and many of her female co-workers would surely swoon if he were lying on their operating tables.

No matter how angry she was with him for deceiving her, she couldn't stop the undeniable attraction she felt for him. He'd been nothing but kind and polite with her the last few days while they made their way through the wilderness, asking for her input in everything from where to set up camp for the night, to whether she needed a rest, to what she wanted to eat. He'd produced some lure and hooks from his pack the second night, and proven himself rather adept at catching fish from one of the many streams that meandered through the valley. He also seemed to know all the edible plants to be found along the way.

Dan fit as easily into this uncharted wilderness as he no doubt did leading a group of modern-day hikers on an expe-dition along a well-marked trail. Often, he would carry on a running commentary about the landscape, pointing out differences in the land in this time from modern times. His continued enthusiasm reminded her so much of Aimee, that Jana often found it hard to hold back the tears. Why did the man she'd thought was Mr. Right less than a week ago have to turn out to be a liar and untrustworthy?

He hadn't brought up the events leading up to their time travel after the first night, when he'd confessed everything to her. He conversed with her about neutral things, acting as if everything was okay between them, and completely ignored the fact that she tried to ignore him. He hadn't made any more attempts to apologize, nor had he tried to touch her.

Jana expelled a loud breath of air through her mouth. It was all so annoying. He was annoying. It irritated her that she was so completely aware of him, and that her emotions were in such a jumble. The fact that he hadn't tried to make physical contact with her, reach for her hand or touch her in a subtle way as he had done on numerous occasions while they were still in the twenty-first century, annoyed her. When he walked ahead of her on the trail, she was preoccupied watching the muscles along his shoulders and arms move underneath his shirt. When he walked behind her, she felt self-conscious, and listened for every move he made.

Jana groaned. Why had she given in and pushed her initial reservations aside, and opened her mind to the possibility of a relationship with him? She'd exposed her heart, and now it hemorrhaged freely.

With jerky movements, she pulled her socks and boots back on. She could survive these few weeks in his company, she told herself firmly. Once they got to Aimee and Daniel's cabin, she would simply have to ignore him. Depending on what date it was, Aimee might be close to giving birth, or maybe she already had her twins and Jana would be too busy helping her friend to even think about Dan.

She refused to allow herself to believe she would never be going home again. The man who had the time travel device would show up. Dan was convinced of it. Somehow Dan would figure out how to stop him from carrying out his intended plan of killing an innocent child. Daniel wouldn't let any harm come to his family, she was sure of it. And after she returned safely home to the twenty-first century, she'd hurry her butt back to California, and put this entire mess,

Dan Osborne included, behind her and out of her mind once and for all.

Tired from a long day of hiking over rough terrain, she sat on the cool ground, and leaned back against the trunk of the tree. She lifted her head to look at the sky. Evening would soon be upon them, and Jana knew she should be gathering wood for a fire. For a moment, she just wanted to sit here, and soak in the peaceful sounds of the forest. Birds chirped loudly amongst the branches of the trees, and the wind rustled gently through the high canopies of the lodge-poles that reached their limbs from the forest floor high up into the sky. Closing her eyes, she inhaled deep breaths of fragrant pine scent, the quiet tranquility of this slot canyon lulling her into a state of relaxation.

Something hard tapped her on the shoulder, and the sudden murmur of deep voices startled her out of her reverie. Her eyes flew open and she stared up into three of the most feral-looking faces she had ever seen.

Jana gasped, and braced her palms against the tree behind her, slowly pushing herself up off the ground. Her shirt snagged in the rough bark as she scraped against the trunk. She swallowed hard, and drew in a deep breath.

"Dan!" she screamed at the top of her lungs.

CHAPTER FOURTEEN

*D*an shook the water from his hair like a wet dog. The cold shower had done little to extinguish the fire inside him. The look of desire in Jana's eyes, although fleeting, stayed engrained in his mind. She might be mad at him, she might not ever forgive him, but she couldn't hide the fact that she was as attracted to him as he was to her. He'd noticed it over the last few days, how she watched him when she thought he wasn't looking. He was acutely aware of everything she did, his entire being tuned in to her. Would her attraction have led to feelings of love at some point? If he hadn't deceived her?

Dan sighed and pulled his hiking pants on. He would probably never know the answers to those questions. The most he could hope for was that she might think of him as a friend after their little sojourn through time ended. Could he settle for a mere friendship with her? He ran his hand through his hair. Not a chance. How could he pretend to feel nothing for her, when his mind was consumed by this one woman?

A sudden loud scream filled the air. Jana's terror-filled

voice echoed through the canyon, reverberating off the cliff walls. Startled ravens took to the air, their loud calls of protest adding to the bone-chilling sound. She'd called his name in terror. Fear pulsed through him.

Dan fumbled quickly in his pack, and pulled out his can of bear spray and the large hunting knife he'd brought with him.

"Jana," he shouted. Barefoot, he raced over the moist earth, leaping over logs and shrubbery. He suddenly wished he had brought his .45 Magnum, a weapon he chose to leave behind in the future. He had wanted to bring as little modern-day equipment with them as possible, and he'd hoped he could ward off a grizzly with bear spray, should they encounter one.

Around a bend in the canyon, three figures suddenly came into view. Dan's mind raced wildly. Over the last couple of days, he'd often wondered if they would meet any Native Americans on their trek through the wilderness. His eyes quickly scanned the surrounding area.

Jana stood backed-up against a tree, the men surrounding her in a half-circle. Their heads turned in unison when he came running toward them. Each man's long black hair hung in two braids past his shoulders. One wore two raven feathers at the back of his head. They were all dressed in leather breechclouts, their legs encased in leggings. Knives and clubs hung from belts at their hips. None of these men wore shirts.

Dan slowed, his heart racing. He knew he was no match against all three of them at once. They not only outnumbered him, they were also well armed. Along with the weapons on their belts, they each carried bows, the quivers on their backs filled with arrows. His hand gripped his bear spray firmly in one hand, ready to release the trigger, his knife clasped in the other. The bear spray might just be his weapon of choice. Much more potent than pepper spray, it could buy him and Jana enough time to escape from these Indians if he needed to use it.

The three stepped away from Jana, their full attention on him. They murmured, and gestured with their hands. Dan shot a quick glance at her, relieved that she didn't appear to be hurt. Her terror-filled eyes sent him a pleading look. He stopped about ten yards from the men, and waited. They hadn't raised their weapons, and stood conversing with each other. They seemed to be as baffled at his appearance as he was about them.

Dan slowly raised his hand in a gesture of greeting. He couldn't be sure, but he was fairly convinced these Indians were not Sheepeaters. He knew enough about their history and customs, even spoke a little Shoshone, to think these were not the band of Indians that made Yellowstone their permanent home. He'd seen bows made from elk antler and mountain sheep horn, and the bows these men carried looked to be made from wood.

Another thought entered his mind. If these were Blackfoot, Jana wouldn't have had a chance to even scream. The Blackfoot were a warring tribe from what he knew, and would most likely kill them before asking questions.

He came to the conclusion that these men had to be from another tribe that traveled through the Yellowstone region. He named off several tribes in his mind. Bannock, Flathead, Crow. His eyes rested on the raven feathers adorning one man's hair. He'd bet money these were Crow Indians. The trouble was, he had no way of communicating with them.

One of the men raised his arms forward, extending his hands in a beckoning gesture. His mouth curved in a slow smile. Dan's mind searched wildly for even the tiniest scraps of information he could recall about the natives of these parts. Chances were good that these Indians had never laid eyes on a white man before, and if they had, it was probably to trade. Most of the historical accounts he'd read of early trappers and the native Indians told of friendly relations between the two cultures. It wasn't until years later, when more trappers and fortune seekers came to the Rockies, that relations between the whites and Indians began to sour.

Dan approached the three. He stuffed the hilt of his knife into his back pants pocket, and clipped the bear spray canister to his belt loop. He held out his own hands, just like the Indian was doing. The three all nodded approval, wide smiles on their faces, and surrounded him. He clasped hands with the first man, while another slapped him on the back like a comrade would do in greeting a long-lost friend. He grinned and nodded at them while they spoke words he couldn't even begin to guess the meaning of.

His eyes darted to Jana, who still stood motionless by the tree. She'd lost some of the terror in her eyes, but fear and wariness remained evident on her face. He couldn't blame her for being scared. She was the only female here, and he was sure she was aware that women were regarded much differently in this time than in the twenty-first century.

After several minutes of friendly handshakes and back slapping, the men moved aside. The one with the crow feathers – Dan assumed him to be the leader – motioned for him to follow. He pointed toward the opening of the slot canyon, from where he and Jana had come earlier. The man held his partly fisted right hand to his mouth and brought it down past his chin, then nodded his head at Dan. He pointed once again in the direction leading out of the canyon.

Dan shook his head, not understanding. The leader spoke to one of the other men, who quickly took off at a fast jog. The man tried again to communicate, repeating his earlier gestures.

Dan's eyes sought Jana, and he finally pointed at her. The

Indian smiled. He gestured at Dan, then made a motion with his slightly hooked fingers down the side of his face along his hair. Then he directed a finger at Jana. Dan could only guess at the meaning, but he assumed that the Indian made the connection that Jana was with him.

"I think they're friendly, Jana. Why don't you come away from that tree," he called to her. He stepped around the man, and headed toward her.

"What if they're not?" she asked suspiciously.

"We'll have to take our chances." Dan tentatively reached for her hand. Would she try and balk at contact with him now? He felt her reluctance when she slipped her hand in his, and he pulled her away from the tree. He offered her a smile of encouragement. She didn't smile back.

Dan led her to the two men standing by, watching him and Jana intently. The leader spoke, and made a sweeping gesture with his hand, out and to the right of his chest. Then he pointed again, first at Dan, and then at Jana. Dan had the distinct feeling he was asking if she was his woman. He nodded firmly, and gripped Jana's hand, pulling her up next to him. He ignored the heated look she shot him.

"I left my pack by the waterfall. If I stay here with these guys, would you mind going and bringing it back?" he asked gently. He didn't want Jana to assume he was ordering her around, and hoped she wouldn't argue with him. It might look out of place if he went to collect his gear, rather than sending his woman to do the work.

Jana opened her mouth, her eyes narrowed on him. She must have thought better of it, and rather than protest or argue with him as he feared she might do, she pulled her hand from his grasp. Skirting around the two Indians, she walked briskly further into the canyon, disappearing behind the bend as the canyon curved to the right.

Time passed excruciatingly slow while he waited for Jana

to return. The Indians pointed at the canister of bear spray dangling from his pants, and Dan offered it to them to inspect. The trigger's lock mechanism was in place, and he was reasonably sure they wouldn't figure out how to unlock it. Preoccupied with the canister, the two men ignored him for the moment. He stood, gazing intently up into the canyon, waiting for Jana to come back.

She emerged at the same time as the man who'd been sent away returned. He carried a small deer on his shoulders. Dropping the carcass in front of them, Dan noticed him glancing at Jana with keen interest when she wordlessly held his pack out for him and dropped his boots at his feet.

The Indian with the feathers in his hair pointed at the carcass, then made the same fisted gesture in front of his mouth as he'd done earlier. He pointed off into the distance again. Comprehension finally dawned.

"They want us to go with them, I think. They're offering food," he said to Jana.

"How do you know they're not wanting to scalp us?" Jana asked skeptically.

"If that was their intent, they would have done it by now. These Indians seem genuinely kind and hospitable. We might even offend them if we refuse."

"Well, I don't like the idea," she said between gritted teeth.

Dan shot a quick glance at the Indians. Their exchange was being watched with some interest. He knew he was about to make Jana mad at him all over again, but he grinned and jutted his chin out at the Crow leader. Everyone smiled, and heads nodded in approval.

The three Indians led the way out of the canyon. Dan quickly pulled his boots and shirt on.

"You'd better carry the gear, Jana," he said, gesturing with his hand at the pack on the ground.

"I can't believe you're going along with them," she hissed. "What if I refuse to come?"

Dan clenched his jaw, and prayed for patience. He'd ignored her anger and sour demeanor over the last few days, knowing he deserved it, but enough was enough. Her stubbornness was not helping them at the moment. He leaned toward her, and grabbed hold of her upper arms.

"Whether you want to believe this or not, I am trying to keep us safe. These people seem friendly enough, but if we offend them in any way, I can't protect you." He paused, glaring at her, and inhaled a deep breath. "I know you don't want to trust me, but you simply don't have a choice right now, Jana. We are in the nineteenth century. In a lot of Indian cultures, a woman is supposed to act subservient to her man."

Jana huffed at his words. "Subservient? If you're expecting me to --"

"Do what I tell you, without arguing, or I will play the role of master as convincing as I need to," Dan interrupted her, his voice almost a growl. The look of animosity she shot him tore at his very soul.

"Fine, *master*. I'll act as the dutiful slave," she said between clenched teeth, and pulled away from his grip. She heaved the backpack onto her shoulders, and marched off, following behind the Indians. Dan stared after her, drawing in a long, deep breath. Enduring the last few days of her anger had been pure torture. Right now, he'd merely succeeded in tossing more salt on her gaping wounds. Self-loathing consumed him. With a heavy heart, Dan picked up the pace to catch up with the group.

CHAPTER FIFTEEN

*J*ana walked silently behind the four men. She was tired, hungry, and her muscles ached all over. If these Indians hadn't shown up, she might already be asleep. The sun was sinking in a fiery red ball into the western horizon, bathing the sky in a palette ranging from reds to orange, and even soft purple hues. She wondered how much further they would be walking to reach their destination, wherever that was.

She'd never been such a moody person, the way she'd been acting the last few days. Her constant anger at Dan, and at herself for harboring feelings for him, left her behaving out of sorts and disagreeable. The fact that he didn't react negatively to her foul mood only served to irritate her more. Dan had come to her rescue without a second's hesitation after she screamed his name. *And it was his name you screamed, Jana.*

He didn't think she trusted him. She didn't want to trust him. He'd already proven himself untrustworthy. But, darn it all, she did trust him. She also knew he was right about how she needed to act more appropriate for a female in this time in the company of other people. That he wouldn't normally ask her to carry the pack, or make a decision without her input and approval was clear to her.

He is trying to keep us both safe. The least you can do is cooperate.

Jana repositioned the pack on her shoulders. It was adjusted for Dan's much larger frame and rode far too low on her back. Gritting her teeth, she kept moving, determined to suffer in silence.

The unaccustomed weight of the backpack on her shoulders seemed to get heavier with each step she took, and her legs felt like anchors trying to root her to the spot. Setting one foot in front of the other became more difficult by the minute. The fatigue in her upper thighs as she trudged on turned to agony. She wasn't sure how much further she could go before succumbing to the urge to drop everything, including herself, and refuse to take one more step. This thought had barely entered her mind, when the sudden unmistakable smell of burning wood filled her nostrils.

A wide clearing came into view shortly after and several campfires glowed in the dim twilight. To her dismay, she counted four more Indians to the three who had found them in the canyon. She hoped and prayed that Dan's assessment was correct, and these people meant them no harm. They were severely outnumbered.

The three men greeted their companions by raising their bows in the air and speaking in their guttural language. Curious eyes darted to her and Dan. He was the center of attention, and laughed and gestured with the rest of them. Jana was left to stand by herself at the periphery of the circle the men had created.

Her back ached from carrying the heavy pack and Jana slid it off her shoulders, letting it drop to the ground. She rubbed at her stiff neck and waited apprehensively. She wasn't as convinced as Dan that these Indians were friendly. Several men shot her curious glances and she caught the unmistakable looks of lust from more than one pair of eyes. She shuddered and hugged her arms around her waist.

She wished Dan was at her side. Instead he had all but abandoned her and acted like a typical guy who'd just met up with some long-lost drinking buddies. Renewed annoyance with him seared through her at the thought.

After what seemed like an eternity, the men dispersed, and several began butchering the deer the three had brought. Jana noticed a few more hides hanging up in trees, stripped of meat. Dan finally came to her side and took hold of her hand. His thumb caressed her palm.

"How are you holding up?" he asked, his eyes focused on her face, a deep concern in his voice.

She shrugged, unable to speak all of a sudden. Her throat constricted painfully and she swallowed several times to dispel the sensation. Tears threatened behind her eyes. She tried to pull her hand away, but he held tight. His genuine concern was too much for her tired mind to deal with at the moment.

"After you get some food in you, you'll feel better," he said. He obviously saw that she was about to lose it.

"I'll be fine," she replied and raised her chin up high.

"I think this is a hunting party. That's why there aren't any tipis and women here in camp."

"*Dah-nul,*" a voice spoke from behind Dan. Jana quickly jerked her hand from his grasp.

Dan turned and nodded at the man who spoke. Jana recognized the one who'd carried the deer carcass. He was also the one whose lust-filled eyes kept seeking her out. He looked at her now, and Jana saw hunger in his dark gaze. She suddenly gained a deeper appreciation for the deer he had killed. Had the poor prey's heart speed up with terror, just

119

before the fatal arrow pierced its throat? She took a hasty step back, trying to conceal her body behind Dan's.

The Indian held out several furs to Dan, along with a leather pouch, and a bow and quiver. He motioned for Dan to take them. To her utter mortification, the man pointed at her as he thrust the items at Dan. He signaled with his hands, running bent fingers down the side of his face, as if he were combing his hair. He gestured at Jana, then back to the items he held.

Dan shook his head. He swept his hand through the air in a gesture of finality, and thrust one hand in a downward motion, palm down, past his hip. He turned halfway and grabbed Jana's arm, pulling her up against him. With his other hand, he roughly stroked her face, pushing strands of hair out of her eyes, and running his hand over her head and down the back to her neck. Jana felt like a dog, being petted by its master. She gritted her teeth, and tilted her head up slightly to flash him a look that told him she was not at all happy about this humiliating treatment. His eyes filled with a fierce possessiveness that caused her heart to flutter uncontrollably in her chest.

Abruptly, he released her, and firmly sliced his hand through the air again. The Indian shot her a final look of longing, then nodded his head in acceptance and walked off with his bundle of offerings. Dan didn't look at her.

"I'll get us some food," he said gruffly, and followed the other man to one of the fires, leaving Jana standing in stunned silence.

She didn't dare follow him. She stayed just within the glow of light from the three campfires, watching the men settle around the flames, pulling chunks of meat from large slabs they had hanging on spits. Conversation was lively, yet carried out in quiet tones. The aroma the meat gave off made Jana's stomach growl loudly.

Dan was welcomed at one of the fires and he sat with the men, who offered him meat and something else from a carved wooden bowl they passed around. Jana's anger boiled to the surface, watching him eat and carry on, communicating with these people using hand gestures. Apparently, she'd been all but forgotten as the minutes dragged by.

To ease the throbbing in her sore feet, she settled herself on the cold, hard ground, and rummaged through the backpack. There had to be at least another power bar left. The surrounding darkness made it difficult to see and she burrowed her hand through the pack by feel. Near the very bottom, she found what she sought. At least it would lessen the hunger pangs a little.

Damn him! He sure slipped into the role of a nineteenth century man with ease. Jana felt sorry for all the women of this time who had to endure being treated like nothing more than a commodity. How did Aimee deal with it? She dismissed her thought. Daniel hadn't treated Aimee like a second-class citizen from everything Jana had seen while he'd been in the future, or from reading her friend's journal.

There's a difference, Jana. Daniel loves Aimee.

Jana blinked back the sting in her eyes as a wave of tears threatened to spill forth. She was bone-tired and still had a long journey ahead of her to reach Aimee's cabin. Her inner strength at the moment seemed to falter completely. She just wanted this ordeal to be over. Her body ached, not only from the difficult hike through the endless wilderness, but also because she hadn't allowed herself to relax in the three days she'd been here. If things were different with Dan, if she didn't feel the need to keep up her angry demeanor all the time, this might all be easier.

Jana tore open the wrapper of the bar, already sick of the smell of peanuts escaping from the packaging. It was protein, however, and she needed the food. She chewed listlessly, and shot another look toward the fire. She nearly choked. Dan stood, facing the same man with whom he'd bartered earlier. With exaggerated and forceful hand gestures, the man offered Dan a pile of weaponry, including a knife, ax, a bow, and a heap of furs and other items Jana could not make out. Talking around the fires had ceased, and all eyes were on the two men.

The Indian pointed in her direction several times, and Dan continued to shake his head and gesture with his hands that clearly communicated the word *no*. Jana had no doubt what the discussion was about. She'd seen the Indian's hungry looks directed at her.

What if the confrontation turned violent? Dan might be putting himself in harm's way because of her. Her mind reeled with a jumble of mixed emotions. Dan could simply hand her over to the Indian if he chose, but he stood his ground, adamantly defending her.

When he turned down a new offer by the Indian, who pulled something from around his neck to add to the growing pile of items, the man tossed everything on the ground and threw his hands in the air before stomping off. There was no doubt he was angry. The rest of the men returned to their conversations, as if nothing had happened. The confrontation seemed to be over and done with. Dan bent toward the ground, and picked up a small bundle at his feet. Even from a distance, she saw the seething anger in his eyes as he made his way toward her.

GLAD TO PUT the confrontation with that Crow behind him, Dan headed toward Jana. His muscles still tensed in anger. He'd seen the man ogle her since he'd first laid eyes on her back in the canyon. His intent had been crystal clear when he offered up those beaver pelts initially.

Never in a million years had Dan ever expected to engage in barter with another man over a woman. It was almost funny. Someday, he was sure he'd get a good laugh out of it. Right now, the situation was much too serious. He had no idea how far the Crow would push him, if he wanted Jana. One thing was clear in his mind. He'd fight to the death to keep her safe.

He hated having to act like some Neanderthal, claiming the prized female. But he would do what was necessary to make sure every one of these men knew he would not relinquish his woman. If he showed any weakness in front of her, he'd look weak in those men's eyes as well. Jana's look of contempt when he'd almost manhandled her in front of her admirer was something he couldn't avoid.

His act might not be over yet. They were in the company of these Crow for the duration of the night, and if Jana remained uncooperative, he didn't know how far he would have to go to show that he was in charge. Dan hoped they could part ways with this group of hunters peacefully come morning.

Jana sat just within the circle of light from the fires, a half-eaten power bar in her hand when he approached. A twinge of guilt hit him. He knew she was hungry, but bringing her food before he had eaten would certainly make him appear weak. None of the men had indicated he should offer her food, or ask her to join the fire. Dan had decided to play it safe and assumed women ate last among this tribe's culture. He caught the frigid stare she shot him, just before she averted her eyes when he approached.

"I brought you some meat," he said, holding out a portion of venison he'd wrapped in a piece of leather. She made a show of taking a large bite of her power bar in response to his words. Dan clenched his jaw, and steeled his heart. He placed the bundle on his backpack, then reached for her arm and hauled her forcefully to her feet. The momentum threw her against him, and he refused to let her pull away.

She inhaled a sharp breath, and raised her head to glower at him.

"Now I know how Aimee must have felt when she stood by as two men bartered for her," she said, her tone icy.

"And I know how Daniel felt, trying to keep the peace and protect his woman at the same time," Dan replied slowly. A lazy grin formed on his lips, hoping to break through some of her cold demeanor. He chuckled softly. "'Course, you're not liking me much these days. Maybe . . .'"

"Don't you even think what I know you're thinking," she hissed. "You're really enjoying that I'm completely at your mercy, aren't you?"

Dan worked his jaw muscles. She continued to believe only the worst of him. He inhaled a deep breath, and quietly answered, "No, Jana. I'm not enjoying this, but I will do whatever it takes to keep you safe."

The uncertainty in her eyes, the hurt, the fear, came crashing down on him. "If you believe nothing else I tell you," he whispered, his face inches from hers, "just know that I would rather die than see any harm come to you."

Her eyes widened, and her lips parted slightly. Dan's restraint faltered. She was too close, and three days of trying to assuage her anger finally took its toll on him. He brought his mouth down on hers, gripping her arms to pull her closer, and groaned as a flood of adrenaline shot through his veins, igniting his heart to beat wildly in his chest.

Jana stood stiffly, her arm muscles tense. He ran his tongue across her lips, tasting the peanuts from the power bar she'd eaten. He softened his assault, slowly gliding his lips across hers, trying to coax a response from her. His grip eased on her arms, and he slid his hands up to her shoulders, following the contours of her neck until his hands cupped her face. With his thumbs, he caressed her cheeks and felt the moisture rolling down her face.

Breaking the contact with her lips, he pulled back slightly, and rested his forehead against hers. He breathed heavily, trying to subdue the powerful jolt of emotions that ripped through his entire being.

"Jana," he whispered. "I'm sorry . . . for everything."

She shuddered against him, and then her body relaxed. Her knees seemed to buckle, and he quickly wrapped his arms around her waist. She fit so perfectly against him, as if she was made for him alone.

"I know," she whispered so softly, he wasn't sure if she even said the words. Her arms slowly rose up, and she placed her palms against his chest. Dan held his breath, waiting for her to push him away. When her hands slid slowly up and around his neck, his heart exploded in his chest.

He expelled his breath of air, and touched his lips to hers again. She sighed, and leaned into him, clinging to his neck. Her mouth moved against his and emotions unlike anything he'd felt before threatened to swallow him up. Possessiveness, protectiveness, desire, and love. For the first time in his life, he could truly claim to be in love with a woman, and the feeling was more potent than anything that came before.

Reluctantly, he drew his head back. He swiped at the tears on her cheeks, and smiled down at her, not sure if she could even see him in the darkness. Shadows from the dancing flames of the campfires behind them distorted both their features.

"I should be angry with you, but . . . I can't be anymore. There's just something about you . . . I can't explain it." She sounded defeated, but not remorseful. His heart suddenly felt lighter than it had in weeks.

"I know, Jana. I feel it, too. I've felt it from the very first time I saw you." He slowly ran his fingers through her hair, hoping she believed him. "I swear to you, I will never lie to you again." Her head moved up and down in a nod.

Jana sucked in a deep breath. "You smell real good," she whispered against his ear. Dan shivered and heat pooled in his gut at her sensual words. With his hands at her waist, he peeled her away from him, afraid she might feel his reaction to her.

"And you smell like you've been out hiking for the last three days," he said lightly. "You should have taken me up on the offer and joined me back there by that waterfall." She could have rolled in a field of bison dung for all he cared; on her it would be the sweetest scent he'd ever smelled.

"The next one we come to, I get first dibs," she said. Dan smiled. He couldn't believe the complete change in her from mere moments ago. Whatever had brought it on, he hoped it wasn't temporary. He took her hand in his, and pulled her to the ground. Reaching for the leather bundle on his pack, he offered it to her.

"You need to eat, and get some rest. Today was a long, hard day."

"Tomorrow won't be any easier," she sighed, accepting the food.

"No, but I'll be carrying the pack again," he said.

"You don't enjoy the power a nineteenth century man has over a woman?" she asked. Dan's eyebrows rose.

"Sure I do, but I'm thinking I prefer my women stubborn and independent." She probably couldn't see the wide grin on his face. Their hike to reach the Madison Valley may not get any easier, but anything they faced from here on certainly would be much more bearable, now that they seemed to have reached an understanding.

CHAPTER SIXTEEN

*J*ana slowly opened her eyes to the crackling sounds of wood burning and the hushed voices of a couple of men mulling about. Other than the faint glow from several campfires, the gray sky barely offered enough light to see by. She inhaled a deep breath, wondering how early in the morning it was. The subtle clean scent of soap suddenly overpowered the smell of wood smoke, and Jana awakened fully.

Her head wasn't resting on her bundle of spare clothes, as it had the three previous nights, but rather on something firm and warm. Awareness seeped into her that she was molded up against a solid, warm body. Her hand rested on top of a man's chest, his heart beating steadily beneath her palm.

She didn't move. Memories of the previous evening came flooding back to her. She'd crumbled, folded like an accordion. She simply couldn't continue being angry with Dan anymore. What he had done - his lies - still stung, but the sincerity in his voice when he'd again told her how sorry he was, had been real.

He'd been foolish to leave Aimee's journal on his desk the day John Hastings had seen it, and then made a terrible mistake in judgment when he'd agreed to the superintendent's offer. Jana could see the turmoil and anguish in his mind over his bad decision. She only hoped they wouldn't be too late to correct Dan's error and prevent the tragedy of Matthew Osborne's murder.

Now she had to struggle with her own dilemma. Her feelings for Dan were more powerful than anything she'd ever experienced. He'd made it quite clear that he wanted a deeper relationship with her than a simple friendship. She couldn't think of anything she wanted more at the moment, either. Dan had proven last night that he would keep her safe and that he cared for her. The Crow who had tried to barter for her had kept his distance.

What would happen when they returned to the future? Was it even possible for them to get back home? Jana didn't want to think about the possibility of remaining here in the past. It was a life that Aimee had wanted, but it wasn't a life for Jana. What about Dan? He seemed to fit into this time period quite well. From what she'd observed, he was enjoying himself here. He was so much like the way she remembered Aimee, she could very well see him opting to stay in the nineteenth century.

If he chose to remain in the past, would she even consider such an option for herself? This was not a life for her. Could she give everything up, just as Aimee had done, and follow her heart? Jana paused. Here, they had no other alternative but to stick together. What about in the twenty-first century? Would a relationship with Dan even work in the future? She had her nursing career in California, while Dan was still finishing school in Montana. He would never want to move away from Yellowstone, not that she could ever ask that of him. But a long-distance relationship wasn't something to consider, either. It would never work.

Don't put the cart before the horse, Jana.

She'd gone out with plenty of men who spouted words of love and commitment, sometimes even on the first date. More often than not, she'd come to the conclusion that men said these things with one goal in mind. Once they realized she wasn't so easily wooed, they'd quickly walked away. She remembered the pact she'd made with Aimee when they were silly schoolgirls to remain pure until their wedding night. It hadn't worked out quite like that for Aimee, but Jana hadn't met the man yet who could wear down her resolve.

Lying here next to Dan, she inhaled deeply of his subtle soapy scent. He hadn't asked for a commitment, and he certainly never said he loved her. Not that she'd expected him to. They barely knew each other. Last night, she hadn't hesitated at his suggestion that she sleep next to him, rather than on opposite sides of the campfire as they had done the previous nights. Dan had built a fire a short distance away from the rest of the group, and she'd gone willingly into his arms when he beckoned to her.

Heat suddenly crept up her neck, burning her cheeks. Wordlessly, Dan had pulled her into his arms, and held her close. He'd simply told her to go to sleep. Nothing else. She remembered the twinge of disappointment that he hadn't kissed her again.

Jana moved her sore and aching limbs. She would never get used to sleeping on hard ground. Leaves and grasses were simply no substitute for her soft mattress at home. She stretched her legs and slowly inched away from Dan. Cold air seeped through her clothes when she lost contact with his warm body and she shivered involuntarily. Dan's arm tightened around her and pulled her back up against him.

"You're awake?" she whispered, her heart rate increasing.

"Yeah," he replied quietly. "Maybe we should get an early start," he suggested, but made no move to release her.

"Maybe we should."

His chest heaved and his arm relaxed. It was still too dark to make out his features, but she could feel his eyes on her. Behind them, the camp was starting to come alive. Men moved about, speaking in hushed tones. Jana had no desire to remain in this camp with the Indians any longer.

"Let's go, then," she said and pushed herself off the ground. Dan followed and headed toward the fires. Jana watched his silhouette as he communicated to the men that he was leaving. One man thrust a bundle at him and Dan removed something from his pocket and handed it to the Indian. After the exchange, Dan called out in a commanding voice, "Come on, woman. Let's be on our way."

Jana sighed. She couldn't help but smile softly. Yup, Dan Osborne would fit into this time period just fine. She groaned and lifted the pack off the ground and heaved it onto her shoulders. So much for him carrying the pack, as he'd said he would do last night. Hopefully they wouldn't have far to go before Dan offered to lighten her load.

THE SUN CREPT slowly above the mountains to the east. With the bright glow to their backs as they made their way further west, Jana didn't have to squint too much. She desperately missed having her sunglasses. About a mile from where they had left the Indian camp, Dan stopped and removed the pack from Jana's back.

She let out a long, drawn-out sigh, and rotated her aching shoulders to loosen the tension in her muscles. A small part of her felt guilty that Dan had carried the pack without complaint for three days.

"Where's the nearest restaurant," Jana said. "I could go for a nice big omelet."

Dan's eyebrows rose and he grinned. "Omelet, huh? All I have is some cold venison and trail mix, but I heard you don't like nuts. We'll stop in a while, and have some breakfast." He shouldered the pack, and his hand reached out to graze her arm. Jana glanced up at him. The warmth and tenderness in his eyes caused her heart to do somersaults.

She quickly turned and continued walking. She sensed he wanted to say something and do more than merely touch her arm. Jana mentally shook her head. She wasn't ready for things to move so quickly. Three times she'd kissed him with more passion than she'd ever kissed a man. Her intense awareness of him and the feelings he evoked in her, frightened her more than the long journey through uncharted wilderness. In the deep corners of her mind, she still held some reservations due to the fact that he was Aimee's descendant. And how much he reminded her of her best friend. And that he'd lied to her.

Dan fell in step beside her. "If we make good time, we might be able to reach the hot springs in three or four days," he said conversationally.

"Hot springs?" Jana echoed.

"Mammoth," Dan clarified with one word.

Jana turned her head to look at him. "We're going to Mammoth? Isn't that out of the way?"

"It's the easier route to get to Madison. We could go over the Blacktail Deer Plateau, but honestly, I've never hiked in that area and I hear the terrain is really rough. In our time, it's a bear management area, and off-limits to hiking. I would assume that even in this time, it's a prime grizzly habitat."

Jana cocked an eyebrow. "You're telling me, Mr. Ranger, that you're afraid of walking through bear habitat?"

Dan grinned. "No, but you'd make a tasty meal for a bear, and I'm not willing to risk that."

"All I have to do is outrun you," she said, a wide smile on her face. It was so easy to tease and banter with him all of a sudden. Jana's heart felt light as a feather, and the strenuous up and downhill hiking seemed far less tiring today.

"Watch it, Miss Evans, or I just might accept the next offer some Indian brave makes for you." He grabbed hold of her hand, and pulled her up against his chest. Jana sucked in a deep breath. His teasing, twinkling eyes suddenly turned dark. Jana recognized the look for what it was. Adrenaline surged through her. She swallowed nervously, needing to get control of her senses.

"Dan, please . . ." she stammered, her voice shaky. "You're moving way too fast for me."

"I'm standing perfectly still right now, Jana," he said, his sensually deep voice sending chills down her back. She pulled her hand out of his grip and took a step back.

"We need to get to Madison," she said firmly. "We need to focus on what to do about John Hastings." She led the way up a steep incline, eager to put a little distance between them. If he held her in his arms again, kissed her the way he had done the night before, she'd be a goner. The hill was steeper than she had anticipated, and she grabbed hold of low-hanging branches of pine trees, and roots that jutted out of the ground to aid her in her struggle.

"You're right," Dan said behind her. "But it's hard to focus on other things with the kind of view I've got directly in front of me." She gasped in surprise when his hands clasped her hips, pushing her onward. Jana redoubled her efforts, glancing upward to see how much further it was to reach the top of this hill. Her thighs and calves burned in protest, but she gritted her teeth and pushed on. If only she could move faster, and get away from Dan's warm hands. Just before they reached the summit, he released his hold on her and sprinted the last few yards past her up the hill. With a wide grin on his face, he waited for her at the top.

"Show off," she mumbled, catching her breath when her feet finally touched level ground.

"What's that you were saying about outrunning me if we meet up with a bear?"

Jana glared at him in response, wondering how to wipe that satisfied smirk off his face. Dan pulled his backpack from his shoulders and dropped it to the ground.

"I think this is a good place to stop and eat something." He paused, gazing out at the vast valley below. "Just look at the view." He made a sweeping motion with his arm in a half-circle. As far as the eye could see, one mountain carpeted with pine trees stretched out before another. In the far-off distance, a river flowed through the valley, twisting and turning like a coil of blue twine. A hawk soared lazily above them in the endless blue sky.

"A man could lose himself here forever," he mumbled, almost to himself. "Leave all his modern-day worries behind."

Jana stood beside him, glancing up at his face. The look of longing in his eyes as he stared off into the distance sent an icy jolt of fear through her heart. She'd been correct in her earlier assumption. Was he seriously entertaining ideas of remaining in the past?

Tentatively, she touched his arm. "Is it really so bad in modern times?" she asked softly. His head turned toward her, as if noticing her for the first time. A slow smile brightened the somber look on his face.

"Not anymore," he said. "Not since I deceived you to come back into my life." The smile disappeared, and his jaw muscles visibly clenched.

Jana avoided his eyes, and gazed at the vast wilderness

before them. Her heart and mind waged war with one another. Her heart told her to let herself go, and just give in to her feelings, while her rational mind warned her to tread with caution. He'd lied to her once already. She had forgiven him, but Jana couldn't help but wonder what it would take for her to cast all doubt aside and trust him completely.

CHAPTER SEVENTEEN

*J*ana stretched her sore limbs, and opened her eyes. Bright sunlight filtered through the canopy of lodgepole pines. Their warm rays couldn't keep her from shivering. There was a definite chill in the early morning air. The loud chirps and calls of countless forest birds announced the new day. After seven nights of sleeping on nothing but bare ground, she thought she would be used to it by now. No such luck. Her aching body parts reminded her of her soft mattress back home.

All things considered, she and Dan had been fortunate so far with the weather. A few afternoon thunderstorms that blew quickly through the mountains had been their only inclement weather. Hovering under some dense spruce trees had been enough during those times to prevent a thorough soaking.

A loud crackling and fizzling sound caught her attention. Dan was up and about before her, as usual. Although he couldn't provide the soft comfort of her bed at home, he did keep her quite warm at night. They no longer slept at opposite sides of the campfire. When he had casually suggested on their first night since leaving the group of Indians that it would serve them both better to sleep together for warmth, Jana had raised a skeptical eyebrow.

Dan's arms shot in the air in a mock defensive posture. A purely devilish grin had spread across his face. "I'll keep my hands to myself. Scout's honor."

To her utmost surprise, he'd remained true to his word. She remembered her heart pounding in her chest that first night, wondering what to expect. Would he kiss her? Would he stop at just a kiss? Would she be able to stop?

Lying down beside her, he'd pulled her up against him, and wrapped his arms protectively around her. He'd told her goodnight, and lightly kissed the top of her head. For hours, she'd lain there, unable to fall asleep while his breathing had been slow and rhythmic. The relief and simultaneous disappointment had kept her awake into the wee hours of the night.

Jana's mixed emotions were thrown even deeper into turmoil over the next three days. Dan had apparently taken her comment that he was moving too fast to heart. Plain and simple, he'd kept his distance. An occasional light touch on her arm followed by a warm smile, or a supportive hand on her back to help her up a steep hill or particularly difficult climb was the extent of his affections. True, he held her in his arms each night, but he may as well have been hugging his backpack to him for the lack of affection he showed her. He seemed completely indifferent.

As the days went by, Jana's frustrations grew. She longed for his kiss, for the smoldering looks of desire in his eyes, even as she told herself repeatedly that she preferred this casual relationship. She often wondered if he'd changed his mind about her. Perhaps he liked his women to be more forward, and the fact that she told him to slow down might have been a complete turn-off for him.

With a loud groan, Jana pushed herself off the ground. A delicious smell wafted to her nose, and although it was a familiar smell, she couldn't quite place the food that would give off such an aroma. She looked up to see Dan squatting by the fire, his little backpacking pot sitting on a flat rock near the flames. She blinked to focus her sleepy eyes, and gasped. Dan's t-shirt was torn at the shoulder and stained with blood, the red in sharp contrast to the white of the cotton. She scrambled to her feet and hurried to his side.

"Dan! What happened to you?" She touched his arm, trying to find the source of the bleeding.

He looked up, a wide grin on his face. "I was getting you some breakfast," he said.

Jana's eyebrows drew together, and she shook her head slightly. "Breakfast? Wha –"

He pointed to the pot. "Not exactly restaurant quality, but I made you an omelet."

Her confusion grew. "Omelet? Why . . . how," she sputtered. Dan stood to his feet.

"Three days ago, you wanted an omelet," he reminded her with a casual shrug of his shoulder. "I couldn't provide you with one then, but I did this morning. Well, if scrambled eggs and some dried meat count as an omelet."

Jana could only stare at him. He remembered her wishing for an omelet? Dan leaned forward, his forehead wrinkling as he looked at her expectantly. "I hope you haven't lost your appetite for one."

Too stunned for words, Jana tried to gather her thoughts. The sudden sensation of warm water lapping at her, seeping into her and wrapping itself around her heart filled her. Here she was, out in the vast wilderness with this rugged outdoorsman, jokingly asking for her favorite breakfast food several days ago, and he'd taken her words to heart and answered her wish.

"Yes, yes of course. I mean, no . . . I haven't lost my appetite." She tried desperately to find her voice.

"There's coffee in the cup. I'm afraid we're almost out."

Jana looked up at him. She raked her teeth across her lower lip. "Thank you, Dan," she said softly and stepped up to him. She placed her hands on his shoulders, intent to reach up and kiss him on the cheek. He flinched, and inhaled sharply. Jana quickly pulled her hand away and jumped back.

"Oh, my goodness," her hand flew to her mouth. "I forgot about your arm. What happened?" She lifted the torn fabric of his shirtsleeve, gently prying it away from a nasty gash in his upper bicep. The blood had dried, making the shirt stick to his skin.

"Goose," he said, glancing down at his arm.

"Goose?" She shook her head in confusion. "Sit down, let me clean that," She pushed him toward a downed log. "That looks nasty."

"So was the goose." Dan held up his hand. "Eat first," he said. "I don't want my efforts to go to waste."

Jana shot him a stern look. "Dan, if that gets infected . . . even a small injury can cause severe problems out here in the wilderness. You should know that."

"Yes, Nurse Evans," he said, a teasing note to his voice. "Eat your eggs, then I'll let you doctor me up."

Jana reluctantly did as he asked. She savored every bite, and even though it lacked cheese and salt, and was otherwise a far cry from a normal omelet, these were the best eggs she'd ever eaten.

DAN WATCHED Jana enjoy her meal. She sat cross-legged by the fire and scraped out spoonfuls of egg from the pot. Her mouth closed around the spoon, and she groaned softly. Her eyes fluttered shut, and pure contentment was written on her face.

He suppressed his own groan. Perspiration beaded his forehead when she languidly pulled the spoon from her mouth. He tried to swallow the lump that had formed in his throat to no avail. Unable to watch anymore for fear he would do something he might regret later, like toss that damn utensil she was making love to in the fire and kiss her senseless, he concentrated instead on a dung beetle as it crawled past his feet in the dirt.

For the last three days, he'd been on the lookout for any kind of bird nests so he could fulfill her wish for some eggs. She could have asked for a bison steak, and somehow he would have managed to bring down one of those massive beasts, just to give her what she wanted. He was convinced he would do anything for her.

What she clearly didn't want was him. Her fleeting looks of desire and her response to his kisses left no doubt in his mind that she was attracted to him physically. However, she acted noticeably uncomfortable around him at times when he wanted to do more than talk about the weather or what the next great obstacle was that they had to navigate. The moment he tried to touch her, she clammed up. Telling him he was moving too fast had to be her way of saying she wasn't ready for a relationship. She may have forgiven him for his deceit, but the rift between them was still there.

Would she ever be willing to surrender her heart to him? She'd told him to back off and he had complied. Holding her in his arms each night to keep her warm had been pure torture. Pretending to be nothing more than her hiking partner ate at his soul. He just wasn't sure how to bridge the gap between them. For now, all he could do was abide by her wishes and simply be her friend and backpacking buddy.

Dan flexed his throbbing biceps. That gander had gotten

him good. The stupid fowl had come out of nowhere when he finally found that nest of eggs hidden among some tall reeds near a pond that was a short walk up ahead. He'd thought he'd seen the pair of Canada geese on the water, but apparently that had been the wrong pair. Geese were notoriously defensive of their nests and if he had paid more attention, the protective male wouldn't have gotten a good bite out of his arm. Dan had finally fought the bird off with several well-placed kicks. He didn't want to harm the animal, but in hindsight, roast goose would have made a tasty dinner.

Jana set the pot down, and licked her lips. She glanced over at him, and the satisfied smile on her face made every gash and cut in his arm worth it.

"All right, where's your medicine kit?" she asked, bending over the backpack. Without waiting for an answer, she unzipped the main compartment, and began to rummage through the pack. Seconds later, she produced a small red satchel with a white cross on it. She unzipped it and studied the contents with a critical eye. Finally, she pulled out some antiseptic wipes, antibiotic ointment, and a bandage.

"I guess this will have to do," she said, and sat beside him on the log. Without any fanfare, she ripped the shirtsleeve of his tattered t-shirt up to the seam along the shoulder, and began to clean his bruised and battered skin with the antiseptic. The alcohol stung and Dan suppressed a hiss, fighting the urge to pull his arm away.

Jana's eyebrows rose and she shot him an amused look. "Don't tell me you're one of those men who turn into complete babies when they have a boo-boo." She said the last part in an overly exaggerated baby voice.

"Maybe if you kiss it and make it better, I won't cry," he said slowly. She froze in her movement. Dan leaned forward, staring into her wide, amber eyes. Fighting the urge to slide his hand behind her neck, pull her closer and press his mouth to her lips took all the self-control he possessed at the moment. Jana fumbled for the roll of bandaging material in her lap.

"Just hold still so I can finish up," she said, all humor in her voice from a moment ago gone. She dabbed some ointment on the gashes, and quickly wrapped the bandage around his arm. He rotated his shoulder when she finished, trying to work the growing stiffness from his injured muscle.

"Good thing I brought along my personal nurse." He grinned, trying to ease the sudden tension in the air. Jana stood and returned the tube of ointment to the first aid kit.

"Thank you for breakfast," she said without turning to face him. Dan inhaled a deep breath. A quick death from an animal or Indian attack was preferable to the slow torturous way Jana was killing him. If he survived the remainder of the journey to Madison with his sanity left intact, he'd consider it a miracle.

It's your punishment for your deception, Osborne.

Heaven stood right in front of him, but he was destined to burn in hell.

CHAPTER EIGHTEEN

"We should reach the hot springs sometime this afternoon," Dan said conversationally after he'd packed everything, and spread the ashes from their campfire. Glancing around one more time to make sure he left nothing behind, he shouldered his pack. His arm throbbed in tune to his heartbeats, and he cursed himself again for not wringing that goose's neck. He still had to come up with something to eat tonight for dinner.

Jana stood ready and waiting to be on their way. Even though it was early morning, she looked tired already. He offered a wide smile and set off heading west. They'd forded the Gardner River the day before and he was glad to have that final major river crossing behind them. He'd been awestruck once again at the sheer number of willow trees near the river, outnumbering the cottonwoods and Rocky Mountain Juniper.

By late afternoon, after a strenuous hike to the top of a sagebrush covered sandstone hill, the first white glimmers of the famous Mammoth Hot Spring Terraces came into view in the distance. No wonder the first trappers called this place White Mountain. The terraces stood out in blinding white against the greens of the surrounding mountains.

Dan had wanted to reach the area sooner. For some reason, time ticked by much too fast and they covered little ground. His legs felt like lead anchors were attached to them, and setting one foot in front of the other became harder with each mile they put behind them. Jana didn't say anything about his slow pace, but she'd cast worried glances at him from time to time.

Dan wiped his good arm across his damp forehead, and rivulets of sweat dripped into his eyes. A cool breeze kissed his heated face and he wondered vaguely why he felt so hot all of a sudden. Clouds had obscured the sun for most of the afternoon and dark thunderheads loomed in the distance to the west. The dull soreness in his arm from this morning had turned into a throbbing ache by mid-day, and each time he moved it even slightly, white-hot pain shot up and down his limb, radiating from his shoulder into his neck.

He eyed the thunderclouds warily and judged the distance to the valley below, spotting large groves of cotton-woods and willow trees. They would provide much-needed shelter. He blinked, and squinted into the distance. Land-marks that had been in focus a moment ago were blurred all of a sudden.

"Dan, I'm not liking those clouds over there," Jana said, echoing his own concerns. Her voice seemed far away, even though she walked right next to him. As if in answer to her words, lightning flashed across the horizon in the distance, illuminating the darkening sky. Seconds later, the loud rolling roar of thunder reverberated through the mountains.

"We have to get off this mountain, Dan." Jana's alarmed voice jolted him worse than the thunder. She was right.

There was no shelter here, only isolated shrubs and junipers. His mind told him they needed to be somewhere less exposed, but his limbs just didn't want to cooperate. He had a hard time concentrating on placing one foot in front of the other. His surroundings began to swirl and Dan felt as though he was floating. His head throbbed painfully, and he touched his hand to his temples.

"Dan?" Jana's voice echoed in his head. Cool, soft hands touched the skin on his face. "Oh, dear God, you're burning up." He heard the words, but they didn't register in his mind.

"Dan, listen to me. You have to move faster. We need to get somewhere less open, less exposed." She wrapped her hands around his good arm, pulling him forward.

"Yeah," he said vaguely, forcing his legs to move. Lightning flashed again, the jagged spidery lines of bluish light followed seconds later by a loud clasp of thunder that made his head throb even worse.

"It's getting closer, Dan. There's an electric storm coming." Jana's voice held an edge of panic. He forced his mind to clear.

"You know what to do, right?" He pushed the words from his lungs. Blinking to focus on his surroundings, he scanned the hillside. "Over there," he said, pointing toward an outcropping of rocks with a shaky hand.

Jana didn't reply. "Answer me, Jana." He looked at her, concentrating to keep his head clear. "Tell me you know what to do when the lightning reaches us." He gripped her hand hard, but kept moving in the direction of the boulders.

"Yes, I think so." Her voice was filled with fear. Dammit! This was a hell of a time to be feeling sick.

"Then let go of me now, and head toward those rocks. Find the lowest spot possible, and get down on the balls of your feet, and keep them as close together as you can. Here."

He pulled off his backpack, ignoring the excruciating pain in his arm as the straps slid over his injury. He thrust the pack at her. "Empty it, and stand on the fabric."

"What about you?" she yelled, refusing to release his arm.

"Jana, we can't stay together. The chances of getting struck are greater if we remain together. I'll find a spot over there." He quickly scanned the hillside and pointed to another set of jutting rocks. "Go! Now!" He shouted at her, and pushed her away.

Jana shot him one final desperate, terror-filled look, then hurried off toward the rocks. Lightning flashed again, followed quickly by more thunder. Dan stumbled toward the boulders on unsteady legs. Crouching between the rocks as he'd instructed Jana to do, he hoped he wouldn't pass out. He looked in the direction he'd sent her, but couldn't see her. The thought of her getting struck by lightning sent a jolt of fear into his chest greater than if a deadly bolt of electricity had seared through him.

JANA CROUCHED low between two large sandstone boulders, balancing precariously on the balls of her feet on the back- pack. She'd managed to hastily dump most of the contents of the pack on the ground in front of her, hoping the rocks created enough of a shelter to keep the wind from blowing most of their belongings away. The less her body contacted with the ground, the less chances of getting hit by a lightning strike. She held her hands protectively over her ears and squeezed her eyes shut.

Fear as she'd never experienced before raced through her. Fear for herself, and for Dan. Not only was he in greater danger of getting struck, his body was also ravaged by fever.

She could only guess that the injury he'd sustained that morning was becoming infected. She should never have listened to him, and insisted on taking care of his wounds immediately. As it was, because of her jumbled nerves when he'd insinuated that she kiss him, she'd done a sloppy job at cleaning the wound.

Jana concentrated on a course of action. Loud cracks of thunder boomed all around her that she couldn't drown out by covering her ears, followed by illuminating lightning strikes. Her body jerked each time she heard the noise. As soon as this storm was over, provided she made it out alive, she would properly dress Dan's wound again. She had no antibiotics to give him. His medical kit was filled with only standard supplies. She hadn't thought the injury was extensive enough to use anything stronger than the disinfectant alcohol wipes, and ointment. She'd apparently been wrong, and now Dan was battling a possible infection.

Jana's mind raced, even as the thunder clapped loudly all around her. She was unwilling to open her eyes, but the bright flashes of light were a sure sign that lightning struck too close for comfort. With her heart beating wildly in her chest, she tried to stay her fear by concentrating on finding ways to properly dress Dan's wound, hoping he hadn't developed septicemia. Dammit! He needed antibiotics. He was an experienced ranger. Why didn't he carry basic antibiotics in his kit?

A sudden heavy weight on her shoulder caused her to jump and let out a startled yelp at the same time. An excruciating pain seared down her oxygen-deprived legs from crouching in a squatting position for – she didn't know how long – as blood rushed to her lower limbs.

"Jana." Dan's labored voice halted her efforts to run before even looking to see what was behind her. She wheeled around, the air escaping her lungs in one quick whoosh.

"Dan." She choked out his name. Relief flooded her, and she threw herself at him. He stumbled backwards, and nearly fell. Jana abruptly pulled her arms from around his neck, and grabbed hold of his hands. She ignored the sensation of thousands of hot needles pricking her legs.

"It's over," Dan rasped. "The storm's passed."

Jana's eyes roamed over his face. His eyes looked glazed and unfocused and beads of sweat covered his forehead and clung to his unshaven chin. His usually olive complexion had a ghostly sallow tinge.

"We need to get to a more sheltered area, Dan," she said, desperately wishing she could tell him to sit and rest right where they were. This hillside was not a good place to spend the night and she needed water to properly clean his wound. If he could make it down into the valley, the willows and cottonwoods would provide ample shelter, and there would most certainly be a water source available.

Jana quickly gathered all of their belongings that she had dumped from the backpack, and stuffed them back in. She flung the pack over her shoulders, and grabbed hold of Dan's arm. He stood, swaying precariously like a tree in the wind.

"Let's go," she said firmly and, staying close to his side, maneuvered him down the incline toward the stretch of trees. Moving forward was agonizingly slow. Dan stumbled several times, and he breathed as if he'd just run a marathon.

"Just a little further," Jana coaxed, out of breath herself. She wrapped one arm around the back of his waist, and urged him forward. If he lost his footing, they would both tumble down the hill.

"I'm sorry, Jana," he rasped, after being silent for a while. "I'm sorry I lied to you."

"I already know that, Dan," she said.

"If anything happens to you . . ."

"Hush. Nothing's going to happen." Jana swallowed back

the lump in her throat. The heat his feverish body emitted, along with the effort to get him safely into the valley, made her sweat. How had his wound become infected so quickly? She hadn't taken the time to peel away the bandage to check the damage. Her primary goal at the moment was to get to shelter and water. If bacteria had gotten into his bloodstream . . . She couldn't complete her thought. Without antibiotics, he might die. She wouldn't even allow herself to think it. He was strong and healthy. He could fight this.

The leaves of a large stand of willows and cottonwoods rustled loudly in the afternoon breeze, their branches swaying and bending in rhythmic time with the wind. Jana focused on a grouping of four old cottonwoods that grew close together, forming a slight arc. It looked like a good place to stop.

Dan collapsed to the ground with a loud groan when Jana stopped. His weight nearly pulled her down with him. Jana shrugged out of the backpack, and fumbled with the zipper. She removed several of her shirts and bunched them up to fashion a pillow for his head. She pulled his windbreaker jacket out, knowing he would need it if he became chilled.

Jana worked quickly, gathering wood, and built a fire. She set the cook pot on a rock near the flames. After she offered Dan a drink from the canteen, she poured the remainder of the water into the pot to boil.

"Jana," Dan murmured, his voice barely audible. His pulse throbbed fast and strong in his neck, and Jana knelt down beside him.

"Once the water boils, I'll remove your bandage and get you fixed up again," she said, biting her quivering lower lip. Her vision blurred as she looked down at the man who, less than a week ago, had adamantly defended her against another man, not knowing if he was putting his life on the line. She gently touched his hot forehead.

"Why did you do such a stupid thing, Mr. Ranger, and tangle with a goose?" she said, and tried to keep her voice light-hearted as she leaned over him. "I should have never listened to you, and cleaned your wound right away."

Dan gave a weak laugh, his glazed eyes staring up at her. His hand reached up, and his trembling fingers lightly touched her cheek. "I wanted to impress the girl I love," he said, his voice labored. "Guess I need to work on that some more."

Jana stiffened. Dan was in love with her? It had to be the fever talking. He couldn't know what he was saying. She blinked, and cleared her throat.

"Let's get you better first," she said, smiling tentatively at him. "I need to unwrap your bandage."

She pushed a clean shirt under his arm, and quickly unwrapped the bandage. Her hands trembled, and her heart drummed in her chest. She shook her head slightly. *Concentrate, Jana.* His words still echoed in her mind.

Dan's arm where the gander had attacked him looked blue and purple, and several gashes had punctured the skin. Jana gingerly touched the swollen area. It felt hotter than the rest of him, and the deepest gash was rimmed by a deep shade of crimson. The entire area looked clean. There was no sign of superficial puss or infection forming, but that didn't mean there wasn't a pocket under the skin.

Jana pulled a sterile gauze pad from the medical kit, and soaked it in the boiling water from the cook pot. Removing it with the tweezers from the kit, she held it up to the air until it had cooled slightly. She squirted some iodine onto the gauze, then pressed it to Dan's injury. He groaned and squirmed, and Jana had to use all her strength to hold his arm in place.

"No time to be a baby," she whispered, leaning close to his face. His eyes were shut, and Jana didn't know if he was asleep or not. She applied several more hot compresses, waiting until one cooled before applying the next. She hoped the heat from the water would draw any infection to the surface.

She didn't know how long she worked over him before she finally rose to her feet. Stretching the stiffness out of her legs, she glanced at Dan. He seemed to be resting quietly for the moment. She needed to find more water. Luckily, she had found some pain medication in the medical kit, and as soon as she filled the canteen, she would wake him and make him swallow some. It would also help to bring his raging fever down.

Jana found a shallow pond a short distance from her chosen campsite, nestled amongst the grove of cottonwoods. A creek gurgled into the pond at one end, but she was too tired to walk around the body of water to reach it. She knelt at the edge of the water, and filled the canteen, then rinsed her hands, using the abrasive silt at the bottom to scrub them clean. When she pulled her hands from the water, she gasped in surprised shock. She shuddered, and fanned her hand quickly in front of her, jumping back away from the water's edge. Several small leeches clung to her fingers.

Chills of disgust seared up and down her spine as she swiped at the repulsive little creatures that looked like tiny black slugs. Putting a hand over her chest, she tried to calm her breathing. She hated slimy crawly things. Bugs she could deal with, but leeches and maggots repulsed her like nothing else ever had. She'd seen patients at the hospital treated with leeches as therapy to restore blood circulation during a limb reattachment. Maggots had been used therapeutically to eat away infected tissue.

Jana glanced over her shoulder toward camp, then back at the pond. A faint memory seeped into her mind. Leeches sucked blood. Dan might have an infection that entered his blood near his wound. In one of her survival courses, the instructor had cited cases where infection had been prevented, and even reversed, by attaching leeches to a wound.

Without a second thought, Jana dashed back to camp, and grabbed the cooking pot and tin cup. Returning to the shore of the pond, she dipped the cup under the water, scooping up the fine silt at the bottom. Sure enough, the mud was teeming with leeches. Swallowing back her revulsion, she picked out the squiggly creatures, and tossed them in the pot. When she had collected about a dozen of them, she rinsed the cup and skimmed the surface of the pond for clean water, adding it to the pot.

Dan slept fitfully when she returned to his side. His body twitched, and he moaned several times. Jana eyed his wound. At a casual glance, it looked rather harmless. The dark bruises could have been caused by a bump or fall. Several gashes had broken the skin, but the one that was deeper than the rest that looked all red and angry, had to be the source of the infection.

Jana eyed the wiggling leeches in the pot next to her. She swallowed back the bile rising in her throat. This had to be done. It might be Dan's only chance. With trembling fingers, she reached into the pot, and pulled out the first leech. The sucker at one end opened into a wide 'o' shape, and the vile creature squirmed and twisted, trying to attach itself to Jana's finger.

She held it to Dan's wound, until the invertebrate latched on. Her spine tingled and she fought the urge to scratch at her suddenly itchy scalp. She reached into the pot again and pulled out the next leech. Moments later, eight leeches hung attached to Dan's injury. They seemed content to do the job she hoped would save his life. All she could do now was wait and see.

Jana added more wood to her fire. She poured some cool water from the canteen onto a cloth, and bathed Dan's feverish face and neck. She wouldn't wake him just yet. Running her fingers along his stubbly jawline, she softly whispered, "I love you, too, Dan."

CHAPTER NINETEEN

*D*an slowly lifted his head up off the ground, squinting into the darkness. A fire crackled close by, illuminating the area around him. He raised his upper body, pushing against his elbows. Hissing as he inhaled a deep breath, he rolled to his side. Pain throbbed in his left shoulder. The memories came flooding back. He'd tangled with a goose this morning, and sometime in the afternoon, he'd felt sick. Then the lightning storm hit, then . . . he couldn't remember anything after that.

"Jana," he called, raising himself to a sitting position. His head pounded, and he blinked to dispel the sudden dizziness. Damn, he hadn't felt like this since the morning after he'd gone out drinking with some college buddies a few years ago. The aftermath of that night had been enough to keep him away from all-night bars.

Where was Jana? And how late in the night was it?

"Dan?"

His head turned in the direction he'd heard her voice. Seconds later, she appeared from out of the darkness, the cooking pot in one hand. A delicious smell wafted to his nose, and Dan's stomach grumbled loudly in response.

"You're awake," she said, relief evident on her face. "Just in time, too. I have some food ready. How are you feeling?" She set the pot down and knelt beside him. Her cool hand touched his forehead.

"Your fever's gone finally," she said in obvious approval, not waiting for his answer to her question. "Your arm looks a lot better, too. I'll unwrap it again in the morning to make sure all the infection is gone."

"Infection?" Dan glanced at his arm. He couldn't see anything, but felt the bandage wrapped snuggly around his biceps.

"Yeah, infection," Jana said. She leaned over him, and jabbed a finger in his chest. Her glare was like a mother hen's. "You scared me to death. The next time you even get so much as a splinter, you'd better tell me right away, so something like this doesn't happen again."

"Why, Nurse Evans, it almost sounds like you're worried about me," he drawled, a wide grin on his face. He pushed himself off the ground, stretching his stiff limbs. It felt as if he'd been lying on the ground for days.

"Yes I was worried, you big dolt." Jana stood, and her hands shot to her hips. "You could have died. And for someone experienced in the backcountry, you sure don't pack the right medical supplies." The intensity of her voice increased with her anger. "You needed antibiotics, but all I had was leeches." She visibly shuddered.

Dan's forehead wrinkled. "Leeches?"

"Since we're in the nineteenth century without modern medical supplies, I had to resort to archaic methods. By attaching leeches to your wound, they sucked the infection right out," Jana explained. "Yesterday, I didn't know if it would work or not. You were barely conscious most of the day."

Dan's brows furrowed, and he shook his head, trying to comprehend. "Yesterday? The lightning storm this afternoon, that's the last thing I remember."

"That was yesterday," Jana said dryly. "After I got you off the mountain, you collapsed when we reached this spot. We've been here ever since."

Dan inhaled a deep breath. Yet one more delay to get them to where they needed to go. He couldn't bear the thought of arriving too late. Hastings couldn't get to Madison before them. Somehow they would have to make up the lost time. He felt weaker than a newborn.

"What's in the pot?" he asked. If he hoped to be fit to travel in the morning, he needed food.

"Fish, and some plants I cooked with it. I think some are wild onions. Hopefully you like the flavor." Her head turned toward the darkness from where she'd appeared earlier. "I cooked away from camp. There's a black bear that's been hanging around all day. I just hope the smell doesn't attract a grizzly."

Dan stared at her. An intense tingling sensation such as he'd never felt before flooded his entire being. His chest warmed. She was such an amazing woman. She'd survived a lightning storm, helped him off the mountain in his feverish state, and no doubt saved his life with her innovative way of treating his infection. And she managed to fend for herself and find food in the wilderness.

"Leeches, huh?" he asked, feigning a grimace.

"They were disgusting." Jana shuddered. "They must have liked your blood. Once they were engorged, I replaced them with new ones. But at least leeches make great fish bait." She smiled sheepishly, and pointed at the pot she'd set near the fire. "Eat. You need to get your strength back. Tomorrow's going to be a long day."

"Yes, ma'am." Dan lowered himself to the ground. He couldn't help but stare at her. The love he felt for her was almost painful. He tore his eyes away when she looked decidedly uncomfortable by his stare. She offered him a spoon, and opened the lid to the pot. Large chunks of fish, and assorted greens floated in a savory smelling broth. He stuck his nose in the pot, and inhaled deeply.

"Smells great," he said, smiling for encouragement. The last thing he wanted to do was make her feel uneasy again in his company. "Sit and join me?" he asked, hoping to dispel her sudden apprehension.

"I already ate," she said hastily.

"At least sit with me, then."

Jana nodded, and joined him by the fire. Neither one spoke while he ate the food. She'd certainly managed to bring some interesting flavor to the fish in the way she prepared it with the herbs and plants.

"There's no water hemlock in this, is there?" he asked jokingly.

Jana's face lit up in a slow, almost evil smile. "You'll never know the difference, will you?"

Dan laughed. She'd thrown his own words back at him, when he'd taunted her a few weeks ago that her burger might be made from marmot meat.

"Don't worry," she said. "I didn't go through all the trouble to get you well, just so I could kill you now."

Dan spooned a big chunk of fish in his mouth to ward off the sudden urge to pull her in his arms and kiss her. He'd be a fool if he acted on his desire. Their relationship was still teetering on a sharp edge, and he didn't want to fall off the wrong side. All he could do was bide his time, respect Jana's wishes to take things slow, and hope that in time, she'd come to love him just a little.

He stared into the fire. *Just tell her you love her.* Now was not the time. Maybe tomorrow. The arguments he waged with himself in his mind were sure to drive him mad. He had no idea how she might react to a declaration of love. She'd told him to back off. When they returned to the future, Jana might decide to do what she'd done the first time they'd met, and rush back home to California. If that was to be her choice, could he let her go? He had no hold on her. Somehow he'd figure out a way to give her reason enough to stay.

"This is such a beautiful area. I've always loved coming to view the terraces," Jana said, shielding her eyes from the brightness of the white view of the mountain before her.

"The early explorers called this White Mountain," Dan said.

"Understandably so," Jana answered. She stood at the base of the Minerva terraces and looked up, in awe at how nature had created these spectacular travertine formations. From a distance the step-terrace formations she gazed at looked like they were carved from granite. Jana knew from earlier visits that the naturally formed steps and terraces, some of which pooled with water, were composed of limestone. Some areas that were dry and without water were so starkly white, she couldn't even look at them. They looked more like a gigantic mountain of cakes layered with heaping dust of icing. Not even snow was so brilliantly white in color.

Some areas had a more grayish hue. In still other parts, water cascaded down from one terrace formation onto the next, which seemed to paint the mountain in brilliant shades of orange, yellows, and reds. The blue pools that formed between steps and layers appeared to have icing laced around their edges.

"Wow," Dan said, next to her, expressing her own sentiments. "Look at the brilliant colors! Minerva is pretty active right now. You can see why this area was named for the roman goddess of artists and sculptors."

"There's so much more color here than in our time. Did some of the areas simply cease to produce water and then just die off?"

"No." Dan shook his head. He turned slightly toward her, while pointing at the formations. Jana smiled to herself. He was back in naturalist and interpreter mode, and she was his tourist audience. "This is such a dynamic area. Underground vents open and close the water supply all the time. Without the water, there's no bacteria which, as I assume you know, is what gives off these brilliant colors. The white terraces are newly formed calcium carbonate deposits, and the gray ones are older."

"I never knew there was so much more here than just this mountain", Jana said, scanning her entire surroundings. The vast valley below her was comprised of many white mounds, and step terrace formations, in stark contrast to the greens of the willow trees and grasses. In their time, this area was a busy tourist hub, with a hotel, gift shops, and the old Fort Yellowstone, which was also the park's headquarters.

"Yeah, the army built their fort right on top of some older formations, right over there." Dan pointed to the north of where they stood, and Jana could picture the stone buildings that occupied the area in the future. As it was now, graying travertine was visible amongst the cottonwoods and green meadow.

"What a shame that so much of this was damaged when tourists first started coming here," Dan continued. "There were no rules and regulations for stepping on these formations, and people used to break off chunks to take home as souvenirs. People used to put objects into the water, to let them get coated with calcium carbonate, which is the compound we call travertine."

"What did they do? Come back a year later to pick up their objects?" Jana asked. She wondered if many of the park's earlier visitors returned year after year.

Dan laughed. "No. It's a really quick process. The hot springs produce about two tons of travertine every day."

"Per day?" Jana's eyes grew wide.

"Amazing, isn't it. One of the few places on earth where you can actually see rock being formed right before your eyes. " Dan paused and his expression changed as if he'd just had a brilliant idea. "Would you like to take a bath? Jim Bridger loved to bathe in these springs."

"What, so I can get coated with travertine? No thanks." Jana waved him off. She'd always been curious about bathing in some of the springs, but this practice was very much illegal in her time. As enticing as the idea was, they couldn't afford to lose any more time, and needed to be on their way.

"If my great uncle hadn't been able to pass the law to protect the park from more concessioners, who knows what sort of damage would have been done here," Dan said, abruptly changing the subject.

Jana gaped at him. He spoke so passionately, it was difficult to believe that several weeks ago, he'd been ready to travel back in time to jeopardize what his ancestors had worked for.

"In the early years, the first hotels here at Mammoth catered to people bathing in the hot springs."

'Yeah, I've heard that," Jana said.

They stood in silence, admiring the beauty of the formations, when Dan nudged her. "Well, since you don't want to take a nice hot soak, we might as well get moving. The next few days might get pretty strenuous. We have to hike up and over Bunsen Peak. We could go through the canyon and save at least a half day rather than go over the peak, but I'm not sure how we'll get out of there. I believe it dead-ends at the falls."

"Let's go over, then," Jana said. "As long as you're well enough for it."

"Fit as a fiddle. Thanks to my wonderful nurse." He grinned, and Jana could do nothing but nod her head. He wouldn't tell her if he was well enough or not.

She followed Dan as he led the way through the travertine area. They followed the Gardner River south until they reached a deep gorge, the sides of which were made up of enormous glaciated rock terraces and cliffs.

Dan set a fast pace away from the canyon, up a steep mountain that leveled out to a flat plateau, no doubt wanting to make up for the time they had lost while he'd been battling his infection. The going was slow and strenuous and it took them an entire day to reach the top.

For the next two days, Jana observed Dan closely to make sure he didn't overexert himself, sometimes feigning exhaustion to slow him down, certain that he would never admit to her that he was worn out. His body still needed to recover from the fever that had raged through him.

"This looks like a good place to stop," she suggested casually the evening after climbing Bunsen Peak, surveying her surroundings. They'd left the canyon and river an hour or more ago, and were traveling through an open meadow. Up ahead stood a large grove of aspens. A wide stream meandered through the tall grasses, and they'd come upon several clear ponds that were hidden amongst tall reeds.

"You sure you don't want to go any further?" he asked.

"We've got plenty of daylight left. We could get a few more miles behind us."

It was probably best to let him think she was tired, rather than suggest that he was the one needing to slow down after the last two strenuous days. "I've had enough for today. We've covered a lot of ground."

Dan smiled softly. He stepped up close to her and touched her arm. Jana's heart reacted instantly to his warm hand. She sucked in a deep breath. This was a different touch than the indifferent way he held her close at night. She swallowed, suddenly nervous. His eyes on her face wouldn't let go.

"I'll admit, I'm a bit tired myself," he said, still staring straight into her soul.

"We'd better not tell anyone that you fought with a goose, and the animal won. Your reputation as a ranger will be ruined." Jana grinned, trying to lighten the sudden tension she felt.

"Oh, yeah?" Quite unexpectedly, he slid his backpack from his shoulders and pulled her up against him. Jana's smile left her face and she gazed up into his intense eyes. "Geese are quite ferocious, you know. Almost as dangerous as a bear." His voice was mesmerizing.

"I'll try and remember that," she whispered. She suddenly couldn't breathe. Dan's fingers brushed against her cheek, just before his hand slid behind her neck.

"I think I'm going to kiss you," he said, his voice deep and husky.

"I think I want you to kiss me," she murmured without a second thought. Dan's eyes widened for the briefest of seconds. His hand at the back of her neck tightened and he cupped her cheek with the other. Slowly, he brought his mouth down on hers. His firm lips moved softly across hers, as his hand kneaded the back of her head. Jana raised her arms to grip his shoulders.

He groaned deep in his chest. His arm wrapped around her waist and he pulled her up against him. The pressure of his kiss intensified, and Jana parted her lips in answer to his demand. She wrapped her arms around his neck, and pressed against him. Suddenly she couldn't get close enough to him.

Dan broke the kiss and brushed his rough cheek against hers. He buried his face in her hair and inhaled deeply. His heart beat wild and strong against Jana's breast, and she hugged him even tighter. His warm, firm hands spanned her waist, holding her flush up against him, and heat seared through her veins.

"I was so afraid you were going to die," Jana whispered against his neck. "Please don't ever do anything crazy like that again."

"You won't mention to Aimee and Daniel that I almost got killed by a goose, will you?" Dan leaned back and grinned. Jana gave a short laugh and released her hold from around his neck. Her hands lingered on his chest, the warmth from his skin radiating through his shirt into her palm. Dan's hand covered one of hers, and he held it firmly over his beating heart.

"Feel that?" he asked huskily. "That's what you do to me." His eyes darkened and the grin left his face. "Jana . . ." He hesitated and gazed at the ground between their feet before his eyes met hers again. "I want more than just a friendship with you. I have no right to ask this after the way I used you, and lied to you, but . . . I love you, Jana. When we get home to our time, I don't want you to walk out of my life again."

Jana's breath caught in her throat. He hadn't been talking gibberish in his fevered state after all.

"Dan, I . . . I think I love you, too, but I don't know if –"

"Shhhh, don't say anything right now." He put a finger over her mouth. "We'll figure out what to do one day at a time."

"Okay," she whispered softly and leaned her head against his chest. He inhaled a deep breath and held her tight. They stood like this for countless minutes, entwined in each other's arms in this wide, open meadow. Jana listened to the evening crickets serenade their confession of love and wondered how to proceed from here.

CHAPTER TWENTY

an sat on the ground with his back propped against one of the countless trees lining the banks of the lake he and Jana had stopped at for the night. He leaned his head back against the trunk, his forearms resting casually on his bent knees.

With his eyes closed, he listened to the swooshing sound of the breeze blowing through the tops of the lodgepoles, some of the trunks groaning and creaking as they bent in the wind. The sounds lulled him into a serene state of mind. From the far side of the lake, the mournful, eerie call of a loon reminded him of a wolf's lonely howl. He should really be building their campfire for the night, but he wanted to savor the peace and tranquility that infused him at that moment.

With his eyes still closed to soak in all of the surrounding sounds, Dan smiled. He was no longer a lone wolf. He'd found his mate, and he would do whatever it took to keep her. Jana still seemed unsure of their budding relationship. Quite frankly, he'd been more than a little shocked at her response the previous evening when he'd told her he loved her. She thought she loved him, too. It was more than he could have ever hoped for.

He needed to tread lightly. He wanted her. All of her. Mind, body, and soul. But he'd be a fool to overstep the fragile new level of their relationship. The previous night, he hadn't merely held her to keep her warm like he'd done during all those other torturous nights. For the first time, they'd lain by the campfire, and he'd pulled her into a lover's embrace, kissing her in a way that had set his soul on fire, not to mention his body.

She'd kissed him back with a reserved passion and the tension in her body had sobered him to the fact that she wasn't ready for a leap to intimacy. He'd forced himself to stop before he lost complete control of his actions. And he had much more respect for her than to take her like some moose in rut.

The splashing of water on the lake brought him out of his contemplation. Jana had been looking for an opportunity at a real bath for days, and he'd suggested she take a swim now, while there was still daylight. The northern shore of the lake was overgrown with tall reeds, and countless lodgepoles that had died ages ago for one reason or another hung into the water.

It was a secluded area of the lake that gave her the privacy she wanted. To assure her that there were no leeches lurking in the lakebed, he'd scooped handfuls of silt to show her it was devoid of the slimy suckers. After his demonstration, she'd been more than eager to grab his bar of soap, but had warned him to stay in camp.

The grin on his face after her stern warning sent her scurrying into the thicket. "I mean it, Dan. You'd better not be a peeping Tom," she'd called to him from behind the bushes

"Scout's honor," he'd promised and turned to head toward

their camping spot, grinning from ear to ear. Her modesty was one more thing he loved about her.

"Dan, I told you to stay away." Jana's voice echoed through the hills in this peaceful little valley. Dan became instantly alert. He was nowhere near her. He leapt to his feet and lunged for his bear spray and knife. Was there an animal at the water's edge that she might have mistaken for him? He hurried along the shoreline. From his vantage point, the reeds and trees gave her plenty of cover, but he could barely see the water.

He scanned the shore through the brush, leery of running headlong into a moose. This was prime moose habitat, and he didn't like the idea of meeting up with one. The outcome of such an encounter would be far worse than his altercation with the goose.

Dan slowed to a fast walk, ducking his head to peer between the tall reeds. Where the heck was Jana? He had to be close to where she'd entered the water. He couldn't see her, but the figure of a man crouching behind a downed lodgepole was the last thing he expected to find. Anger flooded through his veins and overshadowed all sense of caution. The man was dressed in buckskins from head to foot, a fur cap on his head. Several pouches dangled from his side, and in his hand he clasped a flintlock rifle. He was intently staring at the lake.

"Didn't anyone ever tell you it's not polite to watch a lady take a bath?" Dan asked firmly. The trapper had obviously been too focused on what was in the water to notice him standing a few feet behind him. At Dan's words, the man scrambled to his feet, and nearly toppled over the dry trunk of the tree.

"Mon dieu! You put a fright in me." The man raised his flintlock as he spoke.

"Dan?" Jana called from somewhere beyond the curtain of

reeds, while the trapper looked at Dan with wide eyes. The stranger leaned forward slightly and his pupils nearly bulged out of their sockets. His body visibly shook, and he lowered his weapon.

"Daniel Osborne, it is you?" the man said, his French accent so thick, Dan could barely understand him.

Water splashed loudly from the lake. Dan cursed under his breath after the shock wore off that this man spoke his name. Jana needed to get out of that water before she got too chilled.

"Jana, where are your clothes?" he shouted, without taking his eyes off the trapper. His hand was wrapped firmly around his knife handle, his other hand ready to release the safety mechanism on the bear spray canister.

"They're right over here," Jana answered. Dan scanned the shrubbery. He had no idea where 'here' was.

"We have company," he said as calmly as he could. He didn't want to set Jana off into a panic. "Give us a few minutes to head away from this lakeshore, and then you get out of the water."

The only logical assumption he could make was that this trapper had mistaken him for his ancestor. Dan definitely planned to use that to his advantage. "You obviously know who I am. I suggest you and I take a walk away from the shore to give the lady some privacy."

Dan had no idea how his ancestor would have handled this situation, but clearly, he needed to exude confidence in order to maintain some semblance of control.

The trapper's perplexed look didn't leave his face, and he ran a hand over his unshaven chin. He nodded quietly, uncertainty in his expression as he assessed Dan's appearance. Dan motioned with his hand to indicate the trapper should step away from the lakeshore ahead of him.

He stuck his knife in his back pants pocket and extended

his hand. From all of his accounts about nineteenth century fur trappers, he'd read that they were extremely loyal to their own kind, but also very leery and unfriendly to strangers. If this man thought he was Daniel Osborne, it was just as well. Whether he could pull off impersonating his legendary ancestor remained to be seen.

The trapper extended a hand, and Dan clasped it firmly. "I meant no disrespect to your woman," the man said, a toothless smile on his face that didn't reach his eyes.

Sure you didn't.

Dan's anger seethed to the surface again. He clenched his jaw, trying to hide his emotions.

"I am Etienne Bautiste. You do not remember me?"

The man's attempt at sincerity failed noticeably. Dan kept a wary eye on the rifle in Etienne's hand. Besides the flintlock, a pistol hung from a wide belt at his waist, along with a large hunting knife.

"Should I remember you?" *Damn.* If this was an old acquaintance of Daniel's, he would definitely know the difference.

"It has been a long time. You were no more than a boy when my cousin and I visited your father on the Madison. You have grown into a man who has made quite a name for himself in these mountains."

Dan shrugged. A rustling noise behind him made him turn his head. The trapper did the same. Jana walked slowly toward them, concern and apprehension etched on her face. Her hair hung in wet strands past her shoulders, the cotton from her shirt soaking up the water. The wet fabric noticeably clung to her curves. At any other time, this would have been an enticing sight. Etienne Bautiste's eyes held a certain predatory gleam in them as he appraised Jana, and Dan knew exactly what was going through the man's mind.

Dan was overcome with the sudden urge to hit the man, and clenched his hand in a tight fist at his side. This was a much different situation than when he had to haggle over Jana with the Crow Indian. Both men's interest in her was the same, but the Crow had looked at her with admiration, not with raw animal lust so evident in this trapper's eyes.

Jana cast apprehensive glances from him to Bautiste, who turned fully toward her and bowed gallantly.

"Madame, it is my pleasure to make your acquaintance. I have heard rumors of the woman who has become Daniel Osborne's bride, but they pale in comparison to your true beauty."

Dan held out his hand to her, and Jana quickly rushed to his side. He gave her hand a gentle squeeze. As a ranger, he'd gone through law enforcement training, and he had no doubt that he'd be able to disarm this man, if he presented a threat. All he had to do was stick close enough to prevent Bautiste from raising that flintlock.

"Aimee, head back to where I left our effects, while I finish my visit with Etienne." Dan emphasized the name Aimee, hoping Jana would take the hint. She didn't skip a beat.

"Sure, Daniel. Just don't be too long. Would you like your rifle?"

"I'll be along for it shortly. Hunting should be good once dusk settles." She nodded, released his hand, and headed along the lakeshore to where they'd set up camp earlier. Dan watched her disappear through the trees, then turned to Bautiste, who had a look on his face as if he'd just allowed a season's cache of beaver pelts to float down the river.

Bautiste cleared his throat. "I will be on my way," he said. "I do not wish to intrude. A young man needs his privacy with his woman, eh?" He wiggled his eyebrows and smiled.

"Come visit us along the Madison sometime. I'll be able to offer better hospitality then," Dan answered, ignoring the insinuation. He didn't relax his tense muscles. Getting rid of the trapper this easily didn't smell right. After a final handshake, Dan watched Bautiste head in the opposite direction, until he was no longer visible through the foliage along the lakeshore.

"Why didn't you bring a weapon other than your knife?" Jana asked as soon as Dan returned to camp. She looked visibly shaken. He pulled her into a protective embrace. The feel of her soft body against him soothed his own frayed nerves. He'd been thinking the exact same thing. His .45 Magnum sat in the drawer of his nightstand, utterly useless to him at the moment.

"A knife is much more useful and versatile in the wilderness from a survival standpoint. I didn't pack my .45 because I didn't want to bring modern weapons," Dan said, regretting that decision more and more. "Of course, that was also before Hastings showed up at my barrack. Had I known what he planned, I would have brought my pistol. And," he rubbed his hands up and down her back, "I guess my twenty-first century mind wasn't thinking that I had to defend you against every man we meet up with in the Rockies."

"Aimee was kidnapped by a couple of trappers," Jana said quietly. "Daniel killed them."

Dan's facial features hardened.

"I'm not letting you out of my sight," he said in a firm tone. He clasped her head between his hands, tilting her face to look up at him. Although she tried to hide it, he saw the fear and apprehension in her eyes. He softly kissed her lips.

"No one's going to kidnap you," he whispered against her cheek. "That trapper is no doubt long gone from here." Dan spoke the words to reassure her, wishing he believed what he said.

CHAPTER TWENTY-ONE

*J*ana woke early the next morning to the mournful calls of loons on the lake. Out of habit, she reached for Dan, but she only clutched at emptiness beside her. She propped her upper body on her elbows, and squinted the sleep from her eyes. A thick layer of fog hovered over the lake and foliage around the shore. Dan crouched by the burned-out campfire, poking at the coals with a stick. He added kindling, and with each breath of air he blew on the coals, red and orange embers lit up until finally, the kindling ignited in a sudden poof of orange light. The resulting flames licked eagerly at the twigs and grasses, and Dan added larger pieces of wood until a sizable fire crackled where a moment ago only black coals remained from the previous night.

Jana sat up fully and Dan raised his head in her direction, a slow smile forming on his face. The warm look of love in his eyes sent her heart fluttering. How many times in the past had she heard proclamations of love from other guys she'd dated? Not once had those words sounded sincere, until now. She'd never even said *I love you* to a man before, but there was no doubt in her mind when it came to Dan.

Jana inhaled a deep breath of crisp mountain air, the cold rush shooting into her sinuses making her eyes water. She squeezed the top of her nose and took in another breath through her mouth.

"You okay?" Dan left his spot by the fire and came to kneel beside her. He ran his hand over her hair, smoothing it down and away from her face, and gently gripped her shoulder. She glanced up at him, and noticed the dark circles under his eyes.

"I think I'm feeling better than you are," she said. "You didn't sleep last night, did you?"

Dan's jaw clenched. His fingers tightened on her shoulder just before he released her.

"You're still worried about that trapper," she guessed. "Do you think he'll bother us?"

"I don't know," Dan answered, an edge to his voice, and stood. He ran his hand through his hair. "I never thought I'd be this unprepared to come here. There's so much I didn't think about." His voice was filled with anger. He turned his back to her, and kicked at a stick in the dirt.

Jana pushed herself off the ground and came up behind him. She brought her own hand up to his shoulder. The muscles beneath his shirt bunched rock hard and unyielding under her touch. The tension in his body only seemed to mount. Dan scoffed and turned his head to look at her.

"Guess I'm not very good at thinking things through, am I?" The self-loathing in his voice sent a chill racing up her spine.

"What are you talking about?" Jana asked softly, and stepped in front of him. She reached for his hands. His fingers wrapped around hers, almost painfully. His grip was made of iron.

"If I hadn't agreed to Hastings' offer, if I had only used common sense instead of letting my own selfish wants get the better of me, we wouldn't be here right now. My ancestors' lives wouldn't be at risk, and neither would yours. Jana, if anything happens to you . . ." He let the words die off, and pulled her into a fierce embrace.

Jana wrapped her arms around his back, and gave him the time he needed to sort through the thoughts in his head. She was well aware of the harsh reality of their situation. By sheer luck, they hadn't had a confrontation with a grizzly, a terrifying thought even if they did have the bear spray. Dan had nearly died several days ago from a fluke infection. Luckily those Indians they had encountered were friendly. How much longer could their luck hold out? That trapper yesterday had been fully armed. He could have shot Dan on the spot. The thought made her shudder.

Dan gripped her upper arms. "I'll die before I let anyone hurt you," he said into her hair. The raw passion mixed with anguish in his voice was unmistakable. He leaned his head back, and Jana gazed up into those deep brown eyes that were so full of love for her, it made her chest hurt as she drew in a breath. In the next instant, Dan's mouth crushed down on hers, and he plundered her lips as he'd never done before. She wrapped her arms around his neck, drawing him even closer. His intense onslaught, and her equally heated response sent shockwaves of adrenaline rushing through her veins, coiling and entwining in a sweet pain at her very core.

Dan grabbed her waist, and lifted her off the ground. Reflexively, she straddled his hips. He slid one arm beneath her bottom, the other behind her back, and held her close to him. Nothing had ever felt as simultaneously wondrous, scary, and exciting as his arousal pressed up against the junction of her thighs.

No man had ever brought forth such a rush of feelings in

her. Did she want to take the next step? Was it worth the risk? Part of her gave in to the wildly delicious sensations as Dan continued to explore her lips with his own. Her body responded, and she ached for him. That little nagging voice at the back of her mind tapped at her conscience, growing more insistent even as her heart pounded fiercely in her chest to give herself completely to him.

Unable to bear the exquisite torture of unfulfilled longing and desire, she pulled her head away, gasping for air. Dan's chest heaved against her breasts, his breathing as labored as her own.

"Jana," he whispered, and buried his face in her hair. His lips along her neck sent renewed ripples of desire along her spine. She tilted her head back to allow him freer access to the delicate skin along her neck and throat, and moaned from sheer pleasure. *Just one more kiss.* She had to stop this now, or there would be no turning back.

"Dan, please . . ." she gasped, unable to bring forth any other words. He must have understood. His hand relaxed along her thighs, and she dropped her legs to the ground, not sure whether they would support her own weight or not. Dan's arms around her waist kept her from collapsing to her knees. She released her grip from around his neck, her arms shaking.

"I . . . I love you, Dan," she said, her voice hoarse, and stared into his passion-glazed eyes.

He cleared his throat and swiped one hand along her cheek, pushing a few strands of hair behind her ear. "I'll never do anything you don't want me to do, Jana. If you're not ready for . . ."

A slow, loud clapping sound behind them startled Jana out of her dream-like, passion-filled state. Dan immediately tensed. He released her, and quickly pushed her behind him, a string of curses on his lips.

"That was - how shall I say - an arousing performance," a man's voice spoke. He didn't have quite the heavy French accent Jana remembered from the trapper they had met the previous night. She wheeled around and Dan gripped her arm to keep her shielded behind him.

"I cannot wait to try that maneuver myself. Perhaps it would work better with less clothing, no?"

Jana stared wide-eyed, as three men emerged from behind the trees. She recognized Etienne Bautiste, who stood between the two others, his flintlock raised and aimed at Dan. Another man stood to Etienne's left. He looked to be in severe discomfort. One leg was raised up slightly, not bearing any weight, while the trapper leaned heavily on his rifle that he propped in the dirt like a crutch. The man who spoke had a visible sneer on his face, and a predatory look in his beady gray eyes.

"Etienne, you fool. This is not Daniel Osborne. Look at him." The trapper waved a disgusted hand at Dan. "Daniel Osborne dresses like the Snakes who raised him. This man," - he assessed Dan from top to bottom with his eyes – "doesn't even carry a weapon."

"My name's Daniel Osborne, and I'll dare you to disprove it," Dan said heatedly.

The trapper leered at him. "And the woman? Daniel Osborne's woman is said to have hair like gold."

"Then you must not have heard right."

Jana grabbed Dan's arm. The adrenaline rush of passion from a few moments ago was replaced by cold fear. Her eyes darted around their little camp. The canister of bear spray was hooked to the carabiner on Dan's backpack. She had no idea where the knife was.

The trapper who'd been speaking slowly walked closer, his pistol raised at Dan's chest.

"If you are Daniel Osborne, then today is the day you die. I have been waiting for an opportunity like this."

Jana gasped at the man's words.

"I don't even know who the hell you are, so why don't you tell me why you want me dead." Dan seemed much too calm. Jana's own heart was racing. It seemed like their luck had finally run out. She glanced at the other trappers, their weapons raised, ready to shoot. There seemed to be no way out of this situation.

The man smiled, but it was a cold, calculated, murderous smile. "If that is truly the woman the Snakes call *Dosa Haiwi*, she will have the magic of healing." The trapper glanced over his shoulder. "My companion took a swipe to the leg from a bobcat the other day. He needs medicine."

Jana stepped quickly out from behind Dan. His hand reached for her, but she pulled away.

"If I save your friend's leg, you will leave us alone," she called out, hoping her voice didn't betray the fear she felt.

The man laughed. "You are not in a position to make such a bargain, but I will grant you this. Heal Gaston's leg, and we will kill your man quickly."

Jana's heart sank. What had Daniel done to elicit this man's hatred? They had obviously never met the real Daniel Osborne before, or they would have realized that Dan was not him.

"And what if I refuse?" she asked.

"You will not refuse, ma cherie. Unless you enjoy watching this man be tortured to death."

Dan yanked Jana back, and took a step toward the trapper. "She'll not help you regardless," he said roughly between clenched teeth. The man cocked his pistol, and Dan stopped. Jana had no doubt he would have disarmed this trapper in an instant, but Etienne had his own rifle pointed at Dan. There was no way he could fight all three of these men at once.

"After she is done healing my friend," the trapper snarled, "you will have the pleasure of watching her ride me the way she rode you moments ago. Only I will possess her like a real man."

In a move that happened quicker than in the blink of an eye, Dan shoved Jana to the side, then kicked his leg out, effectively dislodging the pistol from the man's grasp. In the next instant, he grabbed the trapper by the front of his shirt, and slammed his fist into his opponent's face.

Jana stumbled to the ground from the momentum of Dan's shove just as a shot fired. Her head darted from Etienne to Dan, but she couldn't tell if the shot had hit its mark. Etienne whipped his pistol from his belt, and ran toward Jana. She scrambled to her feet, but he grabbed her by the arm and held the weapon to her head.

"Release Claude, or this woman dies," Etienne called loudly. Jana gagged at the stench coming from the man's mouth. Out of the corner of her eye, she saw the third man, Gaston, limp quickly toward Dan, his own pistol raised at him.

"You idiot," Claude yelled toward Etienne, gasping and spitting blood that dripped from his mouth where Dan's fist connected with his lips. "You could have shot me." He turned his blood-splattered face toward Dan, who stood frozen in front of Gaston. His eyes filled with fear as he stared toward Jana.

"Leave her be," Dan called. Claude pulled a long strip of leather from the pouch around his neck.

"Do not fight me, or your woman is dead," he sneered. "Put your hands together behind your back," he commanded. With fury in his eyes, and his jaw clenched, Dan complied, and Claude tied the leather around his wrists.

"You," Claude called to Jana. "Fix Gaston's leg. Do it now,

or I will take great pleasure in killing your man as he killed my cousin last summer."

Jana's eyes darted to Dan. Was he thinking what she was? He laughed slowly. "Your cousin? Would that have been one of those stinking coyotes who kidnapped my . . . wife?"

"Pierre Renault was my cousin," Claude barked, advancing on Dan. He pulled his knife and held it to Dan's throat.

"No!" Jana screamed. "I'll . . . see what I can do for your friend's leg. Leave Dan. . . Daniel alone." She glared at Etienne, who still held the pistol to her head. Every cell in her body screamed to rush to Dan.

"When I heard this past winter what had happened to him and to my good friend, Franscoise Chaubelon, I swore vengeance." Claude continued, apparently unmoved by Jana's plea. Abruptly, he pulled the knife back, and stuck it back in his belt. "You will die a slow and torturous death, Daniel Osborne." With those words, he turned toward Jana.

"Fix my friend's leg. We are wasting time." He motioned for Etienne to lower his weapon. Etienne shoved her toward Gaston, who still stood next to Dan, his pistol pointed at him.

Jana looked toward Dan, who nodded his head slightly. There was nothing on his face that gave away what he was thinking. Jana took a deep breath, and motioned for the trapper to sit by the fire.

"Let me look at your leg," she said.

"You have the power to heal?" he asked, an almost fearful look in his eyes.

"Well if I don't, you'll soon find out, won't you?" Jana answered heatedly. She didn't have to look up, but she heard Dan chuckle. Annoyance, mixed with fear, filled her, and made her reckless. If this was going to be the last day she and

Dan lived, what did she have to lose? She didn't need to resort to niceties.

She glanced toward the backpack. "I need my medical supplies," she said, looking over her shoulder at Etienne. "Go bring me that pack."

The man's eyes widened briefly.

"Do it," Claude ordered. Etienne grabbed the pack and dropped it at her feet.

"If you want me to examine your leg, I need you to remove your pants, or whatever it is you call what you're wearing." She looked in disgust at the blood-soaked, ripped leather wrapped around the man's leg. She didn't have to be a medical genius to know that this man's leg was beyond saving. The stench of rotting flesh and gangrene filled the air.

Jana knelt down to unzip the pack, when her eye caught the bear spray canister hanging on the clip. Her heart sped up as a plan formed in her mind. She hastily unclipped the spray, and released the safety.

"Etienne, Claude, come here and help this man cut this leather strip from his leg," she commanded. "How long ago did this happen?" She stood to her feet. While the two trappers leaned over their companion, Jana glanced at Dan.

Close your eyes.

She formed the words with her mouth, hoping he understood. The corners of his lips twitched.

With Gaston on the ground, and the two other trappers right beside him, Jana said, "look at me for a moment, boys." All three raised their heads, looks of surprise on their faces. She quickly held the bear spray in front of her, nozzle pointed at the men, and pressed the trigger. At the same time, she ran backwards to get out of the vicinity of the spray. Luckily, she was facing upwind from them. Dan sprinted after her, his hands still tied behind his back.

The three trappers coughed, gagged, and one even managed to shout.

"Argh, my eyes. I am blind!" Claude screamed. They scrambled to their feet, neither Etienne nor Claude waiting for Gaston to get up off the ground. They stumbled blindly through the camp, their hands on their faces, trying to rub at their eyes.

"You were amazing," Dan said quietly in Jana's ear. They ducked behind some trees, well out of the path of the three blind trappers. Jana shuddered. She could only imagine the pain their eyes and lungs must be in at the moment. Using bear spray on a person in modern times, even in self-defense, would probably be grounds for arrest. And she had sprayed it at such a close proximity, she had no doubt the men would suffer permanent eye damage, and possible lung damage, if they survived.

With trembling hands, she fumbled with the knot that tied Dan's hands together. After he was free, he pulled her into a tight embrace.

"I love you," he whispered huskily in her ear.

"I was . . . am so scared, Dan. They wanted to kill you, and —" Dan kissed her, stopping her from saying more.

The trappers, still howling and screaming, had found their way to the lake, and plunged loudly into the water. Jana's skin began to crawl. All three were destined to die a horrible death, and she was the cause of it. She had sprayed them directly in their faces, and it would take days for their eyesight to recover, if at all. A blind man in the wilderness was as good as dead. She collapsed against Dan's chest, unable to hold back the tears.

"Shhh. You did what you had to do in order to survive," he said, stroking her back. "It was either them or us."

Dan gripped her tightly all of a sudden. His body tensed. Jana's head shot up to look at him. Her heart sped up again.

Something was wrong. What danger could there possibly be now?

Slowly, she turned her head in the direction his eyes pointed. Her heart sank to her belly. Standing among the trees behind them stood four Indians, bows in their hands. One man stood slightly ahead of the others, looking at Dan as if he had just seen a ghost.

CHAPTER TWENTY-TWO

$\mathcal{D}$an slowly released his hold around Jana's waist. He didn't take his eyes off the Indians, who continued to stare at him. In the distance, the howls of the trappers echoed through the valley. They were still in the water. Their attempts to wash away the burning sensations on their faces and in their eyes would be futile. Dan could only imagine the blisters forming on their skin. If one of them came away without serious eye damage, it would be a miracle. In his mind, they got what they deserved.

The Indian at the front of the group leaned forward, his wide, almost terror-filled eyes scanning Dan from top to bottom, then lingered on his face. He stood rooted to the spot. Dan didn't know what else to do, so he took a hesitant step toward him. Jana grasped his arm tightly, and attempted to pull him back.

"It's okay, Jana," he told her quietly. "I don't think we have anything to fear from them." She didn't answer.

Dan eyed the weapons these men carried. Hunting bows not made from wood, but from the horn of mountain sheep.

He'd only seen an authentic hornbow in a museum once. There was no doubt in his mind he stood face to face with a group of mountain Shoshone – Sheepeaters - an indigenous people to the Yellowstone area whose way of life and existence had died out after the government took over these mountains as a national park. The few Sheepeaters who had survived on the reservations had long lost their culture by integration with other, far larger tribes.

Historical accounts of these people painted them as poor beggars, and cowardly. Standing before these four men, Dan could see nothing that would give truth to those words. These hunters, although they were not of large stature, stood tall and proud, their buckskin shirts and leggings made of the finest hides.

Dan extended his hand in greeting, and the apparent leader of the group took several steps back. The other three murmured amongst themselves, nodding with their chins at Dan.

These are your ancestors. The thought raced through his mind. Although he had very little Shoshone blood in him, he could trace a small part of his roots back to these people through his great-great grandfather, Josh Osborne. Dan's interest in the tribe had led him to learn all he could about their culture and language from some elders on the Wind River Reservation in Wyoming. Only a few could tell him about the Sheepeaters, and the dialect they spoke was a lost language.

"*Hakaniyun,*" Dan said, and continued to hold out his hand. The three men behind their leader murmured louder. The one in front cocked his head to the side, his eyes filled with uncertainty.

"You speak Indian?" Jana whispered loudly, and gripped his arm tighter.

Dan turned his head toward her without taking his eyes off the men. "I speak a little Shoshone. I'm not sure if they can understand. The dialect I know is different from these people's. I can only hope it's close enough."

"*Tsoapittsi*," the man said hesitantly. He made no move to shake Dan's hand.

"What did he say?" Jana whispered.

Dan had to think for a moment, trying to decipher the word. "I think he said something like ghost, or spirit."

Jana squeezed his arm even more, surprising him with her strength. "Dan, that guy is looking at you like you're possessed. What if they know Daniel? That's why they're all looking at you like that."

"Do I really resemble him that much?" Dan asked. The trappers, at least Bautiste, had immediately thought he was Daniel. And the way these Sheepeaters were looking at him was downright unsettling.

"You do," Jana confirmed. "Daniel has shoulder-length hair, and there's some minor differences, but it's uncanny how much you look like him."

At that moment, an angry roar reverberated through the trees. Everyone's heads turned. The trapper, Claude, came stumbling through the trees like a rabid dog, his pistol raised. His bloody face and eyes were a gruesome sight. Dan shoved Jana behind him. Without hesitating, the Shoshone at the head of the group raised his bow, and with practiced speed and grace, reached behind his shoulder for an arrow from his quiver, strung the bow, and released the deadly projectile. It happened so fast, Dan barely had time to make out the movement.

The force of the arrow's impact in Claude's chest made him stumble back several steps. He hit the ground with a loud thud, and lay still. Jana buried her face in Dan's shirt.

He put his arm around her shoulders and pulled her up against him, shielding her from the gruesome sight.

The Indian spoke to his companions, and two of them trotted off through the trees in the direction of the lake. Dan could only guess that the other two trappers were about to meet a similar fate as Claude. Dan slowly turned back to the Shoshone. Their eyes met. There was no hostility in the other man's expression, only a sort of awe, and a certain amount of confusion.

Dan nodded his head in a gesture of thanks.

"*Patuhuyaa nuukwi*," the man said, and his eyebrows raised expectantly. "*Samopuu?*" He took a step toward Dan, then first to one side and then the other. He stooped forward, and assessed him again with a critical eye.

Dan's mind was furiously trying to translate what the Indian was saying. The words sounded familiar, even if the dialect was a bit different.

"Brother?" Dan translated out loud. The other words raced through his mind. *Moose, deer, elk... elk running through the forest. Elk Runner!*

"Jana," Dan gripped her arm. "I think I know who this is." She shook her head, her forehead wrinkled with incomprehension. "Daniel's Shoshone brother, Elk Runner."

Jana's eyes widened, and she looked at the Indian, whose expression of bewilderment was almost comical. "Now I understand why he looks so perplexed."

"Daniel Osborne," Dan said, pointing his thumb at his chest. The Indian's eyes widened, and he shook his head in a fierce gesture of denial. Dan slowly spoke in Shoshone, hoping this man could understand. "I come to warn White Wolf of a great danger."

Elk Runner's forehead wrinkled. "What tricks are the spirits playing, White Wolf? Have they punished you?" he

186

asked. "I have warned you many times that you will make them angry. Now they have given your likeness to someone else."

Dan wasn't quite sure what Elk Runner was talking about. "I must find your brother." He wished he could express himself more clearly. He wanted to tell this Indian that he wasn't the Daniel who Elk Runner knew. If he had to guess, it sounded as if Elk Runner believed that the spirits had created another version of Daniel.

"You cannot find your way to your valley?" Elk Runner asked, looking stunned. "I have told you, have I not, that to stay with your wife at this time will anger the spirits. But you would not listen." He threw his hands up in apparent exasperation. "The spirits have even given you a new wife." He nodded toward Jana.

Dan shook his head, and ran his hand through his hair, frustrated that his communication skills were so limited. "No, she is not my wife," he managed to string together.

Elk Runner grinned. "You wish for her to be your wife," he stated knowingly. It almost sounded like a challenge.

Dan glanced at Jana, who listened to their exchange intently. He was sure she had no idea what they were talking about. "Yes, I do," he said, and smiled at her. Her eyes narrowed on him, and he quickly looked toward Elk Runner. The man's grin widened.

"Then do not make the same mistake you made last season, when the spirits gifted you with Dosa Haiwi," Elk Runner said and took several bold steps forward, finally holding out his hand to Dan. They clasped wrists firmly, and the Indian nodded in approval. "Perhaps it is good what the spirits have done with you, White Wolf. You are much more agreeable in your second form, even though your appearance, and your lack of knowledge is not to my liking." He looked Dan up and down, and his eyes lingered on Dan's hair. "You will come with us to our village."

"I must go home," Dan said for lack of words to tell Elk Runner he had to get to the Madison Valley.

Elk Runner shot him a perplexed look. "You will make the spirits angry all over again. You cannot go home yet. You cannot defy the ways of the spirits. Perhaps if you do as they wish, they will return your former self after you fulfill your duty as a hunter of the Tukudeka. Tell me, what has happened to my true brother? Have the spirits taken him away?"

Dan had no clue what Elk Runner was talking about. Apparently, he was under the impression that the spirits were punishing Daniel for something he had done that went against tribal custom, but Dan had no way of asking what Elk Runner meant. For now, he decided to play along and go with the Indians. He hoped to get more information somehow. Maybe the words would come to him later.

"I don't know what happened to White Wolf. How far away is your village from the valley of the Madison?" Dan managed to ask. At least he hoped it was what he'd asked.

Elk Runner looked annoyed. His two companions that he'd sent off earlier came back at that moment, nodding solemnly. The trappers' wails had quieted, bringing an eerie stillness to the valley.

"Our village is close to your cabin in the valley, but you cannot return yet. Our mother will let you know when it is time. We go now," he said. "It is best you come with us. The Sky People have spoken."

"What did they say?" Dan couldn't help from asking. Either he was missing a key point here, or Elk Runner liked to talk in riddles.

"They have sent you here, just as they brought *Dosa Haiwi* to you . . . to your true form, one season ago. You and your new woman have the same manner of dress as she did. Tell me, is this woman gifted with the power of healing as well?"

"Yes, she is," Dan said.

"The spirits work in strange ways sometimes." The Indian shook his head. "They have gifted you with a mild-mannered woman this time. She does not look to be as disrespectful as *Dosa Haiwi*."

Elk Runner abruptly turned and led the way through the forest. Everyone stepped around the dead trapper, and Dan kept himself between the body and Jana so she wouldn't have to take a close look. Dan stopped at the site where they'd spent the night and kicked dirt onto the coals of the burned-out campfire. He grabbed his backpack and nodded to Elk Runner that he was ready to go.

Single-file, the Sheeepeaters walked along some invisible trail heading south, skirting expertly around deadfall. The forest seemed to close in on them with every step they took. The canopies of the tallest lodgepoles blocked out the rays of the morning sun, making it appear almost like nighttime. No one spoke, and the silent way in which these people moved through the brush didn't disturb the loud chirping of countless birds in the trees.

"Where are they taking us?" Jana asked in a hushed tone. She reached for Dan's hand whenever she could. Most of the time, he nudged her to walk ahead of him. The path simply wasn't wide enough for two people to travel side-by-side.

"Back to their village."

"Did you tell him we need to get to Daniel and Aimee's cabin?"

"Yes, but he says I can't go there. Something about angry spirits. I think he believes I am another form of Daniel that was conjured by the spirits. He kept making references to something Daniel did to make the spirits mad, and I am his punishment."

Jana glanced over her shoulder at him. "Sounds like an insult to me." She grinned.

Dan frowned, and swatted her on her rear. "Are you saying I'm the inferior version of Daniel?" he asked in mock anger. "Maybe Elk Runner thinks I'm the new and improved version. He did say he liked me better."

"I like you better, too," she blurted, then quickly faced straight ahead. Dan stared at her backside. Waves of desire rushed through him suddenly, and his blood drained south.

"We have to get to Madison," Jana said almost desperately, and Dan was glad that she was completely oblivious to his thoughts. She didn't turn her head this time, and kept up with the hunter in front of her. Dan gave silent thanks to be bringing up the rear.

"I know. The village has to be on the way. Right now, I'm guessing we're only another couple of days away."

"What if Elk Runner won't let us leave?"

"I'll try and convince him again that Daniel and Aimee are in danger, and we need to see them."

They walked for the remainder of the day. The Indians moved tirelessly through the endless forest, stopping only once along a shallow creek to drink some water and share strips of dried meat and handfuls of a mixture of nuts and berries.

Dan grinned at Jana's dismayed look at the food in her hands. He leaned toward her and whispered in her ear. "You ought to be used to nuts by now." They had eaten plenty on their trek through the wilderness.

"There are some nuts I'll never get used to," she said, and Dan clenched his jaw at the sensual teasing in her voice, and the twinkle in her eyes. He forced himself not to pull her into his arms at that moment. Her unexpected flirty side left his head spinning.

Without a proper comeback, Dan glanced up to distract

himself from the images in his mind, images that included Jana's legs wrapped around him. Elk Runner stared at them from a short distance away. The satisfied smirk on the Indian's face reminded Dan of a fox who'd just raided a henhouse.

CHAPTER TWENTY-THREE

"Are we there yet?" Jana asked listlessly. The sun had almost disappeared behind the mountains, and Dan wrapped his fingers around her hand for encouragement. She looked worn out. It had been one very long day that had started out with a terrifying encounter with those trappers.

Elk Runner and his companions had set a steady pace all day. None of them gave any indication of being tired. Dan was just about to tell Jana it shouldn't be much longer, when his nose caught the scent of wood smoke. Dogs barked in the distance.

"I think we've arrived," he said and gave her hand a light squeeze. Jana's head perked up and she walked a little straighter. Coming out of the forest into a grassy clearing, a group of nine dwellings appeared. Each was constructed of wooden poles erected close together to create a cone shaped hut. Most of them were partially covered with hides, while a few were merely thatched with grasses and leafy tree branches.

Children ran from the village to meet the returning hunters. Soon, chattering kids surrounded the four men. Dan stood off to the side, and slipped his arm around the back of Jana's waist. "Now that's quite a homecoming," he remarked. Several of the children spotted them and stared wide-eyed and open-mouthed. A couple pointed and whispered. Dan distinctly heard the name White Wolf mentioned several times. One little boy, the youngest in the group who appeared to have barely learned to walk, toddled up to Dan, and pulled at his pants. All the other children fell silent.

"*Bia*," the child cried and stared upwards. Dan knelt to the ground to be closer to eye level with the little boy. Chubby little hands reached for Dan's face and the tot smacked them against Dan's cheeks. The little smile suddenly turned upside down and his lips quivered. The boy sobbed, but didn't cry out loud. Dan was lost for words, or what to do. Clearly, this youngster could tell he was not the person he had at first believed him to be.

"My son, Touch the Cloud," Elk Runner said and grabbed hold of the toddler's arm. In one swift move, he pulled him up and set him on his shoulder. The tot grinned again, and grabbed his father's hair.

"He misses his true uncle," Elk Runner said.

"I am not his uncle," Dan said apologetically and stood to his full height.

Elk Runner's penetrating gaze left Dan feeling uncomfortable. These people were strongly rooted in their spiritual beliefs, and Dan had no way of explaining his appearance to them. If Elk Runner believed him to be a copy of Daniel that the spirits conjured up, what did he think had happened to the original? And what had Daniel done to make Elk Runner believe the spirits were punishing him in the first place?

The men dispersed with the children toward the village, where women and other adults waited. Elk Runner's eyes lingered on Dan. It was obvious he was trying to work things out in his mind.

"Come, brother. You and your woman will eat, and I make a gift of my lodge to you. If you keep the Sky People happy, perhaps they will return you to the spirit world and bring the brother I know back."

"And how do I make the spirits happy?" Dan asked.

"By following the customs of the people." Elk Runner looked taken aback. "One season ago, White Wolf refused to take the woman the Sky People brought to him as his wife. When the time came that he realized she was meant for him, the spirits took her away again. He has never told me, but I believe he brought her back from the spirit world. Now he defies the Sky People again. Perhaps they have decided that he is no longer worthy of being a Tukudeka. I cannot explain your appearance. I do not possess the gift to speak to the spirits."

The reaction of all the other adults in the village was the same as the hunters when Dan and Jana had first come upon them in the forest early that morning. Looks of awe and disbelief showed on their faces when Elk Runner led him and Jana through the village. Jana clung to Dan's arm like a tick on a hound.

Elk Runner led them to one of several cooking fires and peeled his son from his shoulders. He set the boy down on the ground, who quickly toddled toward a short woman who held a flat pot made of clay in her hand. Her eyes were full of questions, looking from Elk Runner to Jana and lingering on Dan.

"White Wolf's spirit and his woman will stay in my lodge tonight," Elk Runner said, addressing the woman. She nodded without speaking. Turning to Dan, he said, "This is my wife's sister, Yellow Flower. She will prepare food for you. After you eat, this is my lodge." He pointed to a large wickiup covered in hides. "I will speak to the elders. Perhaps they know the reason why you are here." Without another word, he turned and headed toward several older men who stood in a half-circle, eying them curiously.

"What's going on, Dan?" Jana asked in a hushed whisper.

"I'm not sure," he said, expelling a lung full of air. He ran his hand through his hair.

"Are we prisoners?"

"No." Dan laughed, and touched his hand to her back for reassurance. "We might as well make the best of it for tonight, and I'll try and convince him again in the morning that we need to get to Daniel and Aimee's.

The Indian woman, Yellow Flower, handed him an earthen bowl filled with some sort of soup consisting of chunks of meat and root vegetables. Wordlessly, she walked away, the toddler at her heels. Dan sniffed. The food smelled delicious, and his mouth watered. He wasn't going to tell Jana that she would most likely be eating marmot tonight.

"Let's eat, then you can wash the trail dust off you over by the creek. You might even get to sleep on something other than the hard ground tonight."

While Jana left for the creek, Dan sought out Elk Runner. He sat in front of one of the wickiups, in animated conversation with several older men. They all looked up when Dan approached them.

"Spirit of White Wolf. The elders have agreed to welcome you as a member of our village," Elk Runner said eagerly. "They have never seen the Sky People's power like this before. They all agree that you must do what my brother refused to do, so that my true brother can be returned to us."

Dan's forehead wrinkled. He was more confused than ever. "What do I have to do?" he asked.

"White Wolf must go on a hunt to gift the members of the village. He has refused to do so. The elders say that perhaps you were sent here to take my brother's place."

A hunt? That was it? Daniel had refused to go hunting, and now the spirits were mad at him?

Dan mentally shook his head. There had to be more to the story than that.

"I must get to the valley," Dan said, trying again to communicate that he had to warn Daniel and Aimee.

"You cannot go there," Elk Runner said adamantly. "I have told you this. It is because your other self did not leave the valley that the sky people are angry."

"Your brother White Wolf and his wife, Dosa Haiwi, are in great danger if I do not warn them," Dan said forcefully.

Elk Runner dismissed his words with a wave of his hand. "I will send word to Dosa Haiwi, but she cannot leave her lodge." He paused and smirked. "Knowing that woman, however, she will not do what she is told. Much like my brother." He shook his head.

Dan wanted to hit something. He was frustrated beyond belief. Daniel shouldn't be in the valley, but Aimee couldn't leave? What key piece of information was he missing here?

Elk Runner placed his hand on Dan's shoulder. He looked him in the eyes, smiling. "Spirit of White Wolf. I have made a gift of my lodge to you. Do not make the same mistake my true brother made last season. This time, follow my advice and spare yourself the misery he lived with. Take your woman to your lodge. She is now your wife."

DAN HELD the mountain sheep hide away from the wickiup, and ducked through the opening into the dwelling, letting the flap fall closed behind him. The wooden poles in the center were barely high enough for him to stand up to his full height. He ran a hand through his damp hair, some water droplets falling to his bare shoulders. He wiped at the back of his neck with the shirt he had slung over his shoulder. Washing the trail dust from his body had refreshed his tired muscles.

He squinted his eyes and tried to focus his vision in the dim light. Outside, dusk was quickly giving way to the darkness of the evening and it was even darker inside this hut.

"Dan, these hides are so comfortable," Jana spoke out of the darkness. "I almost forgot what sleeping on something other than the hard ground feels like." Dan followed the sound of her voice, and lowered himself to the ground.

"I hope there's room enough for two," he said, reaching out his hand. He made contact with the top of Jana's head. Her hair was still damp from her own bath. She moved over and Dan settled himself next to her. She was right. The soft furs beneath him did feel mighty nice after weeks of nothing but hard ground. He sighed contently, stretched out on the furs, and clasped his hands behind the back of his head. Jana still sat upright at his side.

He stared up at the darkness for several minutes, listening to the sounds coming from outside. The village was growing quiet. Every now and then, hushed murmurs could be heard, and a dog yipped, but everyone seemed to be settling in for the night. Dan pulled his arm from behind his head, and reached for Jana.

"Come here," he suggested, tugging on her arm. "Tell me what's on your mind."

She resisted for an instant, then lay down beside him, and rested her head on his arm.

"What if we're too late?" she asked quietly. "What if something already happened to Aimee and Daniel? Why would Elk Runner think you're another version of Daniel? Maybe you didn't understand him correctly. Maybe Daniel is dead, and Elk Runner thinks you're his reincarnation."

Dan thought about what she said for a minute. "I don't

think so. I'm not sure these people believe in reincarnation. He simply sees me as someone the spirits conjured to right something that Daniel apparently did wrong, something that supposedly made the spirits mad." He paused for a second. "At least that's how I understood it."

"We have to get to the valley."

"I know. I think we're really close. I saw a bunch of smoke plumes this afternoon to the southwest. I believe that was the Norris Geyser basin. We're less than a day's walk from Madison."

Dan tightened his arm around her, and gave her a reassuring squeeze. Jana lifted her head upwards, and kissed his cheek. "We've almost made it," she said wistfully. "And then we wait for Hastings, right?"

Dan's body reacted immediately to Jana's kiss, regardless that it was just an innocent peck. He suddenly became acutely aware of her hand that rested on his bare chest, and the nerve endings on his skin all around where she touched him sprang to life. He sucked in a breath of air, and his gut tightened at his sudden reaction.

"Yeah, then we wait for Hastings," he managed to say between clenched teeth. He rolled slightly sideways from his back, and wrapped his other arm around Jana's waist.

"You've been amazing these past weeks," he whispered and held her close. He slowly moved his hands up and down her back, and kneaded the tension from the muscles along her spine. Her soft moan of contentment fueled his sudden desire quicker than a raging forest fire. She relaxed and leaned into him, her body molding to his. Heat coursed through him.

Dan leaned over her, kissed her cheek, and let his mouth glide along her jawline until he found her mouth. Slowly, deliberately, he kissed her soft lips, his tongue probing along the seam of her mouth. When Jana wound her arms around his neck, he groaned, and pulled her tightly to him. His hands roamed along her back, and worked their way under her shirt. He wanted . . . needed to feel her bare skin on his.

He slid his hands up along her ribs, molding his palms to her feminine curves. He pushed her shirt upwards, and Jana lifted her arms for him to pull it completely over her head. Dan tossed the cotton garment to the side and a hot wave of desire flushed through him. She'd acted almost flirty with him today, and memories of this morning came rushing back. Her response when he'd held her in that clearing by the lake, the way she'd wrapped her legs around his hips. He'd started to tell her he would never do anything she wasn't ready for, just before those trappers interrupted them. He had wanted to tell her so much more. How much he loved her. How he couldn't envision his life without her.

His mouth left hers to trail kisses down her neck while he fumbled with the hooks on her bra. His lips followed the path of the bra strap over her shoulder and down her arm. With nothing between their upper bodies, he wrapped his arms around her, and rolled onto his back, lifting her on top of him.

"You're beautiful," he whispered, nuzzling along her neck.

"You can't see me," Jana gasped on a sharp intake of breath.

"No, but I can feel you," he mumbled hoarsely. To prove his point, he ran his palms up along the sides of her curves, from her hips to her shoulders, and back down across her back. Jana shivered. "I can feel you, and you feel so good. So beautiful."

Jana stroked her fingers along his jaw, and kissed him tentatively. It was all the encouragement he needed. He entwined his fingers through her hair behind her head, and deepened the kiss. With a throaty groan, he rolled her over onto her back. His heart rate accelerated out of control, and perspiration formed on his forehead and back. He was quickly approaching the point of no return.

"I love you. You have no idea what you do to me," he mumbled against her lips.

She's your wife now. Elk Runner's words echoed in his mind. How simple it was in this time, for these people. Would she agree to marry him when they returned home . . . if they returned home? *You're here, in this time. According to the Sheepeater tribal custom, she's your wife.*

"I love you, Dan," Jana whispered, and tightened her grip around his neck. When she pressed her lips to his, his resolve crumbled, accepting her unspoken invitation. He took command of the kiss, and pulled her closer. She responded to him with a passion that drove him nearly mad. Barely aware of how his pants and Jana's had come off, he leaned over her, and nudged her legs apart. Gripping her hips, he pulled her toward him. Jana arched her back to meet him.

"I love you, Jana," he said again, and slid into her moist folds. He froze. "Jana?" The last thing on earth he expected was the barrier he came up against. *She's never been with a man.*

"It's okay, Dan," she said, her voice quivering. "I . . . I want this. I want you." Her hands pulled his head back toward her, and she kissed him, not giving him a chance to reply. His heart was sure to burst at her words, and it was too late for him to turn back now. Slowly, he pushed past her innocence, and his kiss drowned out her soft cry of pain. He waited for her to relax again beneath him, then moved inside of her, holding her hips, guiding her to move in time with him. He felt her release just before his own, and held her tight while she shuddered in his arms. Rolling to the side, he wrapped his arms around her, too stunned for words that she'd given herself to him, and him alone.

CHAPTER TWENTY-FOUR

*D*aniel Osborne swung his ax high over and behind his head, bringing the blade down onto a round log with a well-aimed blow. With a loud splintering sound, the wood split in half, each piece tumbling off the ancient tree stump that had served him as a chopping block longer than he could remember.

He stood facing an old cabin nestled against several tall lodgepole pines. The structure had been his home for nearly all of his twenty-six years, and his father's before that. Swiping a hand against his sweaty forehead, he pushed some strands of hair from his face and glanced toward the much larger cabin to his left. The corners of his mouth rose in a soft smile.

His new home was nearly completed. The only thing that was missing was the stained glass he had promised his wife, Aimee. The cabin was built in a strategic location to overlook the entire Madison Valley, with the river some fifty yards to the south. She had insisted on large windows, so that she could look out and see the river from their main room. For now, burlap covered the open squares.

By the end of the summer, he hoped to have glass in the windows. When he'd asked his father's old friend and fellow trapper, Josiah Butler, last winter to buy the expensive commodity in St Louis and bring it with him when he returned to the mountains for the fall trapping season, the man had looked at him as if he had taken leave of his senses.

"What ye want glass in the wilderness fer?" he'd asked, wide-eyed.

"My wife wishes it," Daniel had said simply, as if the man was blind and didn't see the answer right in front of him. "She is in no condition to make the journey to St. Louis, or I would go myself. I need your help, my friend."

The grizzled old man had shaken his head. "Women," he'd scoffed and spit tobacco juice at his feet. "Mark my word, Dan'l. Ya start goin soft and coddlin' yore woman, and next she'll be wearin the britches an hen-peck ya mornin' to night."

Daniel could only smile. Little had his friend known that Aimee already wore britches. Not in the sense his friend had implied. Aimee was not a conventional woman, but there was nothing Daniel wouldn't do for her. He considered himself the luckiest man alive. She had made a life-altering sacrifice to be with him. Love for him alone reflected in her eyes, and Daniel swore that he would show her every day how much she meant to him. Sometimes he feared she would regret her decision to leave her old life, and all she knew, behind in order to be with him.

In recent months, Aimee had given up wearing britches. His face sobered and he trained his eyes on his new cabin. Not a day went by when blinding fear didn't threaten to rob him of his sanity. Aimee was due to give birth to their first child any day now. Looking at her, one might think she carried a litter of cubs. These days, she wore a simple buckskin gown that hung down her body. She'd outgrown all of her britches many weeks ago.

Cold sweat trickled down his back. What if something went wrong during the birth? He couldn't bear the thought of anything happening to his wife. His own mother had died in childbirth and the thought of Aimee dying while bringing forth his child was more terrifying than facing down a mother grizzly bear. His foster mother, Morning Sun, and sister-in-law, Little Bird, had come to live with them nearly a month ago in preparation for the birth. Neither one of the women had seen a need to come so soon, but at his insistence, had acquiesced.

Now that Aimee's time was near, the two women scolded him every day to keep out of the cabin and to stay away from her. If it were up to them, he'd be banished to the old cabin, or better yet, away from the valley entirely. They couldn't understand why he would even wish to be here. A man was not present when a woman gave birth. He was reminded of this custom on a daily basis. If not for Aimee telling them to allow him to stay, explaining that where she came from it was all right for a man to be by his wife's side at a time like this, they would have beaten him off with sticks by now like a coyote being chased off a kill by a pack of wolves.

Nothing could prevent him from being near his wife when her time came. He might not be of much help, but Aimee wanted him close by and a herd of bison couldn't make him leave her side. Putting up with the ridicule of two other women was a small price to pay.

Hell, he already faced the scorn of the entire village for breaking with tradition. Although he was a white man, he had grown up amongst the mountain Shoshone who made this wilderness their home. All his life, he had embraced their values and traditions, but this time he would go against everything he'd been taught.

Movement along the river to the west caught his attention. Daniel swung his ax and buried the blade in the chopping block. He groaned silently. The man emerged through the early morning fog that hovered over the meadow and along the river like an apparition. He would most likely be quick to point out what the women had drilled into him for weeks. What was his brother doing here at such an early hour? He must have walked half the night if he was coming from his village.

Daniel straightened his back and headed toward the river. That his adoptive brother, Elk Runner, would even come near the valley at this time was a complete surprise. As a male relative, he would be expected to stay away as well until the child was born. Most likely Elk Runner was here to tell him again that he had a duty to his wife and clan, and leave the valley for a hunt. It was expected that Daniel would provide the village with meat in celebration of the birth.

Elk Runner stopped abruptly when Daniel approached. Daniel frowned. His brother apparently didn't want to come any closer to the cabin than where he already stood.

"It is good to see you, brother," Daniel greeted in the Tukudeka dialect, extending his hand to Elk Runner. The man's eyes widened, and he leaned forward, assessing Daniel as if he'd never seen him before. He did not extend his own hand, but rather walked a slow arc around Daniel, his eyes roaming up and down his body.

Daniel's frown deepened. What was his brother up to this time?

"Explain your behavior," Daniel said impatiently. "I have no time for your practical jokes."

"The spirits have not whisked you away," Elk Runner said. "It is you?" he asked, doubt etched on his face.

What the hell sort of question was that? "Have you taken

leave of your senses?" Daniel asked, not hiding his annoyance.

"The spirits have made it possible for you to be in two places at once."

Daniel frowned. What new ploy had his brother worked up now to lure him out of the valley?

"I feared the sky people had taken you away. I traveled half the night to get here and see for myself. I believed they are angry with you for disobeying tradition. You should be out on a hunt, not sitting in your lodge like a woman."

"I have told you this already," Daniel said between clenched teeth. "I will not leave Aimee's side until the baby is born. Then I will go make meat and present gifts to the village."

Elk Runner's face lightened all of a sudden. "I believed the Sky People took you away and replaced you with another," he said, as if to himself. "Maybe I have mistaken what the spirits have planned."

"Stop speaking in riddles," Daniel said, not bothering to hide the annoyance in his tone.

"The man who shares your likeness, I believed that he was sent here as your punishment, since you are unwilling to act like a proper Tukudeka hunter." He paused and studied Daniel's face some more. Then his lips widened in a grin. Elk Runner walked around him, his hands clasped behind his back, studying him from top to bottom as if he was some prime pelt he wanted to trade for.

"I think I like the other version of you better," he said finally, lifting his chin. "He is not as obstinate as you. At least he follows my advice and is not as foolish as you."

Daniel closed his eyes, praying for patience. His brother made no sense.

"Daniel." A soft woman's voice called from the cabin.

Daniel's head turned instantly, and he watched his wife waddle across the meadow toward him. He left his brother's side, and headed in her direction.

Aimee favored him with a wide smile that never failed to make his heart beat faster. She reached her arms up to his shoulders, and leaned toward him for a kiss. Daniel ran his hand over his wife's swollen abdomen. She looked and felt as if she would burst at any moment.

"Is it all right for you to be out here?" he asked gently.

"Daniel," Aimee huffed, her hands at her sides in the vicinity where her hips used to be. "I can't sit in that cabin all day. Moving around and walking is good for me and the baby."

"Woman, you should be in your lodge, before you curse us all. The spirits will be angry."

Daniel smiled when Aimee rolled her eyes at Elk Runner's words. There was an edge of panic in his brother's voice. Daniel stepped aside to give his wife free access to his brother.

"I believe the spirits cursed me already when you became my brother-in-law," Aimee retorted, a wide smile on her face. Her Shoshone was still a bit stilted, but her meaning was clear. Daniel suppressed a grin. His wife never failed to try and put his brother in his place. The two made it a regular habit to spar with words. "If you are so afraid, why do you come here?" she asked, taking a step toward him. Elk Runner backed up as she advanced.

"I have just finished telling my brother," Elk Runner said warily, "there is another man with his likeness in these mountains. The Sky People have sent him to take your husband's place. That is what I believe."

"What are you talking about?" Aimee asked, throwing her hands in the air, exasperation in her voice.

"A man with the likeness of White Wolf. He has a woman with him who speaks and dresses as you did when you first came to us."

Daniel shot a surprised look at his wife. Her eyes widened as well.

"A man who looks like Daniel, and a woman who talks and dresses like me," Aimee repeated. Then she laughed. "How long did it take you to come up with such a tale?"

"Both she and the man dress the same." Elk Runner scratched the back of his head.

Daniel exchanged a quick look with Aimee. He could see it on her face what she was thinking. Two people, wearing the same clothing as she'd worn months ago. Clothing from a future time. Could it mean two people had traveled through time? How could it be possible? The device that had brought Aimee to him last summer had been disposed of. Aimee was sure that the manner in which they had disposed of it would hide it for eternity. Was there another way to travel through time than with the ancient snakehead?

"Did the woman and man have a name?" Aimee asked slowly.

"The man shares your husband's white man's name," Elk Runner said. No one spoke. Aimee's mouth fell open.

"Daniel?" Aimee addressed him in English. "Are you thinking the same thing I'm thinking? If your brother is telling the truth, how could this happen?"

Daniel merely shook his head. He had no answers. His brother was a known prankster, but how could Elk Runner be pulling a trick on him now. He had no knowledge of time travel. Daniel's mind raced. A man who bore his likeness, shared his name, and wore clothing from the future. What did it mean?

"The man speaks the Shoshone language, but it is difficult

to understand him at times. Some of his words are different," Elk Runner said. "He said he must warn you of a great danger."

"What about the woman?" Aimee asked.

"She does not understand us, nor speaks our language."

"Does she share my name and likeness?" Aimee asked.

"No. The man, I believe, was calling her *Chey-na*."

Aimee gasped, and grabbed hold of Daniel's arm. He quickly wrapped his arm around her back to steady her. Their eyes met.

"It's not possible," she whispered, dumbstruck.

Daniel's eyebrows drew together. Aimee's friend in the future was called Jana. It sounded similar to the way Elk Runner pronounced the name.

"Describe her to me," Aimee demanded, staring at Elk Runner.

"She does not have the yellow color of your hair, but it is not as dark as our own. It is more the color of buffalo in summer. She is perhaps a hand taller than you, and does not share your disrespectfulness toward a hunter. The man has said she has the gift of healing, just as you do." Elk Runner paused, and his eyes narrowed. "Do you know this woman?"

Instead of answering, Aimee looked up at Daniel. "What if it is her, Daniel? What if Jana time traveled? You have to go and bring her here."

"I will not leave you," he said firmly.

Aimee patted his arm. "These . . . this baby isn't coming for several days. You can go and be back before then. Daniel, you have to go and get her."

Daniel clenched his jaw, then glared at his brother. "Why did you not bring these people with you if they are at your village?" he asked.

Elk Runner's face lit up in a brilliant smile. "I have told you, the man is not as stubborn and hard-headed as you."

"Explain yourself." Daniel was quickly losing patience with his brother.

"I asked if the woman was his wife, and he answered no, but he wished it were true. I offered him my lodge." He shrugged his shoulders.

"What?" Aimee asked dumbfounded. She released Daniel's arm, and took a step toward Elk Runner, her eyes shooting daggers at him.

"He seemed quite happy at my suggestion." The grin on Elk Runner's face broadened even as he backed up to maintain his distance from her.

"Jana would never agree to something like that," Aimee said, as if to herself. "Unless . . ." She turned to face Daniel again. "You have to go bring them here, Daniel. Go now, and you can be back by nightfall. The baby will wait." She put her hand on his arm. "Please. I'll be all right. Morning Sun and Little Bird are here if anything should happen."

"What is this danger you speak of?" he asked suddenly.

Elk Runner shook his head. "I do not know. He would not tell me. Perhaps he didn't have the right words. But he said you and Dosa Haiwi are in danger."

Daniel looked into his wife's deep blue eyes. A man and woman from the future, who'd come to warn him of a danger to his wife. He had no choice but to find out more. He would do as Aimee asked. He always did. If she said the child would wait to be born, he believed her. With a reluctant nod of his head, he leaned toward her, and kissed her cheek. "I will go. If Jana Evans truly traveled through time, there must be a very good reason."

Aimee nodded and smiled. He placed his arm around her waist, and walked slowly back in the direction of his cabin with her.

He stopped to glare at Elk Runner, who hadn't made a move to follow them to the cabin. "I will go with you. If you've spoken words that aren't true simply to get me away from my wife, you will have breathed your last breath."

CHAPTER TWENTY-FIVE

*D*ogs barked and children laughed. Other voices mingled with these sounds, and Jana wondered vaguely why there was so much noise around her. For weeks, she'd awakened to only the sounds of birdsong or the gurgling of a creek. She opened her eyes to the semi-darkness, and instead of looking up at the sky or the canopies of lodgepole pines, she stared at narrow wooden poles that were tightly bunched together. Golden light streamed through some of the cracks between the poles and from the ground.

Jana's hand moved across soft fur, the feel shocking her fully awake. She bolted to a sitting position, the warm covering falling away. She gasped at the chill in the air and groped with her hand for the cover, pulling it up and over her shoulders. Awareness that she had no clothes on sent a jolt of adrenaline through her.

Jana groaned. "Oh dear God," she whispered. She glanced around, her eyes adjusting to the dim light in the hut. She was alone. Relief swept over her like a wave of warm water. She couldn't possibly face Dan at the moment. Memories of the night before came rushing back to her. He'd held her and kissed her, and the next thing she knew, she was wrapped in his arms, skin to skin.

A sudden aftershock of desire rippled through her, and she rubbed her hand at the goose bumps on her arms. She couldn't have stopped herself from what had happened even if she had wanted to. She hadn't wanted those delicious feelings he'd stirred in her to end. Her face heated at the memory of Dan's lovemaking. She had told him it was what she wanted, and it was the truth. Just a few weeks ago, she had asked him to go slow in their relationship. She laughed softly. So much for taking it slow. She loved Dan with all her heart, and she'd known all along she couldn't stay true to her childhood vow of saving herself for her wedding night.

A twinge of guilt and shame hit her. She shook it off. She had been teetering on the edge for days, her need and desire for Dan growing stronger each time he held her in his arms and kissed her. She had been able to control those feelings, up until last night.

Jana felt around under the furs for her clothes. What would happen now? Her pulse increased, wondering what Dan would say to her. Had he found her lacking? He'd realized right away that this had been her first time, and he'd acted rather surprised. Jana buried her face in her hands. She'd boldly told him she wanted him.

Oh, God! I can't even face him now. What am I going to say to him?

The thought had barely crossed her mind when the flap to the hut's door opened, and Dan ducked inside. With a pounding heart, Jana clutched the fur covering to her chest. He stopped, bent over, and their eyes met. A wide smile lit up his face.

"Morning," he said and quickly closed the flap behind him. He set a clay bowl on the ground and kneeled down beside her. His hand came up to cup her face and he kissed her. Slowly. Tenderly. Jana leaned forward and into his hand while his thumb stroked her cheek. She cast her eyes downward when he pulled his head back, unable to meet his gaze. He sat down fully beside her.

"Come here. Let me hold you." He wrapped his arms around her and gathered her close to him. "I never want to let go of you," he whispered against her ear.

Jana's eyes filled with tears. His tender words, spoken in a tone that left no doubt he meant them, overwhelmed her. She quivered, and sobbed quietly.

"Jana. Are you sorry about what happened last night?" Dan leaned back, and lifted her chin with his fingers. "I never meant to take advantage of you. I thought you—"

Jana sniffed and gave a short laugh. "You didn't take advantage of me."

Dan caressed her cheek. "Why didn't you tell me . . . you know, that you've never . . ."

"Is that really a good topic of conversation?" she asked.

"And now you have regrets," Dan said stiffly. His jaw muscles clenched and unclenched.

Jana gripped his arm. She shook her head. "Not for the reasons you think," she said quickly.

"I love you, Jana. I think I've made that pretty clear. I don't plan to walk away from you. I hope you don't think this was a one-night fling for me."

Jana sighed. "You're the first man I ever wanted to be with . . . like that. It's crazy how much I love you, how you make me feel. I've been in long-term relationships with one or two guys, and I never had the desire to go to bed with any of them. And now you come along, and in a few short weeks, I'm a goner." She glanced at the furs covering her, absently running her fingers along the soft hairs.

Dan chuckled. "I'll take that as a compliment."

"Aimee and I made a pact a long time ago. We must have been in grade school, two little girls full of romantic notions with ideas of happily ever after in our heads. We vowed we would save ourselves for our wedding night." Jana smiled tentatively. "She broke that vow first. Fairy tales are great for little girls, I suppose. But she did get her happily ever after."

"And you don't think you'll get yours?"

She looked up and stared at him. Oh yes, she wanted her happily ever after. With him. She couldn't bring herself to say that to him, though. She'd made her choice to be with him without the benefit of marriage and she'd bear the consequences if he decided to walk away. She inhaled deeply before speaking. "Dan, I'm not asking for a commitment just because of what happened last night. No worries, okay?"

Dan released her, staring at her dumbfounded. He ran a hand through his hair. "You don't want a commitment," he repeated slowly. "What about me? Maybe I do."

Jana looked up at him. The truth was right there in his eyes. Why did she have a hard time believing him? Dan reached for her hand.

"Jana," he said slowly, pausing as if gathering his thoughts. "These Indians, the Sheepeaters, they have a peculiar marriage custom. It's very uncomplicated."

Marriage. Jana swallowed back the lump in her throat. What was he saying?

"A couple that intends to join in marriage only needs to be seen together in public a few times, and once they share a lodge, it's a done deal." He looked at her expectantly.

"Are you saying we're married in the eyes of these people?"

Dan grinned sheepishly. "One of my ancestors had a Shoshone mother, so I guess that makes me part Indian as well. I'll go with the tradition."

"Why didn't you tell me this last night?"

"Why didn't you tell me you've never been with a man?" He ran his hand through his hair, and inhaled deeply. "Jana, I wasn't exactly in the mood for conversation at the time, and you didn't exactly act as though it would make a difference." The tone of his voice had changed. He sounded angry all of a sudden. He released her hand, and stood. Turning his back to her, he spoke to the wall, his voice full of scorn. "Congratulations, Osborne. You've managed to deceive the girl you're in love with again. Way to go."

He'd misunderstood the reason for her question. The weight lifted from her chest. There was something exhilarating about the thought of him claiming her as his wife in such a way. It wasn't a binding marriage in modern times, but at least while they were here in this nineteenth century wilderness, it felt legitimate enough.

Jana pushed herself off the ground, wrapping the fur covering around herself.

"Dan." She touched his shoulder. His muscles tensed beneath her fingers. "You didn't deceive me last night."

He turned. Slowly. The pained look in his eyes tore at her heart. When would he let go of the guilt he felt?

"Everyone makes mistakes, or loses sight of what's important. You're doing everything possible to make it right again. Let go of your guilt." Jana smiled up at him.

"I'm not losing sight of what's important now," he said huskily, and pulled her to him.

Jana ran her hand along his whiskered cheek. "You're a good man. I love you."

Dan kissed her, first softly, then with greater urgency. Jana wrapped her arms around his neck, not caring that the fur covering loosened from around her, and slid down her body.

"I never thought you'd even give me half a chance, after

what I did . . . after I lied to you," Dan whispered against her lips. "You're the best thing that's ever happened to me."

He bent and hooked his arm behind her knees and lifted her off the ground. His dark eyes locked onto hers as he carried her back to the pile of furs that was their sleeping place. He laid her down as if she was a fragile piece of china, and covered her with his body. Jana lifted her arms, and welcomed him to her, letting him know once and for all that she'd forgiven his deception.

DAN WAITED for Jana at the edge of the village. He'd walked with her to the creek, then left her so she'd have some privacy.

"Don't go too far," she said, perhaps worried that someone would interrupt her. Contentment such as he'd never felt before flooded him. As soon as they returned to the twenty-first century, he planned to ask Jana to marry him in the modern world. Could she leave her job in California and live in Montana with him? He didn't have much to offer her. His school debts would take years to pay off and he didn't have a steady job. Heck, he probably didn't have a job in Yellowstone at all anymore. His future in the park was pretty much over. Somehow it didn't seem to matter. His goals and priorities had certainly changed over the last few weeks.

His confrontation with Hastings weighed heavily on his mind. How was he going to talk this deranged man out of killing an innocent child and get the time travel device away from him? What if Hastings had already beaten them to the cabin? All of this would be moot if he had already accomplished his goal.

Dan rubbed his hand across his face and shook his head.

He couldn't think about that possibility. He'd convinced himself that he and Jana had a good head start on Hastings. He had to focus on facing his ancestors and telling them why he was here, and that because he was here, their son's life was in danger. He certainly wasn't looking forward to that meeting.

If not for his blind and selfish ambition, none of this would have happened. His father and grandfather were probably rolling around in their graves right now. They had achieved their success through honest, hard work. Both of them had worked for the park service. His grandfather had been one of the first rangers after the park service was established in 1916. His father had been a successful state senator after his years of service as a ranger. None of their success had come overnight and Dan had always known it would take him years to achieve his own dreams.

In his teenage years, he had volunteered his summers with the conservation corps, helping to maintain trails in Yellowstone. He'd assisted college professors with their ecological research in the park and had finally applied for a seasonal ranger position four years ago. He'd never used his name as leverage to gain employment in the park. His grandfather had always instilled good work ethics in him. A few months ago, he'd jumped at the chance to reach his ultimate dream quickly, without any forethought to what it might do to the future of Yellowstone. Jana might have forgiven him, but he couldn't forgive himself until things were set right again.

Dan glanced at his surroundings. Standing at the edge of the village, he watched the activities of the people. Women sat working on hides or grinding fruits and nuts, men sharpened knives or worked on arrowheads. Children ran around, chasing each other with sticks. He'd caught the curious stares of some of the younger people from the village earlier this morning, but no one had approached him. After he'd emerged from the wickiup with Jana several hours later, a few older men and women glanced knowingly at them, smiles on their faces.

Dan wondered where Elk Runner had gone. He hadn't seen Daniel's brother all morning, not even when he'd left the hut at dawn, and he couldn't see him now, either. He'd seemed overly eager the day before to get Dan started on making right what Daniel had apparently done wrong to upset the spirits. What if he made things worse, and failed? He shook off his negative thoughts. His main priority right now was to get to the Madison Valley. Once Jana was done washing up, they'd head out. Surely no one would stop them from leaving. It was probably a good thing that Elk Runner wasn't around to detain them any longer.

Jana emerged from behind some trees that led to the creek. Her shy smile sent his heart into overdrive. She was more beautiful today than she'd ever been. Her chestnut hair fell in waves to her shoulders, bouncing lightly as she walked. There was a certain glow to her cheeks, and his body warmed with the thought that he might be the cause of it.

Dan stepped toward her and reached for her hand. He bent forward and kissed her. "Mrs. Spirit of White Wolf, you are gorgeous," he whispered, inhaling deeply of the fresh scent of soap in her hair.

Jana stiffened suddenly. Dogs barked, and the people from the village behind him began to talk excitedly. Dan turned. Two men emerged through the trees at the other end of the village. Dan recognized one as Elk Runner. Walking next to him was a broad-shouldered man slightly taller than the Indian.

The confident, graceful way he moved gave him a commanding presence. From a distance, he could easily be mistaken for one of the Sheepeaters. Instead of a buckskin shirt, however, he wore light tan-colored cotton homespun gathered at the waist by a large belt. A tomahawk and hunting knife hung off the belt on either side of his hips, and he carried a flintlock rifle in his left hand. Various pouches and a powderhorn hung from his shoulders, criss-crossing his chest.

Dan held his breath. He had no doubt who this man was. Not from the stories he'd heard as a child. Looking at him from across the expanse of the village, Dan felt as if he was staring at his own image. The main difference was the man's long, shoulder-length hair, and the hard, penetrating stare of his eyes that he directed first to Jana, and now locked onto him. The moment of truth had arrived.

CHAPTER TWENTY-SIX

*J*ana gripped Dan's arm tighter. He waited, unsure of whether to meet Daniel Osborne halfway, or simply wait for him to approach. He opted to meet him, otherwise he might come across as a coward.

Dan swallowed the apprehension in his throat. He patted Jana's hand and strode toward the village. The people gathered, glancing from him to Daniel. The expressions of disbelief on their faces spoke volumes. Dan wondered what they thought of their Sky People now. Suddenly, both versions of White Wolf were present in the same place. The looks of awe on some faces actually brought a smile to his face.

"Daniel," Dan said, holding out his hand when they stood mere feet apart. This meeting couldn't be any more bizarre. "I'm so glad to finally meet you."

Daniel Osborne stood before him, not a hint of what he was thinking evident on his face. His eyes narrowed almost imperceptibly for a fraction of a second. He held out his hand and shook Dan's in a firm grip. Dan had the distinct impression that in that brief moment, he was being sized up and assessed.

Although they were probably the same age, Daniel's confident and proud demeanor made him seem so much older. There was no arrogance or show of superiority in his behavior, but Dan's feeling of awe in Daniel's presence was akin to meeting some famous movie star. This was his ancestor!

"You're named after the first Daniel Osborne," his grandfather had told him when he was little. *"You're the last of the Montana Osbornes, so wear your name with pride."*

"My brother spoke the truth," Daniel finally said in English, his voice resonating deep and full of confidence. If he was at all unsettled by this encounter, he sure didn't let on. The man must have nerves of steel. Daniel turned his head slightly to his side and glanced quickly at Elk Runner, who stood silently by. "For once he spoke the truth," Daniel added dryly. "When he came to my cabin with a tale of a man who shares my likeness, I believed it was another ploy to get me to leave the valley. I'll wait to hear your explanation for your presence here, and who you are."

And I'm dying to know what the deal is about you having to leave the valley.

Hopefully, this entire mystery could be solved now. Dan wondered vaguely if it had anything to do with Hastings.

Daniel's head turned and he looked at Jana. For the first time, his features softened, and a slight smile formed on his lips. "Jana Evans, I did not believe you and I would ever meet again. You look well."

"Hi Daniel," Jana said quietly. "I didn't think I'd ever see you again, either."

"I am anxious to return to my cabin. It is only because Aimee asked me to come and bring you back with me that I left her side to follow my brother."

"Aimee knows I'm here?" Jana asked eagerly. "How is she?" She released Dan's arm.

"She is well, and looks forward to seeing you. She guessed correctly that it was you when my brother described you to her. This man," he nodded toward Dan, "I am sure you will enlighten me as to who he is and why you brought him here."

"I think we should talk about why I'm here when we're all together," Dan said quickly, before Jana could speak.

Daniel stared at him. "How is it that you and I share such a likeness?" he asked. "You are from the future, are you not? From my wife's time?"

"Yes, I'm—"

"*Bia, bia.*" Elk Runner's toddler son suddenly broke the silence around them and waddled toward Daniel, his chubby little arms outstretched. Daniel knelt, and in one swift move swung the little boy into his arms and over his head, holding him upside down. The toddler laughed with delight.

"You grow fast, little nephew," Daniel said in Shoshone and settled the boy on his shoulder. The smile on the man's face transformed him from the hardened mountain man into someone much less imposing. He turned toward Elk Runner.

"I must return to my wife. I will take this man and woman with me."

Elk Runner's eyes widened. "You cannot take Spirit of White Wolf with you, White Wolf," he said adamantly. "If you refuse to do your duty, he will take your place, so that you may be by Dosa Haiwi's side. It is what the spirits want. That is why he was sent here."

"I do not believe that is the reason he is here." Daniel waved him off with a casual flick of his hand. He turned his attention back to Dan, ignoring Elk Runner's incredulous look. "My brother says you have news of danger?" The smile vanished, and he once again stared with those penetrating eyes.

Dan inhaled deeply. "Yes. I think there's another man here from the future, and your son is in grave danger."

Daniel's eyebrows drew together. "My son?"

"Yes, your son, Matthew." Dan groaned silently. He realized a second too late that he'd said something he probably shouldn't have said.

"I have no son, at least not yet." Daniel's forehead wrinkled. For the first time, his self-assurance wavered.

"Ohmygod!" Jana shot a wide-eyed look at Dan, then at Daniel. "Aimee hasn't given birth yet, has she?"

Daniel stared at her stoically for a moment, then his features softened. Dan was surprised to see something close to fear or panic in Daniel's eyes. "I am glad that you are here, Jana. Your knowledge of medicine eases my worries about my wife. Although my mother and sister-in-law are at her side, I worry about the birth of my . . . son." He shot a quick look at Dan.

Dan kicked himself mentally for sticking his foot in his mouth. "We really need to get to your cabin," he said quickly.

Daniel stared at him, then at Jana, and nodded. Turning to Elk Runner, he said, "I trust you to remain here. Speak to the elders. Perhaps they can tell you why the spirits have sent a man who shares my likeness. Until then, he will come with me, and give me his own explanation. Something you would not allow him to do."

With those words of finality, Daniel set the little toddler on the ground and patted him on the head. He nodded to the people standing around.

"Come," he said with a wave of his hand. Without a backwards glance, he headed into the forest from where he'd first emerged.

"I guess that's our cue to follow," Dan said to Jana. "Go ahead." He nudged her in the arm. "I'll catch up. I have to get my backpack."

~

DANIEL SET a fast pace after leaving the Shoshone village. His silence was unnerving. He picked his way easily through the dense forest, never glancing back to see if Dan or Jana followed. Something told Dan that Daniel knew exactly how far back he and Jana were. In his mind, he replayed his first encounter with the man who'd been painted as someone to look up to by his grandfather's stories. Mountain men were always portrayed as larger than life, and their deeds exaggerated. Dan was sure that the stories about Daniel were closer to the truth than fiction.

His grandfather's tales weren't filled with stories about a man who'd killed a grizzly with his bare hands, or crawled hundreds of miles after being nearly mauled to death, or had defeated an entire war party of bloodthirsty Indians single handed. His grandfather had simply portrayed Daniel Osborne as a man of great integrity, who'd forged a living in this vast wilderness long before many other white men ventured into these mountains.

He'd been brave enough to live here all his life, making his living as a free trapper without joining a fur company. Later on, he'd run a successful trading post to supply others who ventured into these mountains. He'd done all this, and had raised a family that he'd protected with the fierceness of any wild predator, leaving behind a legacy that would forever shape the destiny of the Yellowstone area.

Dan clenched his jaw and cursed silently as he followed in this man's wake. His lack of judgment and his own ambitions might be the ruination of all that Daniel Osborne and his family had accomplished. Dan felt smaller than the cater-pillar inching along on the moist leaf of the wild huckleberry bush he brushed up against. Self-loathing consumed him again, even as Jana's words from earlier this morning echoed in his mind.

Everyone makes mistakes, or loses sight of what's important. Let go of your guilt.

Dan reached for Jana's hand and held on tight. Her eyebrows drew together. She was his crutch, his anchor. As if she'd read his mind, she spoke in a hushed whisper, "The first time I saw him, he was coming out of anesthesia. He fought like a bear. He was scary even then."

He grinned. "So, you don't think I could take him?" he teased. "I'm not scary enough for you?"

"Dan, you and Daniel may look alike. It's bizarre that you two are the same age right now, too. But no, I don't think you could take him. You're a teddy bear compared to him."

"Teddy bear, huh?" He enjoyed the easy banter at the moment. It took his mind off the turmoil within him.

"Yes. And you're my teddy bear," she said and hugged his arm, stumbling over a downed log at her feet. Dan gripped her around the waist and pulled her up. "And I wouldn't want you any other way," she added after she stood securely on her feet again.

"Daniel wouldn't have sold out the park, and certainly not his family," he said before he could hold back what was on his mind.

Jana stopped in her tracks. Her amber eyes searched his face. She reached up and touched his cheek. "Dan, we're not too late. Daniel didn't know anything about Hastings. He obviously hasn't reached the valley yet. We'll make it right again."

"I sure made a mess of things when I said his son was in danger." Dan shook his head.

"It's probably a good thing you didn't mention the other baby." Jana whispered almost imperceptibly, and smiled.

"What happens if Hastings shows up and Matthew isn't

even born yet?" Dan asked suddenly. He spoke in hushed tones, wondering how good Daniel Osborne's hearing was. He certainly didn't want to give the impression of talking behind the man's back. He glanced at the figure walking some twenty yards ahead. He couldn't possibly overhear them.

No sooner had the thought entered his mind, when Daniel stopped abruptly and turned, waiting for them to catch up.

"Do you need to rest?" Daniel asked, directing his question at Jana.

"Am I holding you up?"

Daniel's lips raised in a grin. "There was a time when Aimee said the same thing to me. I should have learned by now not to question a woman from the future's abilities. They take offense much too easily." He directed his grin at Dan.

"Twenty-first century women are a bit harder to handle, I would imagine, than a nineteenth-century woman," Dan said.

Jana shot them both an annoyed glare. "I see you two are going to get along just splendidly. How much further is it to your cabin?"

"Perhaps another hour," Daniel answered. "If you are not too tired, we should keep moving. I do not like leaving my wife. Her time is close."

Daniel started walking again, but he didn't move ahead of them. The forest wasn't as dense in this area, and they could all walk side by side.

"Elk Runner said you refused to leave the valley, and it made the spirits angry. My Shoshone is a bit sketchy, so that's what I understood," Dan said, eager to engage Daniel in conversation. There was no doubt Daniel would be a fierce adversary, but Dan was also curious about Daniel as a person, not just the legend.

Daniel smirked. "The Tukudeka are a highly spiritual people," he said. "You understood him correctly."

"But you were raised by them. Don't you share their beliefs?"

Daniel turned to look at him. "I do share their beliefs. I believe that everything we see before us," he swept his hand in an arc in front of him, "is connected. Without the trees, there can be no birds in the sky, or beaver in the water. Without the beaver, the trees become too numerous, and grasses will not grow to feed the elk, which in turn feed the wolves, and the people. This is the way of the spirits. They connect everything from the smallest fish to the fiercest predator."

He paused for a moment, and his chest heaved in a visible sigh. "Then there are the things we cannot see or explain. I am alive because of the gift of the Sky People. Because of this gift, my wife would not be here, also."

"So, what did you do to make the spirits angry?"

"Just as everything you see before you is in balance, so are the traditions of the Tukudeka. I am choosing to ignore one of the traditions in favor of remaining at my wife's side when she gives birth. It is customary for a father-to-be to go hunting to supply his clan with meat as a gift in celebration. I have explained to my brother, and to the elders of the clan, that I will do what is required after my child is born. The elders have accepted this. My brother has also accepted it, but he enjoys tormenting me."

"Siblings like to do that to each other," Jana chimed in. "Don't you think, Dan? Some things are just timeless."

"I wouldn't know. I'm an only child," Dan said, and his eyes met Daniel's. It was another thing they shared in common, Dan suddenly realized. His ancestor's gaze revealed nothing of what he could be thinking.

"Oh," Jana said softly. "You never talked about your family. I didn't know."

Dan laughed. "I'm the last Osborne in Montana," he said quietly, and met Daniel's penetrating stare.

"Perhaps you should tell me who you are, before we reach the valley, and why you are here." Daniel said suddenly. "I do not wish to upset Aimee."

Dan ran a hand through his hair. How much should he tell him? This was not going to be easy. He glanced briefly at Jana. Her eyes widened.

"Your wife, Aimee, writes in a journal."

"Yes." Daniel nodded.

"Several years from now, she will leave that journal for Jana to find."

"I remember her telling Jana this on the day I came for her in the future," Daniel said, looking at Jana.

"Well, I met Jana right after she found that journal and she guessed right that I am one of your descendants."

Daniel's features softened. He looked Dan over out of the corner of his eyes. "I have assumed as much," he said, the hard edge to his tone gone. "But how is it that you are here? Aimee and I made sure the time travel device is gone forever."

"We found it with the help of the Sky People, I think," Jana chimed in. "An old Indian came to me in a dream, telling me where to look for it."

Daniel's eyebrows rose. "The Sky People wanted you to come here? Why?"

"Because I made a terrible mistake," Dan said solemnly. He stared at the ground as he walked, unable to look his ancestor in the eye.

"When a man realizes he has made a mistake, it is the first step to undo what he has done wrong," Daniel said, as if he spoke from experience.

Dan scoffed. "Yeah. Well, because of my mistake, I've put your child's life in danger. Someone else from the future has found out about the time travel device, and has come here to kill your child because of something one of his children will accomplish in the future."

Daniel tensed, and his eyes hardened. "Where is this man now?"

"We don't know. We assume he came here after we did. He has the time travel device. I don't know how long it took him to figure out how it works, but I'm sure he will come here, if he isn't here already. And without that device, Jana and I can't return home."

Daniel stopped, and faced him. Holding out his hand to him, he gripped Dan's arm with the other. "This man won't have the opportunity to harm any member of my family. We'll find him, and you can return to the future."

Daniel pointed with his rifle straight ahead. "Keep walking east. This forest will open up into the valley of the Madison very shortly. Follow the river, and you will come upon my cabin."

"Where are you going?" Dan asked, perplexed.

"I must get to my wife. If you say there is a man here somewhere who wants to do harm to my family, I need to get back home quickly." He nodded briefly, then took off running through the trees and was soon out of sight. Dan stood with Jana, and clenched his jaw. Daniel wouldn't be so welcoming once he found out about the events that had led him and Jana to come to the past. Once Daniel knew that it was he, Dan, who had brought danger to Daniel's family, he might not live to return to the future.

CHAPTER TWENTY-SEVEN

*J*ana's heart sped up with excitement. She knew they were getting close to Aimee's home. The forest had given way to a narrow, steep-walled canyon some time ago, and the Madison River flowed beside them. She and Dan walked along briskly, following the river's banks. The sweet smell of the grass that grew green and tall in this area was intoxicating and lifted her spirits. All these weeks of trekking through harsh wilderness, they had finally reached their destination. And they had surely beaten Hastings here.

Jana hadn't realized how fast she was walking until Dan grabbed her by the arm and held her back.

"Slow down," he said, a lazy grin on his face. "If you're in such a hurry, you should have gone running off with Daniel."

"Sorry." She couldn't suppress a giggle at the image coming to her mind of trying to keep up with Daniel running through the forest. "I'm just anxious to see Aimee."

Dan pulled Jana to a stop. He stepped toward her, close enough for their bodies to touch. His eyes darkened and the soft smile from a moment ago vanished, to be replaced by a serious look.

"I know how much you miss her," he said, his voice deep and sensual. Ripples of desire ran up and down Jana's back, and a knot coiled in her stomach. It was almost frightening how she responded to his nearness. She inhaled deeply of the clean masculine scent coming from his skin, watching his pulse throb along his neck.

"Our time alone is over," he said, brushing his fingers against her cheek. "And I've enjoyed every minute of our adventure together. You can be my backpacking partner any day."

"First we have to get back home to the future," Jana whispered and raised her head to look into his eyes. "What if Hastings doesn't come?"

The muscles in Dan's jaw clenched and unclenched. "He's here. I can feel it." He looked up, his eyes scanning into the distance, as if expecting the man to materialize from the forest. Abruptly, Dan cupped her head between his hands, and kissed her. Jana leaned into him, and wrapped her arms around his middle.

Sucking in a deep breath of air when he broke the kiss, she rested her head against his chest. His heart beat loud and strong against her ear. Dan held her to him, stroking the back of her head and running his fingers through her hair. He kissed the top of her head and his chest heaved.

"How will you explain us to Aimee?" he asked quietly.

Jana pulled away from him. "What do you mean?" she asked tentatively.

"You know. Girl talk. What am I to you? A casual friend? The guy you just met and are having a summer fling with? Or . . . your husband?"

Was that uncertainty she saw in his eyes? Hadn't she

convinced him that she loved him? *A summer fling?* Jana's eyes narrowed.

"You didn't want to go out with me because of my relation to Aimee, remember?" he reminded her when she looked at him, too dumbstruck to speak.   His eyes roamed over her face, as if looking for answers. When had Dan become so unsure of himself?

What was she going to tell Aimee about her relationship with Dan? Jana hadn't really thought about it. After Daniel had shown up at the Indian village, there hadn't been a whole lot of time to think about it. She was sure Daniel knew that they were more than casual friends. There wasn't much that slipped past him and surely he had seen them hold hands.

Perhaps Elk Runner had even told him that she and Dan had spent the night together in the lodge. Obviously he knew that they had been alone together since coming to the past. She hadn't noticed any signs of disapproval from Daniel. And why should he care? It was none of his business.

What Aimee thought about her relationship with Dan mattered more to Jana. Aimee would be happy to hear that Jana had finally found someone she wanted to have a long-lasting, if not permanent relationship with. How she would react to that person being her descendant, and looking a lot like her own husband, would remain to be seen. Oddly, Jana didn't think about it with trepidation like she had weeks ago when Dan first asked her out.

"I haven't really thought about it," Jana finally answered, looking down at her feet. What did he want her to say to him? Dan had told her he considered them married in the Indian tradition, but did he seriously consider her his wife? He hadn't said anything about when - if - they returned to the twenty-first century, what kind of relationship they would have then. He'd hinted that he wanted a commitment, but he hadn't asked her to marry him, either. The rules were different here than they were two hundred years from now. Surely he realized that.

Dan released her. He stepped to the side and wordlessly continued walking toward their destination, running his hand through his hair. It was a sure sign that he was mad or frustrated about something. Jana jogged to catch up to him. She hooked her arm around his.

"I'm going to tell her we've become very close," she said when he finally glanced down at her. His impenetrable expression made him look more like Daniel than ever before. It suddenly became clear to her why he had this need for acceptance from her. He'd been so self-assured since she'd first met him, but today, he acted more like a little kid looking for validation.

"Daniel can be quite . . . intimidating, can't he?" she asked casually, hoping her hunch was correct.

Dan scoffed. "When I was little, my grandpa told me stories about Daniel Osborne, the legendary mountain man. A man who wasn't afraid of anything, and held his family above everything else. I didn't pay too much attention to the stories before, because the deeds of the mountain men have always been exaggerated. Now that I've met him, I know that the stories about him are all true." Dan stared straight ahead.

He lifted his face to the sky for a moment and laughed, sweeping his arm in front of him as he spoke. "And here he thinks I've done this noble thing by coming to the past to warn him of a threat to his family." He kicked at a rock on the ground. "And what do I do? I lie and deceive, and I'm to blame for this entire mess. Can't wait to see his reaction when he learns the truth," he added, his voice full of self-loathing.

"You're his family, too. He'll understand you made a mistake, and are here to correct it," Jana said softly. She

233

didn't know what else to say to him to make him feel better about himself.

He turned his head to look at her. "I meant what I said this morning, Jana. You're the best thing that's ever happened to me, in this time and in the twenty-first century. If I die tomorrow or the next day, I just want you to know I love you."

Jana's forehead wrinkled, and she shook her head.

"Stop talking nonsense," she said uneasily. "Why would you die? You survived a goose attack. You can handle anything." She hoped her attempt at humor would snap him out of his bad mood.

"Daniel's going to kill me when he finds out my part in the danger to his son." Dan's voice was firm, as if he truly believed what he was saying. Now that he'd met his ancestor, Dan seemed more remorseful than ever about his mistake. Jana wondered what it would take for him to truly forgive himself.

THEY CONTINUED their journey in silence. Jana thankfully left him alone with his thoughts. Dan's heart and mind were in turmoil. How Jana presented him to her best friend seemed to be important all of a sudden. He couldn't explain his sudden need for total acceptance. It had been Jana who had reservations about their relationship, but she seemed to be comfortable with the idea now.

Meeting his ancestors, and the fact that he was to blame for the trouble that was descending on them weighed heavily on his mind. Daniel was a force to be reckoned with, and Dan found himself severely lacking in his ancestor's presence. Try as he might, he couldn't shake off his irrational sense of insecurity, accompanied by a feeling of doom.

They'd been following the river for the last half hour, and the Madison Valley widened ahead of them. The heavily forested mountains to the left became sparser with trees, and a dark-colored straight-faced mountain loomed ahead in the distance. The river veered slightly to the left around a low-rising butte. Once they rounded the bend, Jana expelled a loud breath of air.

"We're here," she said in awe. The valley stretched before them and what looked like a newly built cabin came into view to the north of the river. Another, smaller cabin stood a short distance further back, nestled against a grove of lodgepoles.

A woman knelt by the river, dipping something into the water. It looked like she was washing clothes. It was obviously not Aimee. This woman looked short and rather plump, her long black hair hanging in straight strands freely down her back. She wore a simple tan-colored buckskin dress. Her head turned suddenly in their direction, and she jumped to her feet. Shouting excitedly, she ran toward the larger of the two cabins.

"I guess we're being announced," Dan said lightly, trying to hide the heaviness he felt in his chest. Now that they had reached the end of their journey, he already missed the solitude and closeness he'd shared with Jana over the weeks they'd spent in the wilderness. A sense of possessiveness took hold in him. He knew he was being unreasonable in his thinking, but he didn't want to share her attention with others just yet. Not since they'd made love so recently. Combined with his sense of inadequacy around Daniel and the reason for being here, his mood had slipped into a quiet sulkiness.

The front door of the cabin opened and another woman emerged, she being even rounder than the Indian woman who came to meet her.

"Aimee," Jana whispered, and her pace increased. Despite his mood, a slow smile formed on Dan's face. Jana's happiness made him happy. The short, petite blonde stepped from the cabin and waddled as fast as her heavy bulk allowed toward them.

"Jana, ohmygod! Jana," she called.

"Come on, Dan," Jana urged and grabbed for his hand. She pulled him along, nearly breaking into a run.

When they reached each other, Jana awkwardly threw her arms around Aimee's neck, trying to stand away from her swollen belly as best as possible. Dan wondered quietly how she hadn't exploded yet. *She's carrying twins*, he reminded himself, and wondered what today's date was. The journal had mentioned July 20th as the birthday of Zach and Matthew.

Both young women sobbed and cried, and laughed all at once.

"What on earth are you doing here?" Aimee asked between sobs, after they both released each other. "And how did you get here?"

"I'll tell you everything, but first I want you to meet someone very special." Jana stepped away and looked at Dan. He'd remained a few steps behind her. The soft, loving look in her eyes beckoned him closer.

"It's an honor to finally meet you, uh . . . Aimee," Dan said, unsure whether to extend his hand to her, or try and embrace her. He wasn't sure how to appropriately address her.

"Oh . . . oh my," Aimee said, her eyes widening as she assessed him from top to bottom. "Elk Runner sure wasn't embellishing the truth this time," she said, and stepped toward him. Her arms reached up and around his neck, and he bent forward to give her a light hug. Her taut stomach pressing against his was a strange feeling.

She smiled warmly up at him, her deep blue eyes sparkling with joy. Her pretty face was framed by her free-flowing blond waves of hair that hung loosely past her shoulders and halfway down her back.

"Daniel said you're our descendant. Genetics can do funny things, can't it?" She glanced at Jana, and her smile widened. She clasped his face between her hands, tilting his head first one way and then the other, examining him.

"Your resemblance to Daniel is absolutely amazing. After my experience with time travel, I thought I'd seen pretty much everything." She studied him for another minute, then said, "Come on. Let's get you two to the cabin before Morning Sun comes and locks me in my room for being out here." She laughed, and pointed a finger at Dan. "And don't you dare call me grandma." Turning to Jana, she hooked her arm through Jana's and they turned to head toward the cabin. "When we get to the house, you're going to tell me everything."

"You're huge," Jana commented. She touched Aimee's stomach, and they both laughed.

Aimee glanced around quickly, as if looking to make sure no one else was within earshot. She leaned toward Jana. "I know I'm carrying twins," she said in a hushed tone. "But I didn't dare tell Daniel. He's already scared to death of this birth." She glanced toward Dan. "I think seeing you is giving him courage that I might actually live through it."

Dan couldn't picture the idea of Daniel being afraid of anything. He did notice the hand Aimee held pressed to her back.

"What's the date today?" he asked impulsively.

"July 20th."

CHAPTER TWENTY-EIGHT

"So, Jana, tell me about Dan." Aimee didn't waste any time the moment she was alone with Jana. Daniel had met them in front of the cabin and after the introductions were made with Daniel's sister-in-law Little Bird and foster mother Morning Sun, the two women were now alone in Aimee's bedroom. Daniel had wanted to talk to Dan about Hastings, and Aimee had said her back ached and she needed to lie down. Full of concern for his wife, Daniel had ushered Aimee to their bedroom, and asked Jana to sit with her.

Jana exchanged a quick glance with Dan before following Aimee, and she could see it on his face what he was thinking. Today was July 20th. The day of the twins' birth according to the journal. It was already late afternoon.

"Are you feeling okay?" Jana asked, instead of responding to Aimee's demand.

"My back hurts worse than usual. I think I might be in early labor. I can't wait to get these babies out of me."

"Have you had any contractions?"

"A few false ones this past week." Aimee stared at her, and

her eyes widened. "You know when these babies are going to be born, don't you?"

Jana simply nodded. She didn't know what to tell Aimee. There was a lot of stuff she could tell her about the future.

Aimee waved a hand in front of her. "Don't tell me anything. If you've read my journal, I'm sure you must know my life's history, and I'd rather not be told anything." With a groan, she eased herself onto the fur-covered large bed in the center of the room. Afternoon sunlight brightened the room from the open square that served as a window.

"So, what's going on with you and Dan? And how did you ever meet him?" Aimee prodded again, a wide smile on her face.

"The day I found your journal, I met him. He's a park ranger, and at first I couldn't believe my eyes," Jana said, sitting down beside her friend.

Aimee laughed softly. "I bet. There's no question those two are related. What's he like?"

Jana smiled up at her. "He's like you. Full of passion for Yellowstone."

"And you're in love with him." It wasn't a question, just a simple statement of fact. Jana's eyes widened, and Aimee beamed. "It's pretty obvious. And it's obvious he absolutely adores you." She leaned over and put her arms around Jana's shoulder. "Now we can really say we're related, don't you think?"

Jana just stared at her friend. Aimee had accepted her relationship with Dan without question. She had known without being told.

"And Elk Runner was happier than a bison wallowing in the mud when he came here this morning, announcing he had successfully played matchmaker." She leaned back, her eyebrows raised, and studied Jana's face. "Obviously the two of you spent quite a bit of time together before now, but did you know that in the Tukudeka tradition, you're considered a married couple if you spent the night with him?"

Jana could feel the heat rising in her cheeks. She studied her hands in her lap, and tried to work some dirt out from under her fingernails. "Yes, Dan told me about that," she mumbled.

"Did he ask you to marry him?" Aimee's voice was full of excitement. For a moment, Jana and she were back home, sitting together after school, talking about boys.

"He says he wants a committed relationship, but he hasn't asked me to marry him." Jana looked Aimee in the eye. "I've only known him for about a month, Aimee. How can I have such strong feelings for him in such a short amount of time?"

Aimee laughed. "I think I knew I was in love with Daniel a few weeks after I met him. When it's the right man, it can happen fast."

"And you're okay with me . . . and Dan? I mean, he's your descendant. You're his ancestor. I have to tell you, it was weird for me at first. I resisted the idea that I was attracted to him."

"Stop being the serious Jana I know, and let yourself go. You found a good man, it seems. Hold on to him. Why should his relation to me have anything to do with it?"

"That's what he wanted to know, too." Jana laughed. The weight was fully lifted from her shoulders.

Aimee eased herself back against the headboard of the bed, groaning softly. She rubbed her hands across swollen abdomen, and Jana lifted her friend's feet onto the bed. Her fingers made indents in the skin of Aimee's swollen ankles.

"I'm glad you're here, Jana, even though I still don't know why."

Jana was glad she could talk to Aimee in private about why they had come. Explaining it all in detail with Daniel present, or even Dan, would have made the telling a lot more difficult. She wondered what Dan was telling Daniel at this very moment. She started at the beginning, when she'd first met Dan, and how he'd called her months later. She told Aimee about Dan's lies and motives, and how remorseful he was now, and of their journey these last few weeks since coming to the past.

"Sounds like he made an impulsive, stupid mistake. You made him see that there are more important things than his ambitions," Aimee said. Her forehead wrinkled. "What I don't understand, though, is how the time travel device sent you to Lamar Valley. Daniel and I never went there, certainly not with the device."

"And shouldn't we have stayed together after we traveled?" Jana wondered. "We were split up until Dan found my tracks and followed me. I was scared at first that I had come here alone."

Aimee shook her head. "I don't know. It sent Daniel and me back here together, but we were also holding the device. If Dan touched the snake eye when he tried to take it from Hastings, and you touched Dan at the time, it explains how you two traveled. I wouldn't expect Hastings to have traveled at the same time."

Aimee paused, her face contorted in concentration. Then she continued. "That's how Daniel's father sent me here without him traveling along with me. You have to touch the snake's eye, but unless you're also holding the device, or the person holding the device isn't touching the person touching the eye, you stay behind." She laughed again. "I know it's a bit confusing. Dan touched the eye, and you touched Dan. Therefore, the two of you traveled. Hastings was only holding the device. It's not the device itself that is the time travel vessel, if you will, but the snake eye."

Jana nodded in understanding. "Dan is convinced Hastings will follow once he figures out how it works. I'm sure he's already figured it out, and is somewhere close. We couldn't have that much of a head start on him." Jana clutched Aimee's hand. "He's here to kill your baby, Aimee," she said urgently.

Aimee nodded. "We'll just have to be ready for him," she said, unusually quiet.

"How are we going to be prepared? A single shot flintlock rifle is no match against a modern day gun, Aimee." Jana couldn't understand why Aimee seemed so calm about all of this.

"We'll have to let Daniel and Dan worry about that," Aimee said, a sudden look of surprise on her face. Her body stiffened, and she sat up a bit straighter. "Because I have other things to think about right now. My water just broke."

DAN STOOD in front of the hearth, his hand gripping the edge of the mantle above his head. He stared into the crackling fire. The dancing display of the orange flames as they eagerly licked the logs he recently added had an almost hypnotic effect on him. Perspiration formed on his forehead from the heat.

His mind kept replaying his discussion with Daniel from earlier in the evening. They'd walked along the riverbank together, Daniel questioning him about Hastings. He'd asked for descriptions of the man, what sort of weapons he carried, and what his motives were for coming here. All strategic questions to get to know an enemy's weakness.

Dan had cautioned Daniel about modern-day weaponry, and how the old Kentucky flintlock Daniel carried would be no match against a repeating rifle. At the very least, Hastings would carry a .45 Magnum, but Dan suspected he would most likely have a hunting rifle to boot.

Luckily, Daniel hadn't pressed him for more information about his role in Hastings coming to the past. Daniel seemed to be focused only on how to prevent Hastings from harming his family, and the reason for his appearance was unimportant.

"If anything happens to Aimee or your child, I am to blame," Dan had finally said. He had to get it off his chest. The guilt drove him insane. "I was caught up in my own ambitions, and didn't see what harm would come from my actions. I was told to bring documents that would benefit Hastings in the future. When he told me he wanted me to kill one of your children, I refused."

Daniel walked silently beside him. Whatever he'd been thinking, he hid it well. He'd stopped walking abruptly, and turned to face him. Dan had met his stare. They were almost the same height, although Dan guessed he stood slightly taller that his ancestor. They might be evenly matched in a test of strength, but Dan held no illusions that Daniel could take him down in the blink of an eye. Even though he'd had defensive training, he could never go up against Daniel's years of experience living in this harsh environment, where life and death were tested daily and a man depended on his wit and brawn to survive.

"I could easily kill you for bringing this evil upon my family," Daniel had said quietly, breaking the silence between them and echoing Dan's own thoughts. "Your mind was led by greed and ambition. That is what you are telling me." His eyes had bored holes right through Dan, but he hadn't taken the coward's way out and looked away. He'd nodded, unable to deny Daniel's words. He'd felt about as low as a man could get.

"But you are also telling me that this man, Hastings, asked

you to do something that would not cause harm to anyone, but would aid him in the future to fuel his own greed. You have been deceived by this man. Only after you found the device did he tell you of his true intentions. You refused to do what he asked."

Dan had scoffed. "If I hadn't been so selfish, none of this would have happened in the first place."

The corners of Daniel's lips had curved upward, and he'd actually grinned at him. "Sometimes it takes a good woman to help us let go of the demons we carry inside us. It is something I had to realize myself."

Dan had blinked, his forehead wrinkling. Jana's face flashed before his eyes. When he was with her, he could forget his troubles. But until this current situation was resolved, the guilt would remain with him.

"I'll do whatever it takes to make this right again," he'd said. "Then I can think about Jana."

Daniel had resumed his walk along the riverbank. "Jana Evans is like a sister to me," he'd said. "She and my wife regard each other as such. Because of their bond, I must also keep her safe. What are your intentions toward her?"

"I love Jana, and hope she'll consent to marry me. Eventually."

"My brother Elk Runner has already proclaimed the two of you wed. You are aware of the Tukudeka custom?"

Dan had smiled, despite himself. "Yeah. I'm aware of the custom. I studied a lot about the Sheepeaters because one of my ancestors . . . " He'd stopped. He'd put his foot in his mouth again. "I have a special interest in them, so I learned the Shoshone language and some of the customs."

"I do not wish to learn about the future, but I am glad to see that Aimee and I have left something of us for future generations."

"You can be proud of what the two of you left," Dan had

said. "I am the end of the line, though. My father was an only son, and so am I."

"I see many sons for you and Jana in the future," Daniel had said, and grinned. His head had turned abruptly toward the cabin. The woman he spoke of had come running from the house, frantically waving her hands in the air.

"It's time." Dan had heard her call repeatedly, and he'd known exactly what that meant.

CHAPTER TWENTY-NINE

*J*ana emerged from Daniel and Aimee's bedroom, closing the door softly behind her. Dan glanced up from staring into the fireplace for so long, he had to blink to adjust his vision. Their eyes met from across the room. She swiped her hand across her forehead, reminding him that he was covered in perspiration as well. She looked worn out, her eyelids heavy from lack of sleep, but a bright smile lit up her face.

"The proud parents are finally resting," she said quietly, and walked into Dan's open arms without hesitation. He inhaled deeply of her subtle flowery scent, pulling her close to him.

The two Indian women, Morning Sun and Little Bird, had retired to the little cabin shortly after the birth, commenting that Aimee was in good hands with her knowledgeable white sister.

While Aimee had labored, Dan had quietly tried to put Daniel's mind at ease that everything would be all right. Daniel had paced the main room of the cabin like a caged lion, until Jana had finally come from the bedroom, calling him into the room. Aimee had wanted him to be with her during the birth. Dan had almost laughed at the look of sheer panic on Daniel's face just before he followed Jana into the room. Dan had slapped him on the back with a wide grin, which had earned him a murderous glare.

"It's okay, Daniel. Modern men are frequently present when their wives give birth. You can do this. Just hold her hand, support her back, and let her tell you how much she hates you for putting her through such agony."

Jana's eyebrows had shot up at his words, and she glared at him. Dan had shrugged. "It's what they say in the movies."

"I can't believe we got here on the day Aimee has her babies," Jana said, bringing Dan's mind back to the present.

"Fate wanted you to be here," Dan whispered, kissing the top of her head.

"Or the Sky People," Jana said quietly.

A sudden loud banging on the front door made Jana jump. She pushed away from Dan, a fearful look in her eyes. Dan knew exactly what she was thinking. Hastings! The bedroom door opened seconds later and Daniel emerged, a rifle in each hand. He shot a quick look at Dan and Jana, and motioned with his hand for them to move to the right of the room toward the bedroom he'd just come from. He tossed one of the rifles to Dan, who caught it with a reflex he didn't know he possessed.

"You know how to fire this rifle?"

Dan stared at the Hawken rifle. He'd only fired a flintlock once or twice before, and wasn't at all sure if he could do it if called for quickly. He nodded slowly. A baby began to cry loudly.

"Go in there with Aimee," Dan whispered, and pushed Jana toward the bedroom. She grabbed hold of his arm, her eyes wide with fear.

"Go," he said forcefully. She hesitated another second, then disappeared through the door.

Whoever was outside banged on the front door again, and a man's voice shouted. Dan couldn't understand the words, but relief swept over him. It wasn't Hastings. Daniel yanked the door open, and three men stumbled in. Two Indians supported a third man, his arms draped around each of their shoulders. He was unable to stand on his own, and a loud moan escaped his lips. His eyes were closed and his buckskin shirt was soaked with blood.

Daniel spoke to the two other Indians in quick, hushed tones, and motioned with his hands to lay the man on the ground by the hearth. Dan couldn't understand what they were saying. They were not speaking in Shoshone. He noticed both of the other men were bleeding as well, one from his upper thigh, the other from his arm.

"Jana, come out here," Dan called. He rushed to the Indian, and knelt to the ground. Blood had soaked his entire buckskin shirt. It was torn in several places where bullets had entered his chest and abdomen. Dan was amazed the man was even alive. Only a modern-day rifle could have put so many bullets into this man.

Everything seemed to happen at once. Jana dropped to her knees beside him, checking the wounded man's pulse. Daniel stood beside Dan, telling him these were Absarokas who had encountered two white men before dark, who then shot at them with magical weapons. Three of their companions had died instantly. These three had fled, and were here to seek aid from Aimee.

"This man isn't going to make it," Jana said frantically. Aimee called from the bedroom, wondering what was going on. She could hardly be heard over the loud cries of both babies.

"I've got this," Jana said, looking up at Daniel. "Aimee

needs to stay in bed. I need any medical supplies she might have. Water. Bandages. Dan, sterilize a knife for me and bring me your medical kit."

Dan rushed to do her bidding, thrusting a knife into the hot coals of the fire. He ripped open his backpack that he'd tossed in a corner of the cabin when they'd first arrived and pulled out his medical kit. There was no hope for this man. He knew that, and Jana knew it, too. Pride swelled in him, even during these frantic moments to save a man's life. The way she took charge of the situation, tossing out orders at him and Daniel. It was a side of her he hadn't seen before.

Dan handed her the medical kit, when the man on the ground gasped. His body went rigid, just before his limbs relaxed again in death.

"No, dammit." Jana immediately began chest compressions. Dan reached for her and tried to pry her away. She pulled away from his hold, refusing to give up her life-saving measures.

"Jana, he's gone." Dan hooked his hands under her arms, and hauled her to her feet. "There's nothing you can do for him," he whispered, and pulled her into his arms. She trembled, and sobbed into his shirt.

"There are two other men here who could use the attention of a good nurse," he reminded her gently. "Why don't you see what you can do for them."

Jana straightened, and he released her. She picked up the medical kit and knelt beside the man with the gunshot wound to his leg, making gestures with her hands to get him to remove his leggings so she could examine the wound.

Dan watched her for a moment, then turned to look at Daniel. He was conversing with the other warrior.

Two men. Daniel said these Indians told him there were two men. Hastings had brought someone else with him. Dan cursed under his breath. Hastings and his accomplice were obviously well armed.

"This attack occurred not far from here to the east. Less than a half day's walk," Daniel said, moving around the table to stand next to Dan. "You only spoke of one man, but Broken Lance says there were two. Two men with weapons that can do this kind of harm," he pointed at the dead Indian on the ground, "make this far more dangerous. What do you suggest we do?"

Dan stood there, speechless for a moment. Daniel asked for his advice?

"I'm wondering if Hastings didn't attack these people to draw you out, get your attention," he thought out loud. "I wonder if he thinks I have found you by now, or if he believes I never made it this far. If the attack occurred to the east, he didn't come the same route Jana and I did. He may have come from the canyon."

"Then we must use the element of surprise. If I go now, I can find their camp by dawn." Daniel headed for his bedroom. The babies had quieted down again, and Dan heard Aimee's soft voice raise when Daniel spoke to her. She apparently didn't like what he had in mind to do.

Daniel reappeared, a bow and a full quiver of arrows in his hand.

"I'll go with you," Dan said, when Daniel headed for the front door. Daniel halted in his tracks, and turned to face him.

"I leave you to watch over my wife and sons. If all goes well, I will be back before the end of the night. I cannot allow this man to come to the valley. I must meet him out in the open, but I can't leave my wife unprotected." He pointed to the Hawken propped against the wall.

"Do what you must to protect the women. I will send Morning Sun and Little Bird to help Jana care for these men,"

Daniel said with finality. He didn't wait for an answer, but turned and headed out the door.

Dan could only stare after him, dumbfounded. He slowly turned his head in the direction of the bedroom. Daniel had left him in charge to protect his wife and babies. What had he done to earn such trust and respect?

Dan clenched his jaw. He picked up the Hawken, and checked to see if it was loaded, even though he had no doubt that it was. He swore under his breath. Whatever it took, this time he would not fail his ancestors.

JANA CRADLED the little infant in her arms, rocking him gently back and forth. The baby was almost asleep, content with a full belly and a clean change of a cloth diaper. She lightly touched the blond fuzz on top of his head, and stroked his rosy baby cheek with the back of her finger. She glanced over at the bed where Aimee sat, feeding her other son. She looked worn out, her eyes almost closed and her head resting against the bed's backboard.

Jana didn't know which baby she held in her arms – Zach or Matthew. Daniel and Aimee had not named the infants yet. If Hastings showed up, how would he know which baby to murder? After everything she'd witnessed, the dead and injured Indians, the man would have no trouble killing both infants.

Aimee didn't show it, but she was worried. Jana knew her too well. Her friend always put up a good front, but the haunted look in her eyes said she was afraid for Daniel. As if she knew Jana was thinking about her, Aimee looked up, and her lips curved in a weak smile.

"Everything's going to be okay," she said, her voice hoarse from lack of sleep.

The early morning sunshine filtered just enough light through the burlap covering over the window to cast the room in a dim glow. Jana nodded in agreement, although she didn't feel as if everything would be okay. Daniel had left in the middle of the night. How was he going to track two men in the total darkness? He only roughly knew where Hastings and his accomplice might be camped, based on what the Crow had told him.

Morning Sun and Little Bird had taken the injured Indians to the small cabin to finish tending to their wounds after they helped Dan remove their dead companion outside.

"You should get some sleep, Aimee," Jana said. She placed the baby in her arms into the wooden cradle that looked newly made. Luckily, it was big enough to hold both babies for now. Daniel would have to carve out another one soon. Reaching for the infant in Aimee's arms, she laid him next to his brother. When she turned around, Aimee was asleep. Jana rubbed at her own tired eyes, and quietly left the bedroom.

Dan sat on a chair at the table, the rifle draped across his lap. His arms were propped on the table, his hands supporting his head. He looked just as worn-out as Jana felt. His head turned when she entered the main room. Quietly, she closed the door behind her and offered him a smile. He sat up straight and laid the rifle on the table, holding out his hand to her, beckoning her to him.

Jana came to him and he pulled her onto his lap, wrapping his arms tightly around her waist. She rested her hands on his shoulders, and smiled softly.

"Kiss me," he said in a low tone. Jana bent her head without a second thought, and pressed her lips to his. Dan held the back of her head, deepening the kiss, exploring her lips with his tongue. Jana wrapped her arms fully around his neck, and leaned into him. Deep ripples of desire flowed through her, and she gave herself over to the wonderful feelings Dan's touch and kiss evoked deep within her.

"I love you so much," she whispered, touching her hand to his whisker-roughened cheek.

"You're my whole world, Jana." Dan ran his fingers through her hair. The smile on his face couldn't betray the apprehension in his eyes.

"What's on your mind?" she asked gently.

"You are," he answered.

Jana scoffed at him. "I hope I don't put that worried look on your face."

"I know Daniel can take care of himself and Aimee, but even he's no match against a man with a twenty-first century gun or rifle. Let alone two men."

"Daniel knows what he's doing. And he obviously holds you in high regard." Jana could see what a heavy weight rested on Dan's shoulders. He was held responsible for the safety of Daniel's wife and children.

Dan shifted his weight underneath her. "Have you had any sleep at all?" he asked.

Jana took the bait that he wanted to change the subject. "No, and neither have you. At least Aimee and the babies are asleep."

"Why don't you try and get some shut-eye then," he suggested.

"I'd rather just sit here with you."

Dan nodded. He hugged her to him, and Jana rested her head on his shoulder. They sat in silence for some time. The room of the cabin lightened as the sun climbed higher over the mountains to the east. The burlap covering the window opening could only filter out part of the brightness.

"When is he going to be back?" she murmured.

"I don't know," Dan answered. His chest heaved. "The

element of surprise is on his side. If he found their camp in the dark, it'll all be over real quick."

Jana shuddered. She could never live in this world. The harshness of the land, the violence that was required in order to stay alive, was too much for her.

The cabin door suddenly flew open with a loud bang, and Jana screamed. Dan bolted from his seat, throwing her off his lap. She stumbled, but caught her balance.

"Get to the bedroom," Dan ordered in a harsh tone before she could even look up. When she did, the gasp caught in her throat. John Hastings stood just outside the door, a rifle pointed into the room. Gone was the cleanly dressed man she had seen briefly in Dan's room all those weeks ago. This man looked like he was on safari, dressed in khaki cargos, a green shirt, and a tan hunting vest.

A triumphant smile erupted on his heavily whiskered face, and he pointed the rifle directly at Dan as he stepped into the cabin. Dan had the old flintlock raised, and both men stood facing each other.

"I was wondering if you'd be here, Osborne," Hastings said, almost as if greeting a friend. "I have to tell you, your little disappearing act was quite impressive. Took me a few days to figure it all out."

"You're not going to get away with this, Hastings," Dan said, a harsh edge to his voice. Jana had never seen such intense hatred in his eyes. She darted nervous glances from him to Hastings, not daring to move from where she stood. Dan slowly moved sideways, stepping in front of her. He positioned himself to stand between Hastings and the door that led to Aimee's bedroom. "Why don't we all just go home, and forget about this entire episode."

Hastings laughed harshly. "I've come this far, I'm not about to change my plans now."

A baby began to cry from the other room, and Jana groaned in despair. Hastings' smile brightened even more.

"Step aside, Osborne," he commanded, and motioned with his rifle for Dan to move out of the way. "See, the beauty here is that I don't have to kill you now. You could even live for a little while longer if you just cooperate."

"What the hell are you talking about? You're not going to kill anyone." Dan clenched his jaw, and raised the rifle in his hand a few inches higher. Jana wished he would just shoot. Her heart pounded fiercely in her ears, and her constricted throat burned.

Hastings laughed. Dan was now standing directly in front of her, blocking her view of the deranged madman.

"Do you really think that antique you've got in your hand can hurt me? I'll blast you so full of bullets before you even pull the trigger. I wonder if you'll die instantly when I kill the woman and her kids, or if you can live out your life here in the past."

Jana gasped. He intended to kill Aimee!

"Your plans have changed again, I see," Dan said. Jana realized suddenly that he was trying to keep Hastings talking to divert his attention. Maybe he was hoping Daniel would show up.

"When I kill her, your entire family will be wiped out. My way will be free and clear." Hastings moved a little further into the cabin.

Dan laughed. "Do you realize what that will do to the future of the park? There may not even be a park for you to rule over when you go home. You've gone completely insane."

"I'm done talking, Osborne," Hastings bellowed.

He stepped closer, and adjusted the butt of his rifle against his shoulder. The muscle in Dan's arm flinched and he fired the flintlock. In the same instant, the cracking sound as several bullets fired deafened Jana's ears. She didn't hear her own screams, and the world moved in slow motion. Like in a surreal dream, she watched Dan collapse to the ground in front of her. Her arm felt like lead, reaching for him. Her lungs filled with air, taking in the acrid odor of black powder from Dan's rifle. The weapon hit the floor with a loud thud, and Jana screamed Dan's name.

Her knees hit the wooden floor, but she ignored the pain shooting up her legs from the impact. Her vision blurred when she grasped Dan's heavy, limp arm. A dark shadow nearly drowned out the light coming through the cabin door, and in the next instant, Hastings dropped to the ground, blood spewing from his neck. Daniel loomed over him, a large hunting knife in his hand. Her heart pounded in her ears, drowning out all sound.

With a trembling hand, Jana swiped at the tears in her eyes. She tugged on Dan's arm. Blood soaked his shirt. "No!" she screamed again and again. She leaned over him, and fresh tears streamed down her face. She hastily blinked them away.

"No. Dan . . . nooo. Please, . . ." she pleaded. Her hands were sticky with his blood, and his lifeless eyes stared up at her. Jana frantically searched for a pulse, then leaned her head against his chest. Her mind refused to believe what she knew was the truth. He was gone. Dead. She cradled his face between trembling hands. "No, Dan. Please, . . . don't leave me. Please . . . I love you." She kissed his lips.

The world around her ceased to exist. Jana fought the arms that pulled her away from him and carried her some-where away from Dan. Muffled voices spoke in the back-ground, and infants cried loudly. Aimee's familiar voice close to her ear didn't quite penetrate her mind. Dan was gone. It was all she understood.

Jana didn't know how much time had passed, when

Aimee spoke to her again. She looked around, her eyes unfocused, not really seeing anything. Her hands touched soft furs beneath where she sat. A lamp was lit in the corner of the room, casting a warm, dim light around her.

"Dan?" she called, the sound of her voice foreign to her own ears.

"Daniel found their camp, but Hastings was already gone," Aimee said, her arm around Jana's shoulder. "He hurried back home, but he didn't get here in time, Jana. He was a second too late." Aimee's voice cracked. She pulled Jana into an embrace, and Jana clung to her. They both trembled and cried in each other's arms.

"He died, protecting you and me," Aimee whispered.

Dan was dead. He was lost to her forever. The finality of that thought was too much for her to bear. Her mind conjured his smiling face, his passion-filled eyes, the tender touch of his hands, and she squeezed her eyes shut. All gone.

THE NEXT SEVERAL days passed in a blur. Jana couldn't think, couldn't eat, couldn't sleep. She merely existed. The day after Dan's death, Aimee asked her the question that made his death final.

"Do you want to take his body home to the future?"

Jana shook her head. "No," she sniffed. She stared across the valley to the east, to the dark mountains stretching high into the sky.

This looks like a spot I'd want to be buried at.

Dan's words echoed in her mind. "He wanted to be buried on Purple Mountain. Right here, to overlook the valley. This is where he wants to be."

Daniel carved his and Aimee's names in a rock, and dated it 1811. Underneath, he carved the words, *Dan Husband to*

Jana. Jana stared at the rock when he showed it to her. A shiver raced up her spine. The grave Dan had found on Purple Mountain, the one he'd shown her, thinking it was Aimee's, had been his own! Age had weathered away all of the inscription except for Aimee's name and the date.

Daniel had found the time travel device in Hastings shirt pocket. Aimee had handed it to her a day later, and had asked if Jana wanted to stay with her and Daniel in the past.

"I can't," she answered. "I can't live in this time. This is your world. It's time I returned home."

Her life was forever changed, but she couldn't remain here. She would do what she had planned to do all along. Go home to California, and try and forget all that had happened. Try and forget the man she loved above everything else. She knew it would be impossible.

Kissing each of the twins on their cheeks, Jana hugged first Daniel and then Aimee in a warm farewell.

"Yellowstone exists because of you," Jana said, smiling softly at both of them. "This was your destiny all along."

She stepped out of the cabin and walked across the meadow. Looking to the east, she gazed up at the purple-hued mountains. She could almost feel Dan looking down at her, and she blew a kiss in his direction. A soft breeze lifted her hair and swept softly along her cheek. Jana closed her eyes, and raised her chin into the wind, imagining Dan's fingers caressing her face.

"Keep a watch on the valley, my love," she whispered, and with the tears flowing freely from her eyes, touched the right eye of the snake.

CHAPTER THIRTY

*J*ana's head spun dizzily. The echoes of many people talking at once all around her pounded her mind. Groaning, she raised her heavy eyelids, holding a hand to her temple to ease the dizziness. Without even looking, she knew that she was back in her own time.

"Dan," she whispered his name. "Dan, I love you." She sniffed, and reached into her pocket. Startled, she realized she held the snakehead in her hand.

Quickly, she returned the time travel device to her pocket. She didn't want anyone to see it and perhaps comment on the strange object. The device had caused enough trouble already. It would be up to her now to dispose of it, she realized. Jana ran her hand over the soft leather that bound Aimee's ancient journal. Strange that she should have it with her now.

An icy breeze touched her face, sending a shiver down her spine. Glancing up, a large crowd of hikers entered the lobby of the inn. In the back of her mind, Jana thought the scene looked oddly familiar. An overwhelming feeling of déjà vu hit her. It was as if she had lived this moment once before. No. It couldn't be possible! The time travel device didn't work that way. Past events could never be repeated.

A tear hit the leather of the pouch clasped in her hand, leaving a dark spot on the tan colored hide. Jana sniffed, and she wiped at her eyes.

"Now what would cause such a lovely woman to cry on such a beautiful day here in Yellowstone?"

Jana looked up, startled by the ranger who had sat down next to her on the couch she occupied. A split second passed, and Jana shrunk back in shock. Her hand flew to her mouth, and she gasped.

"Dan?" she whispered in disbelief. For a moment, she was frozen to the spot. She couldn't move, or think. He was here, alive and well. Her eyes roamed quickly over his uniform. There wasn't a drop of blood in sight. He sat down beside her, a wide grin on his face. She sobbed again, ready to throw her arms around his neck, when his next words stopped her cold.

"Yeah, my name's Dan," he said, pointing to the name badge on his uniform. Jana clearly read the name, Daniel Osborne.

Her mind raced for comprehension. He didn't recognize her. He didn't know her. Her hand shot to the time travel device in her pocket. She had come back to the future, but not to the time she'd left. It was the only explanation. The device had sent her home, but two months prior to when she'd left, to the time when she'd first come to Yellowstone to search for Aimee's journal. She glanced down at her hands. That's why she had the journal with her now.

"You look like you've seen a ghost," the ranger flashed her a radiant smile. "Are you okay?"

"Yeah, I'm fine," Jana replied slowly. "You . . . you remind me of someone."

Dan, don't you remember me? Don't you remember anything that's happened? I love you.

Why was she the only one who remembered?

"Well, I hope that's a good thing," he grinned. His sensual voice penetrated her thoughts. "So, you didn't answer my question."

"Huh?"

"What is a lovely lady doing in this grand park, crying. There is no such thing as a bad day in Yellowstone."

"I was reading." Jana shrugged, fingering the pouch with the leather bound journal in her hands.

"Tell you what." Dan patted her on the knee. "I just got back from a six hour hike, and I'm real hungry and thirsty. Would you care to join me for dinner and a drink? I'm off duty as of now."

"Sure, I'd love to." She was still staring at him, disbelief on her face.

You've been given a second chance, Jana. Don't walk away this time.

She searched her memory, trying to remember their initial conversation when he'd first approached her, and asked her to dinner.

"Can I ask you something?" she asked tentatively.

"Sure."

"Has your family lived in this area long?"

Dan laughed. "My family has roots here since time began. I think my great, great, great, great, something great-grandfather was one of the first fur trappers in this region. I was named after him. Legend has it he fell head over heels in love with a woman who appeared out of nowhere in the Yellowstone wilderness, and they lived happily ever after. What a weird question to ask, though."

"Well, Dan." Jana stood up. "It's about to get a lot weirder."

He stood to his feet as well and led her toward the lodge's restaurant. "Ok, now I'm mighty curious."

"Not only are you named after your ancestor, but you could be his twin brother." Jana smiled at the perplexed look on his face. Not giving him a chance to react further, she held up Aimee's journal, and continued, "I hope they serve something pretty stiff to drink here, because you're going to need it after I'm done with the story I'm about to tell you."

He responded to her odd statement with that grin she'd come to know and love. Would he have the same feelings for her now as he'd had the first time they'd met?

Dan led her through the lobby to the Inn's restaurant. After they were seated, he leaned forward, still smiling broadly.

"Do you have a name?" he asked, his eyebrows raised expectantly.

"Jana. Jana Evans," she answered quickly, and took a hasty drink from the water glass next to her place setting.

"So, tell me Jana . . . Evans, how long are you here in Yellowstone?" His voice had gone deep and sensual, his eyes darkening from the chocolate brown they'd been a moment ago to an almost midnight black. He reached a hand across the table, softly covering her own. Jana sucked in a deep breath and closed her eyes. Memories of her weeks spent with him flooded her mind. Memories of their night under the buffalo robes in an Indian wickiup, when he'd made her his wife in the Sheepeater tradition.

Dan, you have to remember.

"I'll be here as long as it takes," she whispered and opened her eyes. This was not how she remembered the conversation from three months ago.

Dan cleared his throat. "You know, I've changed my mind about dinner," he said and, to her surprise, stood. Hesitantly, she pushed her chair back from the table and rose to her feet.

"There's still a lot of daylight left. Would you care to take a walk with me?"

Lost for words, she merely nodded. Dan took her hand. He pointed at the leather pouch on the table.

"Don't forget your book. That looks to be quite rare. Not something you'd want to leave lying around, I bet."

Jana hastily grabbed the journal, and allowed him to lead her out of the building into the bright, late afternoon sunshine. Too baffled by his behavior to speak, she kept pace with his leisurely stride as he navigated his way through the parking lot toward the geyser basin, past Old Faithful, and across the Firehole River.

"Have you ever seen Old Faithful go off from Observation Point?" he finally asked when they reached the familiar trail-head leading up the steep incline to the spot of their first unofficial date over a month ago.

"Yes, I have," Jana said, blinking back the tears that threatened. It was as if she was reliving different parts of different first dates with Dan.

He smiled at her and motioned for her to head up the hill ahead of him. In much better shape to climb the steep switchbacks this time than she had been six weeks ago, Jana reached the top without being winded. She gazed out at the vast expanse of the Lower Geyser Basin below. Castle Geyser spouted water high in the air in the distance, putting on a nice display for a group of eager tourists. The water runoffs and pools of hotsprings glistened as the late afternoon sun shimmered down on them.

"It's really beautiful up here," she said quietly, and turned. Dan stood inches behind her. That look in his eyes, the look he reserved only for her when he held her close, when he'd made love to her, shone in their depths. Jana's heart sped up. Would he fall in love with her a second time?

"Yeah, nothing beats the view from up here," he said

huskily and wrapped his arms around her, pulling her close to him. Jana didn't resist. Her arms reached up of their own will, snaking around his neck, pulling him to her.

Dan lowered his head and their lips met, pressing against each other first slow and soft, then with an urgency neither of them could hold back. Jana moaned. He pulled his head back slightly and cupped her face between his hands.

"I kissed you like this in a Crow hunting camp two centuries ago," he whispered. "I remember making love to you, claiming you as my wife under the covers of a Sheep-eater wickiup. Tell me you remember it, too, Jana."

Jana sobbed and wrapped her arms around him tightly, breathing in his scent as if she wanted to burn it into her memory forever.

"You remember?" she sobbed, her words barely audible. "I didn't think you remembered. I remember everything, Dan. I love you." She pulled his face toward hers and kissed him again, slowly and tenderly. "I thought I lost you. I thought you were dead."

"Everything is blank in my mind after Hastings' bullets hit me. I woke up here, ready to take my group of hikers to Shoshone Lake. At first I thought I had dreamt everything, but the more time went by, the more vivid the memories became. When I walked into the Old Faithful lobby and saw you sitting there, in that same spot you were in before, looking as sad as the first time I saw you, I had to make sure you remembered, too. That it was real and not just a dream."

"We have a chance to start over," she said hopefully.

"Yeah, we do." He held her close and smiled down at her. "The mistakes I made, deceiving you, I'm getting a do-over. And I'm planning to do it right this time."

A disturbing thought entered her mind. "If you're here, alive, then Hastings must be here as well. Daniel killed him and his accomplice in the past. They'll remember everything, too."

Dan laughed softly. "Who's gonna believe them if they bring it up? Hastings'll never see the journal this time around. I may not have a seasonal job here anymore, but Hastings won't be superintendent forever. I can wait, and bide my time."

"I have the time travel device," she said, reaching into her pocket. "Just like Aimee and Daniel, let's get rid of it so it's never found again."

"We'll do what Aimee intended the first time. We'll toss it over the falls again, but I'm adding some extra weights for good measure. There's still plenty of daylight left. The canyon is spectacular in the setting sun."

"Since we've come back two months before our trip into the past, does that mean the events we experienced, being with Aimee and Daniel, didn't happen?"

Dan's forehead wrinkled in concentration. "I don't know. But I do know this. Even if they didn't experience it, we did, and we'll always have that as a memory."

It took them a little less than an hour to reach the parking lot leading to the Brink of the Lower Falls trailhead. Dan held tightly to Jana's hand as they walked briskly down the half-mile of switchbacks to reach the viewing platform. Just before they reached the bottom, Dan pulled her into an embrace.

"I have something to say before we do this, and we can't hold a conversation over there," he said, motioning to the wire-meshed safety fence. The roar of the river was loud where they stood now, but it would be deafening at the brink, and conversation would be impossible. Jana raised her eyebrows expectantly, and waited for him to continue.

"I have a year left in my master's program. I'm planning to earn my teaching credential during that time as well. Next summer, I'm not sure if I'll get another seasonal position if Hastings interferes." His hands slid up and down her back while he spoke. Jana wondered why he was telling her this.

Dan cleared his throat. "I have a lot of student loans to pay off. It will take me years to clear my debts."

Jana shook her head, and smiled up at him. "No, it won't. You have an inheritance now."

Dan's eyebrows drew together.

"Aimee left a lot of money behind when she went to live with Daniel. She inherited it from her parents when they died. It's been sitting in an account we shared. When we moved to California together after we graduated from nursing school, we pooled our money, just in case something happened to one of us, the other would have full access. It should rightfully belong to you now. I'm sure there's more than enough to cover all of your loans."

Dan's shoulders visibly relaxed. "Jana," he said slowly. "You and I . . . I claimed you as my wife in that Sheepeater village. I think of you as my wife. Would you . . . could you consider a marriage to me in this time? Can you see yourself married to a simple schoolteacher and seasonal ranger?"

"That is the strangest marriage proposal I've ever heard." Jana beamed.

"I can get down on one knee if you prefer." Dan released his hold on her, and was about to do just that, when Jana grabbed his arm.

"I don't need that kind of proposal," she whispered. "I like the one from two centuries ago."

"Jana, will you marry me again, in this time? Officially?"

"Yes, you big dolt. I'll marry you." She wrapped her arms around his neck. Dan lifted her at the waist, and spun her around.

Hand-in-hand, they walked toward the brink of the falls. Jana pulled the device from her pocket, and Dan found a few rocks that he added to the leather pouch. He tied a secure knot, and together they reached over the fence. Jana glanced down the gaping canyon, a small rainbow arching amidst the spray and mist from the water as it caught the evening sun.

She gasped, and clutched Dan's arm. Standing at the base of the falls, as he had in her dream so many weeks ago, was the old Indian. He stared up at her, holding his hand out in a gesture of good-bye, his leathery face smiling brightly, nodding his head in apparent approval. Turning toward Dan, Jana hugged him close and gazed up into his soft brown eyes. She released the pouch with the time travel device. Within seconds it disappeared from view as the waters of the Yellowstone swallowed it up. The Indian smiled, and nodded in satisfaction just before he disappeared from view, the only one other than them who would ever know about Dan's Yellowstone Deception.

IF YOU ENJOYED THIS STORY, please help others discover the book, and consider leaving a short review on Amazon. Reviews are extremely helpful to authors and let other readers discover new books.

THE ADVENTURES in the Yellowstone Romance Series continues with Yellowstone Promise.

DEAR READER

I hope you enjoyed this installment in the Yellowstone Romance Series. Perhaps you've visited Yellowstone, and have seen first-hand some of the places that my characters have experienced. Maybe you've never been to this wonderful park, and might want to go see it now. I hope I was able to entertain you for a few hours with my spins on some of the historical events in and around Yellowstone.

The true-life senator who became my fictional character Robert Osborne (Dan Osborne's great great-uncle), was a man by the name of George Vest. He was a US Senator from 1879 to 1903. He is best known for his "a man's best friend" speech that he gave in 1869 during the closing arguments in the trial in which damages were sought for the killing of a dog named Old Drum.

In 1882, Vest became aware of concession abuses in Yellowstone National Park. Railroads and other businessmen made outright attempts at uncontrolled monopolies in the park. Vest introduced and helped pass legislation that required the Secretary of the Interior to submit concession and construction contracts to the Senate for oversight, in order to prevent corruption and abuse. From then on, he was called the *Self-appointed Protector of Yellowstone National Park.*

Dan and Jana's journey from Lamar Valley to reach the Madison Valley was probably not the quickest route. My intent was to "tour" the park a little and highlight some of the features and landscapes, such as Mammoth Hot Springs, that I didn't get to explore in previous books. Dan's chosen route roughly follows a portion of the Howard Eaton Trail in the park today (with a few detours).

Please join my list of awesome readers, and get exclusive content, such as the unpublished Prologue, and first three chapters that were cut from the original manuscript for Yellowstone Heart Song just for signing up! Find out about Aimee's encounter with Zach before she time traveled.

You'll also be kept up-to-date with the characters from the Yellowstone series in my popular exclusive monthly "Aimee's Journal" entries, sneak peeks, free book offers, behind the scenes info, latest releases, and much more!

Go to: http://www.subscribepage.com/j3x0h0 on your web browser to sign up.

Yellowstone Romance Series:

Yellowstone Awakening
Yellowstone Dawn
Yellowstone Deception
A Yellowstone Promise
Yellowstone Origins
Yellowstone Legacy
Yellowstone Legends

Many of my readers have asked for a timeline for both the **Yellowstone series** as well as the **Teton Trilogy** and the **Wilderness Brides Series**, since the three series are related (by setting and time period) and characters from one series make cameo appearances in the other. Please email me, and I will get you a download link.

peggy@peggylhenderson.com

Special Thanks to:

My editor and beta readers

Cover Design: Carpe Librum Book Design

Also, the guys and gals who were gracious enough on the Yellowstone Up Close And Personal Forum to give me their input when I posed the question "if you could go back in time 200 years to change something in Yellowstone then that would have a negative impact on the park today, what would it be?" I'm sure I caused some raised eyebrows, but the answers and suggestions were not only entertaining, but also very educational. You all know your Yellowstone inside and out! Thanks to Randall for mentioning a name I had never heard of, which gave me the idea I needed.

ABOUT THE AUTHOR

Peggy L Henderson is an award-winning, best-selling western historical and time travel romance author of the Yellowstone Romance Series, Second Chances Time Travel Romance Series, Teton Romance Trilogy, and Wilderness Brides Series. She was also a contributing author in the unprecedented 50-book American Mail Order Brides Series, contributing Book #15, Emma: Bride of Kentucky, the multi-author Timeless Hearts Time Travel Series, and the multi-author Burnt River Contemporary Western Series.

When she's not writing about Yellowstone, the Tetons, or the old west, she's out hiking the trails, spending time with her family and pets, or catching up on much-needed sleep. She is happily married to her high school sweetheart. They live in Yellowstone National Park, where many of her books are set.

Peggy is always happy to hear from her readers!

To get in touch with Peggy:
www.peggylhenderson.com
peggy@peggylhenderson.com

Lightning Source UK Ltd.
Milton Keynes UK
UKHW041830120320
360251UK00001B/65

9 781096 697732